D0912619

Love and Lore

A Samhain Publishing, Ltd. publication.

Samhain Publishing, Ltd.
512 Forest Lake Drive
Warner Robins, GA 31093
www.samhainpublishing.com

Love and Lore
Print ISBN: 1-59998-723-6
A Fairy Special Gift Copyright © 2007 by Gia Dawn
Heart of the Sea Copyright © 2007 by Sela Carsen
Wildish Things Copyright © 2007 by Carolan Ivey

Editing by Angela James
Cover by Anne Cain

First Samhain Publishing, Ltd. electronic publication: November 2007
First Samhain Publishing, Ltd. print publication: November 2007

Contents

Acknowledgement

Special thanks to Rebecca Goings for the title of this anthology *Love and Lore*.

A Fairy Special Gift

Gia Dawn

Dedication

For Poppy. I miss him.

Chapter One

Meara hated fairies. She tried her best to ignore them as they pressed against her window—talons tapping and snouted noses squashed tight against the glass. The slightest encouragement from her would have them swarming into her house in a rush of feathers and fur, destroying anything and everything that happened to stand in their path.

The creatures had plagued her since she was a child, tormenting her with their childish pranks, their pleasure made all the greater because no one else could see them. She had suffered untold embarrassments at their hands and now detested them with a fierce and unmatched enmity.

She reached beneath her chair for her fairy-swatter. Well, it was actually an ordinary flyswatter, but she bought the biggest ones she could find, and kept several hidden away in her house. They found them and stole them whenever they could, so Meara always made damned certain she had plenty of extras on hand.

Their fairy-agitation grew worse the more she continued to ignore them, but she wasn't the least bit fooled. She kept her gaze glued solidly to the television, hoping against hope she could finish her favorite show.

Fat chance. Suddenly the window burst open and a swarm of bodies rushed inside, twirling and swirling through the air.

Shimmering wings knocked over pictures, and frantic claws tore up the curtains. Her cat, Duchess, hissed and arched her back, fluffing her fur until she was nearly twice her normal size as she jumped to the back of the couch, her shrieks of outrage adding to the din.

One lovely sprite dove at the cat, biting her tail as Duchess twisted in fury. Meara swung her swatter in futile rage, swearing she would kill them all if she ever found a way. Although they were too blasted fast for her to squash, she occasionally managed to damage one or two.

"Get the hell out," she ordered, pointing to the window. "Now."

They rushed to the ceiling like a flock of birds and smirked down at her from above.

"Gift," one trilled, raking a claw down Meara's wallpaper. She swatted at it, barely missing one iridescent wing.

"I have no gifts for any of you miserable little horrors," Meara shouted, pointing to the window again. "Out."

"Nooooo," purred a second "Giffftt for you."

Meara had to laugh. The last time they'd brought her anything, they left a stolen horse at her doorstep, the poor beast so winded from the wild night ride she thought it might drop dead by morning. It took her several days to find the horse's owners and have it settled safely back home. Anything they gave her was certain to be tainted.

"I don't want it. Whatever it is, take it back." Meara managed to grab Duchess by the scruff of the neck and tossed her into the bedroom, pulling the door shut tight. The cat yowled in protest, sharpening her claws on the wood. Meara shook her head; that was another repair she'd have to add to her list. Too bad they didn't make fairy catastrophe insurance.

One of the more misshapen monsters dove down to pull her hair. Meara managed to land a good swat and it tumbled to the floor. She smiled in satisfaction.

It gave her a toothy grin. "Man," it muttered.

Man? Meara felt her hackles rise. Had they actually gone out and stolen a man? Or had they found one walking alone in the dark and driven him loony with their wicked games?

"You found a man and brought him here?"

A hundred heads nodded in unison.

"Is he injured?" Or worse, she added to herself.

"Yesss." The beautiful butterfly wings surrounded the ugliest fae Meara had ever seen. It looked like a tiny pig, with a broad snout and beady eyes.

"Did you do it?"

They all shook their heads at once.

"Nots hurts mans. Finds mans," came the answer. Several flew to point out her window.

"Come, come, come," one urged.

Meara didn't have a choice. If there really was an injured man out there in the night, she had an obligation to find him. "I'll put on my sweater, but out you go, the lot of you." She breathed a heavy sigh of relief as they finally obeyed. When the last one had gone, she pulled down the window and locked it tight, wishing she knew some banishing spell to keep them away forever.

After grabbing a flashlight and turning off the television, Meara stepped out into the night. It was magical. A crescent moon hung low on the horizon, the rest of it barely visible behind the earth's shadow. A breeze blew the smell of salt from the sea and she could hear the crash of waves on the rocky coast below the cliffs. She really didn't need her flashlight. The glow of the fairies lit the twisting path, sparks of color that shone like jewels. She wished they were either as beautifully magical up close or that they would always stay this far away and let her admire them from a distance.

They were in rare form tonight. Several darted back to hover at her side, whirling up and down and round about until Meara grew dizzy watching their dance—like she was having some bad flashback or epileptic seizure.

"Fasterrrrr," ordered a bright pink light drifting close to her ear. She batted it away before it could fasten its teeth on her skin.

She didn't bother to fight them as they urged her toward the coast. "What did you do, push him down the cliffs?" How she wished she had thought to bring the swatter.

"Bad, Mearee girl," scolded a ghoulish golden blob buzzing across her nose.

Dogs howled in the distance, the lonely sound haunting in the dark. The path grew precarious as she climbed down to the sea, and Meara had to turn on the light to pick her way along the rock strewn trail. She loved this part of her world, the stark beauty of the New England coast. Her family had lived here for generations. Legend had it that an ancestor brought a band of fairies with her from Ireland, and they so loved this wild and open land they decided to stay forever.

Too bad, she thought with a grimace, trying not to curse her long dead relative.

"Are we there yet?" Meara was beginning to think they were playing some huge and elaborate joke, planning to leave her alone in the dark while they giggled and moved on to newer sport.

"Yes, yes, yes, yes, yes," they answered.

As Meara watched, they gathered in a circle on the beach, their light combining to illuminate the dark form of a man. "Is he dead?" A shiver crawled along her spine. She jogged the last few paces and knelt on the sand, reaching out a hand to feel for a pulse. Her breath blew out in a sigh when he groaned and tried to roll over.

"Can you hear me?" Meara aimed her flashlight's beam just over his shoulder, trying not to shine the powerful light directly in his eyes. "Are you conscious?"

When he groaned again, Meara set down her light to help him turn over. A clot of blood smeared his forehead, trailing thickly down his cheek. He probably had a concussion, but hopefully no bones were broken.

She looked up at the crowd of fairies. "How did he get down here?"

They moved several yards away, circling a motorcycle halfway buried in a dune. So he was on some wild night ride and crashed, she thought with a frown. And no helmet either. Typical.

She motioned the fairies back again. "You found him, you'll have to carry him." She stood and brushed the sand from her pants. "I'll hold his head up. Hop to it, half on either side. Grab his clothes and lift."

To her utter amazement they did as she asked, managing to float him fairly steadily from the ground. The journey home was quicker than Meara expected, and soon she had the man stretched out on her couch while she swallowed her pride and thanked the unruly sprites for their assistance. After they actually left her in peace, she grabbed what bandages and ointment she could find, debating whether she should call the paramedics right away. She had just picked up the phone to dial nine-one-one, when his voice made her jump.

"Please. No need to call an ambulance. I'm okay." He grimaced and tried to sit, forcing Meara to hang up the phone and urge him to lie down again.

"Um...I really think you should see a doctor. That's a pretty nasty gash on your head. Hang on a sec and I'll clean it up. Do you know who you are?"

"I'd rather know who you are," he replied easily.

She couldn't suppress a snort. "Are you trying to hit on me with all that blood running down your face?"

"Hmmm, not working?" His expression was so woebegone, Meara almost giggled.

"Meara Magee," she told him, going into the bathroom to run some hot water and find a couple of washrags.

After wiping off his face, she realized the cut was not as bad as she expected. What had looked like pints of blood pouring from a massive slash turned out to be only a halfway decent wound. "It should probably have stitches," she remarked, cutting a butterfly bandage to hold the skin together.

He grinned, propping up on one elbow. Pretty, pretty, Meara realized as his clear green eyes fastened on hers. With thick brown hair, bad boy leather riding jacket, and at least six feet of tall, muscled flesh, he was a force to be reckoned with. Not to mention his perfectly beautiful smile.

"Got any aspirin? Or a bottle of bourbon? Or both?"

Meara chuckled despite herself. He was obviously incorrigible. "How about some warm milk?"

His face fell in utter disappointment. "Will you put a slug of whiskey in it?"

"As long as you let me drive you home."

"Deal. By the way, how did you find me?" He watched her closely.

"Would you believe I just happened along?"

He shook his head.

"I didn't think so. How about the fairies told me?" She asked the question flippantly, figuring he would laugh the comment off, but to her astonishment he heaved a great sigh of relief.

"Wow, they really did what I asked them to."

Meara blinked stupidly. "Asked who?"

"Uh..." Now it was his turn to look dumbfounded. "Nothing...never mind." He sat up and propped his head in his hands. "I could use that aspirin."

"Right. Sorry." Meara rushed into the kitchen, her thoughts whirling. Had he been serious when he said he'd asked the fairies for help? Did he see them too? And did she have the nerve to broach the subject again?

She had just found the aspirin and nuked him a warm glass of milk—with a decent shot of peach brandy—when she heard a soft knock on the door. What now? Deciding to ignore the interruption, she sat in her armchair and watched him sip tentatively at the drink before winking at her in appreciation.

"Very good."

The knock came again.

"You gonna answer that?" He nodded to the door.

An ear-piercing shriek caused them both to jump.

"What the—" He stood shakily and scanned the room. "Do you have a gun? Baseball bat...anything?"

Meara felt her heart sink. Could this night possibly get any worse? "She's not dangerous."

"She? You know her?"

"Not personally." Damn, how was she going to explain this? The shriek sounded again. "Give me just a second, I'll send her home." She walked wearily to the door, hoping against hope her new visitor would go away.

The shrieking built again...impossibly high, and Meara was forced to put her hands over her ears until the sound faded slowly away. Then she wrenched the door open.

"Begone. He's not dead!"

The pale woman sniffed, bloodshot eyes weeping long trails of tears. Her hair stuck out in all directions, a knotted mass of silver and grey. "Ohhhhhh, nooooooo, he must be d-dead. I have to do my j-j-job." She twisted her hands together in dismay.

Just then the man poked his head into the hall. "What the hell?"

When she started to scream again, Meara clamped her hand over the other woman's mouth. "Shhhh, you'll wake the whole town. Get in here and listen. This is—" She motioned for the man to come closer.

"Jamison. Jamison Murphy," he said.

Well, that explained a lot, Meara thought. His ancestry was as Irish as hers. "Jamison had an accident...nothing major...and I was just getting ready to take him home."

The pale woman's shoulders slumped. "He's really not dying?" She sounded so upset, Meara made her sit down.

"No, dear. I'm sorry."

Jamison stared with his mouth open. "Is she what I think she is?"

Meara was beyond coming up with a suitable lie. Maybe when he woke up tomorrow he would think he'd been having delusions. "Banshee."

He seemed totally fascinated by this bit of information. "And you were coming for me?"

Banshee nodded, her tears starting once more. "You probably think I'm h-h-horrid," she hiccupped.

"Oh, no." Jamison took her hand. "I am honored to meet you."

"You are?"

"Absolutely. My family was always proud we could claim our very own banshee. This is fantastic."

Now it was Meara's turn to stare. "It is?"

"But you're not dead." Banshee's tears actually stopped.

"I promise you I will...someday." Jamison gave her an amazing smile and Banshee almost smiled back.

"Oh, you are right! Do you think it might be soon?" she added hopefully.

Jamison winked. "You never know."

Banshee stood and smoothed out her tattered skirt. "Then I guess I should be going, I might be needed somewhere else tonight. Very nice to meet you, Jamison," she said, practically floating out the door. "I'll see you again."

Meara had never seen the likes—the man had actually charmed a banshee and acted as if he'd done it every day of his life. She watched him lean against the doorframe and cross his arms over his chest. His hair had fallen down to cover the gash on his head, and he was as handsome a man as she'd ever seen. Her breath quickened as she realized this was someone who could actually understand the complications of her life. He was dealing with the exact same situation.

"You tried to fool me before," he accused, stepping away from the door. "You do see them, and they did tell you where to find me."

The closer he came, the larger he loomed, and Meara suddenly found herself pinned against the wall with his body practically touching hers. Forgotten needs washed heavy over her skin. Heat and want and delicious desire. Meara fought back the urge to trail her hand across his chest. It wouldn't do to be too needy. She'd seen women who were needy—cloying, desperate things who gave up all life of their own and bent over backwards to do their husband's will. Not her style, no matter how appealing...despite the perfect mouth that hovered so close to hers and the muscled arms that rested easily against the wall.

Not good, not good at all.

"I think I should take you home." She ducked beneath one arm and went to find her keys. It didn't help that he followed her around the room like a stray puppy, wiggling his perfect ass, making her want nothing more than to pet him the rest of the night.

"You still haven't answered my question." He gave her a lopsided grin and Meara found him even more attractive—as if that were at all possible. "Tell the truth."

Attractive and annoying, she corrected. "Yes, all right, I do see the miserable little horrors."

"How does it happen in your family?" He smiled smugly and batted his lashes. "In mine it's tied to the green-eyed thing."

"My grand-mother said her mother saw them. Just my luck I got some freaky recessive gene that hasn't shown up for generations. I'd rather have a great big wart on the tip of my nose. I could get rid of that."

His laughter filled the room. "They can be a bit of a challenge. You just don't know how to play their game."

Meara's attraction lessened as her annoyance grew. "I have no desire to play their games. All I want is for them to leave me alone. If you can find a way to manage that, I'll owe you big time."

He stepped toward her, his eyes taking on a wicked gleam. "What would you owe me?"

Meara's mouth dropped open.

"I know their secret," he continued in a na-na-nanana voice.

The man really was outrageous. "Of course you do." But Meara's mouth curved up despite herself. Okay, why not? She hadn't had a conversation with a gorgeous man in ages and she was enjoying every minute of it. "So, if I actually believe one word of what you say, what would I owe you?"

"Interested, huh? Now we're making progress." He stepped toward her again until there was barely a space between them.

Meara stood as tall as she could and looked him straight in the eye. "Go on, but I warn you, this better be good."

His mouth hovered a hair's breadth from hers. "Kiss me," he said. "One kiss and I'll tell you everything."

Chapter Two

Jamison couldn't believe his luck. Here he was, standing toe to toe with one of the most lovely women he had ever met...and she saw the same things he did. Not to mention, she took it as a daily occurrence when a banshee came to call. What he had thought was going to be a miserable night spent in pain on the beach had now become one of the better moments of his life. Granted his head still pounded like he'd been hit with a rock, and muscles he never knew he had were beginning to scream in protest—but he wouldn't have changed a thing if it meant not meeting the fascinating, freckled female.

Her strawberry blonde hair hung just past her shoulders, with wisps of bangs that tried to tangle in her lashes. Her eyes were the color of good brandy, soft and brown with just a hint of stubborn. She was tall and curved in all the right places, places he would love to touch and fondle and—

Ah, hell, he was already growing hard. Not that he minded. It had been a while since he'd been well and truly aroused. It had probably been a long time for her, also, if their fairy buddies meddled in her affairs as much as they did his.

"Well?" he demanded when she made no move to press her mouth to his. "I'm getting tired of waiting."

"Unh, unh." She shook her head and chewed her bottom lip. "Not until you tell me something I don't already know."

"I sleep naked."

She choked on a laugh, her eyes brimming with mischief. "So do I, but we both know that's not what I meant."

Now it was Jamison's turn to chuckle. They had another thing in common. Very nice. "You drive a hard bargain. Still, never let it be said that Jamison Murphy doesn't play fair. I bribe them."

"You bribe them. That's your big announcement."

"Works every time." He moved his mouth smugly closer, but she pushed him away with a grimace.

"Not good enough. What do you bribe them with?"

"That will take a second kiss." Before she could protest, he wrapped one hand around her nape and pulled her face to his. He was hungry and she was the only thing that would sate him. He'd imagined she would taste as fiery as she talked, but he was startled to find she was sweet like cherry wine or fine mead—one of his personal favorites.

Her hair slipped through his fingers, thick and straight. He thought nothing would feel better than to have that hair spread over his thighs while her soft sweet mouth wrapped tight around his cock.

Shit. He thrust his tongue between her lips, stiffening even more when he heard her moan of acceptance. Her arms curled around his waist, her fingers stroking his back, clawing into his skin when his tongue delved even deeper.

He took a chance and nibbled at her lip, using just enough pressure to make it sting, and almost spent in his jeans when she dug her nails into his back. So, she liked it a bit on the rough side. That suited him just fine...he liked it a little rough, too.

He thrust one knee between her legs, rubbing it against the heat of her mound while his hand traced the curve of her breast. Her nipple was already swollen. He rolled it hard between his fingers. She whimpered and pulled her mouth away.

"You said kiss, not groping," she accused in a shaky voice. He noticed she still kept her arms wrapped around him.

"You didn't like it?" He bent and nuzzled her neck.

"That's not the point. You were trying to take advantage. Bad, bad boy." Her smile was naughty.

His grin matched. "I could be even badder...if you gave me another chance?"

She shook her head, but there was interest in her eyes. "Not tonight. Time to go home."

With a heavy sigh he stepped back, only to stumble and fall to his knees. His head spun and his legs had grown alarmingly weak. "I guess you got to me more than I cared to admit," he managed ruefully. "Maybe I do need to go home."

"Probably more to do with the accident than my womanly charms." Her laugh was gentle as she helped him sit back on the couch.

"Don't be too sure about that, Meara, me girly," he answered, running a finger down her cheek. "Don't be too sure about that at all."

ৎ০ৡ০৩

They were waiting for her when Meara got home, still remembering the last kiss Jamison planted on her lips before he thanked her again for coming to his rescue. Their wings buzzed in the dark like a plague of locusts ready to swarm.

"I know you're there," she yelled, opening the car door and sticking the swatter out. "The first one I catch gets locked in with the cat. Have you ever seen what a cat does with a trapped fairy...it's not pretty."

She fumbled for her key, making sure she had the right one before she made a mad dash toward the house.

Instantly the night was ablaze with light, mad orbs of color rushing toward her at dizzying speed. She struggled with the lock, dropping the key as the first wave of bodies dove toward her. They landed on her back, their nails scratching holes in her sweater. Good thing Meara had taken to buying all her clothes at the local Goodwill. She couldn't afford to have cashmere or silk torn into shreds the first day she wore them.

She swatted blindly at the stinging hoard, grinning in evil delight when she felt her blows connect. "Take that, you miserable creatures."

But they were winning, they always did. Her hair was already being twisted into knots, and she could see the scratches running down the length of her arms. In desperation she found her key and rammed it into the lock, heaving a huge sigh of relief when she heard the bolt slip free.

She even managed to slide through the door without any following her inside, before she threw the swatter down in absolute frustration.

She couldn't take them anymore. Something had to be done.

Meara sat down at her computer and scrolled through the search list. Somehow, somewhere, there was a way to rid herself of the meddling fae once and for all.

Some of the Wiccan sites seemed promising. They advertised a spell for everything—including banishing and protection from evil. Were the fairies really evil? Granted they were winged monsters, tiny demons of the air, but evil?

The spell called for a black candle, saltwater, ground cinnamon and sage. You were supposed to ring your space with the ground herbs, light the candle, then wash all your windows and doorways with saltwater. Evil was guaranteed never to bother you again.

Meara looked at the mass of lights hovering over her herb garden and decided the spell was not nearly strong enough. She tried her favorite search...pest control.

Flypaper. Already done that, the fairies paid no attention to it at all. Bug spray—too messy. She didn't want poisoned fae gasping for breath on her doorstep. Roach motels? Nope, needed to come in much bigger sizes.

Oh, this looked good. A big plastic ball filled with honey. Well, it was actually a wasp catcher, but the logistics looked right. Fairies flew in, but they couldn't get out. She ordered two and had them shipped overnight express. If she managed to catch enough, the rest might just take the hint and leave her in peace for a change.

She heard Duchess hiss at the window and watched her cat paw frantically at the glass, trying desperately to reach the smirking fairy hovering on the other side. The cat jumped, slid down the window and knocked off an entire shelf of books and magazines.

Meara dropped her head on the computer keys, praying the catchers wouldn't get lost in the mail. She could see the headline now. "Woman driven insane...claims fairies won't leave her alone."

Grabbing her sketchbook, Meara funneled her fury into her work. The drawing took shape with little effort on her part, and in less than an hour she was looking happily at her latest creation. A tiger-striped cat sat licking one paw, a fairy wing sticking out of its mouth. The other paw held a struggling fairy in its out-stretched claws.

Meara wrote the caption in satisfied amusement. *Fairies, you can't eat just one.*

She liked this picture enough she decided to paint it before putting it up for sale on her website. It ought to bring in a decent price. She had quite a few fans who loved her work.

Her anger appeased for the moment, Meara studied the creatures gaping at her through the window, remembering that they had brought her the fabulous Jamison Murphy. Okay, score one point for them, but the tally was still miles from being even. Nonetheless, she was smiling as she pulled the curtains shut and got undressed for bed...until her eyes fell on the letter she'd left sitting on her dresser.

She didn't have to pick it up to know what it said. She'd been offered the job she'd applied for in Nevada—advertising designer for a new line of fantasy toys. The money was decent, and she'd be stuck somewhere in the middle of the desert...a place she felt certain the fairies would despise so much they'd stay here and leave her in peace. She'd jumped at the chance when she'd first heard about the job, but suddenly Nevada seemed barren and bleak. There'd be no sound of gulls crying in the morning, no foggy nights or maple trees draped in dew.

No Jamison Murphy lying on her couch bargaining for a single kiss. Her timing had always been bad, Meara realized as she fought the curtains shut and threw her clothes on the floor.

෴෴

Jamison hit the beach well before dawn and frowned at his half-buried bike. He hadn't been on a joy ride last night...not really.

But he had been blowing off steam. Furious that a known drug runner had slipped through his fingers again, Jamison had raced along the shore like a man possessed, his rage and frustration egging him into realms of stupidity he rarely visited.

Missing evidence. The same thing that had happened his last three busts. And it was beginning to look more and more like a deliberate sabotage. If he ever found out who was tampering with his evidence, he would hang them from the highest tree and dare anyone to be brave enough to get past him and cut them down.

Just remembering the entire situation set his blood on fire again. He deliberately turned his thoughts to the beautiful Meara Magee. His blood still burned, but the new fire was much more palatable. Delightful, he thought, running his tongue over his teeth as he dug out his bike and brushed off the clinging sand.

His gaze drifted to the horizon, watching the sun come up. There was nothing he adored more than the ocean. It was in his blood. His father and his father's father, and generations of his ancestors before them had all earned their living on the sea. She was their mistress, their lover, the one woman they felt understood their restless souls.

He ran his hand through his hair and glowered at the dawn. Some days he didn't know why he bothered—the drugs kept getting deadlier, the stockpiles kept growing, and the amount of money involved was mind-blowing.

A sappy poster sprang to mind, the one where a boy stood on a beach littered with stranded starfish and threw them one at a time back into the ocean. While he couldn't save them all, he could make a difference to a few.

That difference was why he stayed.

His cell-phone rang and he flipped it open. "Murphy."

"We've got a new lead," came the voice of Chief Chambers. "The DEA has an informant who works on the docks. Another shipment is due in very soon. They'll put a tracker on the boat and let it head back out. Then it'll be up to you to find their main warehouse."

Jamison allowed himself a thin smile. "Thanks, Chief. Has anyone else been assigned to watch the evidence lockers?"

"The DEA has promised us an extra hand...if you find what they're looking for."

"Don't worry, I'll get the information if I have to track them all the way to South America." He closed the phone with a satisfied snap. Just a few days until show time. And the lovely fairy queen to keep him company until then.

His mouth actually turned up into a grin as he started the bike and rode into town.

৪০৪০৫৪

Meara woke early, struggling to keep her spirits up when she saw the storm clouds rolling in from the sea and the fairy heads trying to peek at her through the curtains. After giving the sprites a mocking wave, she shrugged on a thick terry robe and made her way to the kitchen, refusing to let thoughts of the delicious Jamison turn her away from the plans she'd made. She plugged in the coffeepot and was just deciding what to eat for breakfast when she heard a knock at her door. Jamison's voice called out her name and she ran to greet him, her move to Nevada forgotten in the thrill of the moment.

"Top o' ta mornin' to ya, Miss Meara Magee," he said in a decent Irish brogue. "Will ya be lettin' me in? I have a special gift ta tank ya fer rescuin' me last night."

Meara giggled and stepped aside, slamming the door shut behind him when she saw several fairies dive-bombing toward her. They slammed into the wood with series of thumps that made Jamison shake his head.

"No wonder they don't like you. You're mean."

"You don't know the half of it." Meara dug a swatter out of the closet. "Want one?"

"Not me. I'd rather stay on their good side." He sniffed appreciatively. "Coffee?" He followed her into the kitchen and set a package on the table, his eyes never leaving the opening of her robe. "I like it here."

Meara watched him prowl around the small room with its bright yellow paint and white lace curtains. She thought a home should be cheery, and she'd decorated her small cottage accordingly. The bathroom was eye-glaring turquoise, her single bedroom a pretty peach, her office was wild-rose pink and her main living room was apple green. Ireland in the spring.

"There used to be a lighthouse on that small outcrop." She pointed out the window toward a tiny peninsula. "This was the caretaker's house. The lighthouse was torn down almost seventy years ago and my family bought the land. We've been here ever since. My grandparents built a bigger house in town and my parents still live there."

Jamison leaned in too close, his hips pressing into her bottom and his mouth almost nipping at her ear. "So we're all alone, out here on the seashore?"

Meara frowned at the pixie crawling on her window ledge. "Almost."

Jamison chuckled, a rich sound that caused her blood to heat. "That's why I brought you the present." He took her hand and pulled her back toward the table. "You open it and I'll pour coffee."

Meara was too entranced by the sight of the fabulous man being all domestic in her kitchen to argue. It seemed right to watch him poking through cabinets to find the cups before rummaging in the fridge.

"Milk?"

Meara nodded. "No sugar. I have some pop-tarts—first door to the left over the sink."

"Nothing like a healthy breakfast. What flavor do you want?" He opened the cabinet and took down several boxes. "Good Lord, do you have every flavor?"

"I think so, but I ate all the strawberry ones." She looked at the gaily wrapped package, wondering what on earth he'd brought her.

"You can open it anytime." He was watching her in amusement.

She tore into the paper delightedly. It wasn't every day a gorgeous man gave her a present. He brought two cups of coffee and sat next to her, his eyes glowing with mischief.

Meara tore off the top of the box and frowned. "What's this?"

His laughter echoed around the room. "I promised you my secret. Fairy dust."

"Fairy dust." She snorted. "You've got to be kidding me." She took out the bags of glitter, sequins and tiny bits of confetti. "You bribe them with junk?"

"Not just any junk." He tore open a bag of glitter and poured it into the box. "Sparkly, gaudy, fascinating junk. They love it. Come on, help." Jamison opened another bag. "I mix it up and keep some in my pocket all the time. Whenever I need them gone...I just throw a handful out."

"Uh, huh." Meara ran her fingers through the sparkly mix. "It is pretty, I'll grant you that."

Jamison captured her hand in his. "Not nearly as pretty as you."

Desire hung thick between them. Meara remembered the way she'd felt in his arms last night. The way her body still thrummed in need as she'd tossed and turned for hours, the ache between her legs almost more than she could take. Eventually she'd pulled her vibrator out of the drawer, but it had been so long since she'd been interested in using it, the batteries had gone dead.

Then again, who needed a toy when she had the real thing stroking her fingers right now? He leaned forward, his lips nearing hers. He had great lips. Fabulous lips. Lips that were made for pleasuring a woman. Meara swallowed, suddenly nervous. She was certain those lips had seen more action than hers. Hell, the whole world had seen more action than she had. She drew back and took a sip of coffee, choking on the drink when he tucked a finger into the opening of her robe.

"Meara, if you let me, I would take you to bed right now and spend the entire day making you scream my name." His eyes were dangerously beseeching. His finger tugged her robe looser.

"You don't waste any time," she somehow managed to squeak out. She tried to stand, but he refused to let go of her robe. If she moved, he would pull the entire thing off.

"Do you think I act this way with every woman I meet?" His face had grown serious.

Meara tried to laugh. "Only the crazy fairy-seeing ones."

"There are no other crazy fairy-seeing ones."

"That's just my point. What makes you think we're compatible based on just that?"

"What makes you think we're not? I already love your wicked sense of humor, the way you don't care if your hair is mussed or if your make-up is on perfect. I feel more at ease with you after one day than with some women I've known for months. Life is short. I don't believe in wasting time." He ran his hand down her hair, brushing some wayward strands from her cheek.

Meara knew her indecision was written on her face. When Jamison sighed and leaned back in his chair, she felt like her world had come to a stop. His grin was sheepish. "Okay, okay, I know I'm pushing. How can I convince you my intentions are honorable?"

"Let me brush my teeth and we can start with a kiss. See how things go from there?" Meara felt herself blush all the way from her toes when he slipped his tongue over his teeth.

"You've got two minutes before I come looking for you." He tapped his watch. "Better hurry, I'm already counting."

Meara bounded to the bathroom. She finished her teeth and even managed to run a comb through her hair before she heard Jamison's voice counting down the seconds.

"Ready or not, here I come."

Meara giggled when she heard his footsteps crossing the floor. But her smile faltered when someone knocked at the door. Who could that possibly be? She'd had more visitors in the past twenty-four hours than she usually had in weeks. "Don't answer it," she whispered, meeting Jamison in the hallway.

"If you say so." He took her hand and pulled her close. "Now, about that kiss…"

Chapter Three

"Meara, darling," called a too cheery male voice from outside. "Open up and let me come in."

Meara froze, her heart racing. Damn, damn, damn. And just when she thought this day might actually turn out well. She gave Jamison a pleading look. "Do me a huge favor and just play along," she whispered before heading to the door. "This shouldn't take long."

A blond giant stood on her small porch, a bouquet of wilting flowers held stiffly towards her. "For you, light of my life, my love, my heart, my—"

"Okay, I get the picture." Meara made no move to take the flowers. "Lugh, come in. We have to talk."

He had to duck to fit his seven-foot-plus height through her doorway.

Meara swallowed and introduced the two men. "Jamison, this is Lugh, Celtic god of fire. Lugh, this is Jamison...my fiancé."

The god's face crumpled. "Fiancé? Maybe I should sit down." He moved to the living room and folded himself onto a tiny hard-backed chair.

Meara thought she'd never seen a more pitiful sight in her life. Jamison, however, looked as if he'd rather be tied to a stake and burned alive than here facing the immortal giant.

She gave him a nasty look that said you'd-better-not-screw-this-up, and Jamison finally managed to speak. "Nice to meet you," he said holding out his hand.

Lugh gave it a perfunctory shake, his own fingers completely dwarfing the other man's. "I'm not really happy to meet you," he replied. "Sorry." He looked like a puppy who had just been scolded for chewing up the carpet.

"I completely understand. Why don't I get us both a drink. Meara, do you have any beer? I know it's early, but given the circumstances, I could use a good stiff belt."

"Beer's in the fridge. There's also that bottle of brandy on the counter."

"Right." Jamison left the room so fast she thought he'd actually break the sound barrier.

She turned to Lugh. "I'm sorry I didn't tell you sooner, but you know as well as I do this would never work out between us. You're a god, for heaven's sake. Can't you find some nice immortal goddess to fall for?"

Lugh sighed. His breath blew two paintings off the wall. Meara cringed when she heard the glass shatter.

Jamison poked his head around the corner. "You two all right in there?"

"Fine. But you'd better make that three beers." She focused her attention back to Lugh. "Have you asked any of them out on a date? Or sent a note telling them how you feel?"

Lugh shook his massive head. "All the goddesses I know are spoiled and silly. Who wants to get blasted just for trying to steal a kiss? It's not like in the old days when you could carry them off to your palace and live happily ever after. Now they want to talk about how they feel, and what they want, and whether or not I think they're fat. It's too much like work."

Jamison returned, a dark grin spreading across his face. "Here you go, buddy. And let me tell you, you aren't the only man who doesn't understand women these days."

Lugh's face brightened just a bit. "I'm not?"

"Nope, not even close." Jamison took a long slug of beer and motioned for Lugh to do the same.

Lugh downed his can in one drink and politely asked for another.

"Not too much," Meara warned as Jamison headed back to the kitchen. "The last thing we need is a soused god on our hands."

Lugh puffed out his chest. "I never get soused. Except for that one time about two thousand years ago...I was helping fight off the Romans—nasty little men, but they brought with them shiploads of very nice wine. Have you ever had Italian wine? It is some of the best ever made."

"Here." Jamison shoved another beer into Lugh's hand and handed one to Meara.

She toyed with the can as the men raised theirs in a salute. "Isn't there even some nymph you're interested in?" she finally asked Lugh.

"I've dated every sprite or muse I could think of in the last several centuries or so. That's why I was counting on you." He raised pleading eyes to hers. "You were my last chance at love."

When she frowned, Jamison chuckled. "Sorry, old man," he offered. "But she's mine and I plan on keeping her. Besides," he added in a just-between-us-guys voice, "you'd get tired of her after a few years. She doesn't do that adoration thing very well."

Lugh's face brightened. "I never thought of it that way. It would be hard to live with a woman who didn't absolutely worship me."

"Well, there you go." Jamison clapped Lugh on the back. "Glad to have helped you sort this whole thing out."

Lugh jumped to his feet. The small cottage shook alarmingly. "Forgive me, my lovely, beautiful, delightful Meara for breaking your heart, but it wouldn't be right for a fabulous god like me to be seen with a simple mortal woman like you. You do understand...don't you?"

"I'll do my best to get over it," Meara mocked, watching him bang his head as he ducked back out the door. She raced after him and turned the lock before Lugh could change his mind. She thought if he stuck his smirking face back in, she'd have to use the swatter. She took it out of the closet just in case.

"What was that all about?" Jamison was sitting on the couch with his arms stretched out and his legs spread wide in invitation.

Meara groaned. "He found out I could see him about six months ago. He swore it was fate and has been bugging me ever since. Do you believe he actually wanted me to kneel at his feet the first night he came over?"

Jamison chuckled. "Maybe I should've tried that approach." He laughed harder when Meara stuck out her tongue. "Come here and do that," he said. "Jees, what does a man have to do to get a kiss around here?"

Despite his flippant tone, his gaze was heavy where it raked across her skin. Meara shivered in answer as she let him settle her on his lap. Before she could say a single word, he tilted her head back and brushed his mouth over hers. It was a gentle kiss, asking rather than demanding. He teased her, drawing her out of her tentative response until she was the one who begged for more.

It would be easy, so easy, to do as he'd requested—let him lead her back to bed and show her what she'd been missing for so long...the warm and expert touch of a man. The heat rose fast between them and Meara surrendered to the need as his mouth became more demanding, his tongue sliding between her lips.

When someone else knocked on the door, Meara wanted to scream her frustration. "What now? If we pretend there's no one home, do you think they'll go away?" She snuggled deeper into his lap, letting the warmth of him wrap deliciously around her.

He nuzzled her neck, his fingers slipping through the opening in her robe. Meara trembled when she felt him stroke one nipple, teasing it into a pearl of sensitive flesh. She laid her head on his shoulder, biting her lip against a cry of want as he rolled her nipple between his fingers, the swift sting of pleasure hitting hard between her legs. She could feel his cock swell against her bottom, proof that his arousal was growing to match hers. She wanted to touch the length of him, stroke her fingers around his shaft while he begged her to not to make him come too soon, his groans of hunger harsh and heady in her ears.

The knock came again, followed by the beginnings of a high-pitched scream. Banshee.

"What could she possibly want?" Jamison frowned. "I'm not dead again, am I?"

Meara smiled. He was beginning to realize just how annoying the magical creatures could be. "God, I hope not. Cover your ears," she added as the shrieking rose to a head-pounding roar.

"Nothing like a good banshee wail to get one out of the mood," Jamison grumbled, dumping Meara on the sofa. "I'll go see what she wants."

Meara smooched at him as he crossed the room. "I'll be waiting," she promised, assuming a seductive position...until Jamison returned with a clearly upset Banshee in tow.

"She, uh, asked to talk to you."

Meara hurriedly drew her robe together and sat up straight. "I'm not dead, either," she said. "Go away."

Banshee opened her mouth to scream, but Meara stopped her with a slice of her hand. "No more shrieking."

Banshee settled for sniffling and hiccups. "W-w-was he here?"

"Who?"

"L-l-l-uuggghhhhh."

"Shhhhhh. No crying or wailing either."

Banshee sniffed one last time and Jamison handed her a box of tissues. "Th-thank you."

"What about Lugh?" Meara asked.

"I...I-I love himm."

"You love that blond egomaniac?" Well, now this was very interesting. "Have you told him?"

Banshee shook her head. "He is so handsome. What would he ever see in me?" Her mouth started trembling again.

Meara considered. With some decent make-up, a new hairstyle and something sexy to wear, Banshee could be the answer to her prayers. If Meara fixed her up with Lugh, they might leave her and Jamison in peace.

She smiled at Banshee. "I have a plan. But it's gonna take a lot of work. Jamison, we need you to go to town. I'll make a list."

℘ℛℛℭ

Several hours later, Meara stepped back to survey her handiwork. "Almost," she said, adding a final touch. "Are you ready?"

Banshee twisted her hands in her lap. "I-I think so. Will this really work?" she added in a hopeful tone.

Meara gave her shoulder a squeeze. "If it doesn't, Lugh is a bigger dope than I imagined. You look beautiful. Really. Okay, do you remember how to do this all yourself?"

"Yes."

"Then let's have a look."

Jamison poked his head in the room. "Can I watch?"

"Absolutely. We need a man's opinion." Meara motioned him closer. "Here goes." With a great flourish, she spun Banshee around so she could see herself in the mirror.

For long seconds the fairy stared at her appearance in stunned silence. "Is that me?" she finally asked, running a hand down her cheek.

"Yep." Meara couldn't help but grin as she watched the other woman's expression. "Isn't it amazing what a little make-up and a good hair style can do?"

Jamison whistled his approval and Banshee actually blushed, the pale pink lighting up her perfectly formed face.

Truth was, Meara was a wee bit jealous. The fairy had a fragile bone structure that a human woman could not possibly match. High cheekbones, huge uptilted eyes, cupid's bow mouth and alabaster skin. A good concealer hid the shadows beneath her eyes, and waterproof black eye make-up made her look mysterious and haunting. Her untangled hair was soft as spun silk, the silver strands spilling over her shoulders, while a splash of rose lip gloss made her mouth glisten.

Meara had loaned Banshee a push-up bra and slinky gown to complete her new look. The whole effect was ethereal and otherworldly.

Banshee sniffed, huge tears welling up in her eyes. "I don't know what to say."

"Do not cry," Meara warned. "Even waterproof make-up has its limitations."

Banshee blinked back the flow. "What now?"

"Now," Meara waved them all into the living room, "you go find Lugh."

Banshee looked like she was about to be fed to the lions. "I c-can't do that."

"Why not?" Meara balled her hands on her hips. "Just go up to him and tell him that you absolutely worship the ground he walks on. He'll like that...trust me."

Jamison nodded when Banshee turned pleading eyes to him. "Meara's right. Just this morning he was telling us how he wished he could find someone to adore him. You, lovely Banshee, are exactly what that god is looking for."

"Take a deep breath, stand up tall and go get him," Meara ordered. "Wait, don't forget your make-up, hair brush and detangling spray." She placed a brightly colored cosmetic case into Banshee's hands. "And whatever you do, don't let him see you without your war-paint...at least for a few hundred years."

"War-paint?"

"Never mind." Meara led her to the door. "Good luck, okay? I mean that."

Banshee came close to smiling. "Thank you. Very much." She gave Meara a quick hug before flying out the door and into the evening shadows.

Meara grinned at Jamison. "You do good work."

"I didn't do anything."

"Oh, yes you did. When she saw the way you looked at her, she really believed she was beautiful. Should I consider her a rival?"

He grinned from ear to ear. "Only if I have to compete against Lugh. Otherwise, I am perfectly content to have a warm, human, Irish princess in my arms." He stalked her across the room. "We never did get to finish our morning kiss."

"We finished several as I recall." Meara ran into the kitchen, giggling as Jamison followed close behind. He had her trapped against the sink, his mouth barely touching her cheek, when her stomach rumbled loudly. "Suppertime. What should we have?" She turned to check her cabinets, pleased when he ground his hips against hers.

"Let me take you out to dinner."

Meara was already shaking her head. "I don't think that's such a good idea."

"Why not?" He curled his arms around her waist.

"You know why." Meara pointed out the window where several fairies were buzzing against the glass. "Do you know what havoc they cause if I go into town? I've been thrown out of more places than I can count because of their damned pestering."

Jamison's smile broadened. "But I have the fairy dust. I can keep them occupied for hours—plenty of time to have dinner and get you back home. I promise," he added, planting a small kiss on her neck.

Meara couldn't resist. If he really could make the capricious fairies leave them alone, this might be a night made in heaven. "Let me get my coat. It's getting cold today." She even managed a quick swipe of mascara and lipstick before she returned. "You brought your car, right, not that silly motorcycle?"

He had the grace to duck his head. "Maybe you should drive."

She chuckled. "Are you gonna pay or is this Dutch treat?"

He pulled a wad of bills from his pocket. "I'll buy and get rid of the fairies. Fair enough?"

"Deal." Meara grabbed her purse and keys. "You first," she ordered when they reached the door. "Show me this great fairy magic." She resisted the temptation to snatch up her swatter.

"Watch." He placed his finger to his lips and walked into the yard. Almost instantly he was surrounded by the blurry bodies of the fairies. They swarmed around him like flies, picking at his clothes and hair.

He winked at her as he reached into his pocket. Then he flung a handful of his magical mix high into the air. It caught on the wind and blew in all directions, the sunlight glinting off it as it dazzled and sparkled overhead. Jamison was completely forgotten as the fairies chased their new amusement, the sounds of their wings growing fainter with every second.

"Works every time," he said smugly. "So, my lady, drive us into town."

Chapter Four

It was a peaceful drive along the coast road, no winged monsters mugging up her windshield or hanging onto the rearview mirrors until she couldn't see a thing behind her. The ocean sighed peacefully against the shore, its salty smell comfortingly familiar. In winter when the Nor'easters brought their wind and snow and ice the sea danced as if possessed, but today the sun sank slowly beneath a bank of shadowy clouds while the water glowed as if littered with diamonds.

Jamison whistled a lilting tune, content to watch the world flow by, and Meara let herself relax, lulled by his nearness and the blissful peace he'd brought her.

They ate at one of the best seafood restaurants in town, by big glass windows that gave them a spectacular view of the coast. They both licked their fingers after the meal, lingering over a bottle of champagne while the crowd thinned until only a few other couples cuddled in the shadows.

Meara didn't know when she'd had so much fun. The food was perfect, her companion was perfect, and there hadn't been one sign of fairy trouble all night. This was a life she had long given up on—a normal, sane life with a normal, handsome man. Well, not normal, she amended as sparkles of fairy dust glinted in his hair. Maybe normal wasn't all it was cracked up to be.

"So, what do you do for a living?" Jamison leaned back in his chair and watched the play of candlelight on her skin. She looked as ethereal as ocean mist, as beautiful as moonlight on the waves.

He wanted to see her spread out across the bed, watch her eyes turn stormy with desire, feel her body hot and tight around his length. He stiffened at the thought, the pulse of need flowing hard into his cock. He smiled at the pleasure and continued to imagine her sweaty and whimpering in his arms.

He could tell she didn't have much experience with men...he liked that idea more than he should have. The truth was, he'd never had much experience with women until he'd found how to bribe the pesky fairies and keep them away from his dates. But it could be a crapshoot. Some days the fae were more inclined to stay and interfere with his life no matter how many handfuls of glitter he threw. Of course, he wasn't about to give Meara that tiny bit of information.

"I'm an artist. I do fairy drawings." Meara toyed with the stem of her glass. Jamison pictured her fingers playing somewhere completely different. "I torture them hideously in paint and ink and make quite a decent living at it. I have an online business."

Jamison chuckled. "Fairy therapy?"

Meara nodded. "Absolutely. What about you?"

"Coast Guard."

Her eyes widened and a smile tugged at the corner of her mouth...her beautiful, tempting, very sexy mouth. "So it's true? They don't follow you over water?"

Jamison smiled back. "Every now and then one gets brave and decides to hop on board. After hours spent on deck while the boat rolls and dips, it's pretty much cured of the need to bother me at work again."

Her laugh tinkled across the air. "You are good, I'll give you that."

He leaned forward and captured her hand in his fingers, his eyes never leaving hers. It was time to make his move. "I am good at other things, Meara. I want to teach you, show you the pleasure you've been missing."

She snatched her hand away. "What makes you think I'm so ignorant?"

He pointed out the window to where a single fairy snarled at them through the glass. "I am the same as you. I know how it is. The first time I ever kissed a girl one of them flew down and bit her on the ass. She thought I'd pinched her and smacked me for my trouble." He chuckled at the memory, encouraged when Meara smiled with him.

"One time a boy asked me to dance and several tied his shoelaces together. He tripped and knocked us both down, somehow managing to break his wrist." She sighed and her expression dimmed. "Not much action after that." She watched several fairies join their companion outside. "Looks like time's almost up."

"It doesn't have to be. Let me stay with you tonight. I'm off until tomorrow afternoon. We can make love for hours and sleep in as late as we want."

Her head shot up when he said "make love". But he needed her to know exactly what he was asking. If she took him home with her, he didn't want to leave anything to chance. He fully intended on making her scream as he discovered every inch of her...and let her discover every inch of him.

"I have been very patient," he added. "All day long."

"You're not supposed to have sex on the first date."

"Says who?"

Gia Dawn

"All the experts." She crossed her arms over her chest.

"What do the experts say about seeing fairies?" he countered. "We have to decide what works for us...and you have to decide what works for you." He tucked her hair back from her cheek, barely resisting the urge to beg her to say yes. "I said make love," he added softly. "We both know there's a difference."

A crease of worry tried to form between her brows. He smoothed his finger down the wrinkle. "I intend to love you, Meara, whether you believe me now or not."

He could still see her doubt. Taking her hand, he pulled her to her feet, throwing a stack of bills on the table. "Back to your place so I can get my bike." He didn't try to hide the disappointment in his voice, and was completely astounded by her next words.

"I think my bed's big enough for two. You don't snore do you?"

ಖ಄಄ಚ

Jamison led her to the bedroom and closed the door behind them. Meara trembled when he turned to her again and she saw the hunger simmering in his eyes. She took an involuntary step back and he smiled at her softly.

"Come here." He held out his hand and leaned against the door, legs spread wide as he waited for her to obey. His gaze narrowed when she still hung back, but his hand didn't drop an inch. "Do you want me to go home? Last chance to back out."

Meara tried to return his smile. "I just don't want you to think I'm too easy."

His chuckle would have charmed a nun. "I know you're not easy. How long has it been? Tell the truth. No smart-ass answer, not this time."

Grinning despite her nervousness, Meara glanced at him through her lashes. "Figured me out already, huh?"

He shook his head. "Not at all. But I intend to spend the next several years making strides in that direction. Tell you what, forget the true confessions bit. How about I'll take off my shirt and you take off yours." He pulled his tee shirt over his head. "Your turn."

Meara swallowed, the atmosphere suddenly grown dark and dangerous. He was more beautiful than she'd imagined and she wanted him with a fever. However it ended up in the morning, she needed to be with him now. Taking a deep and calming breath, she unbuttoned her blouse, wishing she had on some frilly bra and panties. Not that she thought he'd let her keep them on long.

She saw the appreciation on his face as she stepped closer, thinking he was every bit as glorious as any Celtic god or hero of old. Muscled and tanned from the hours he spent on the ocean, his body invited her to run her hands across it, feeling the heat of his skin, tasting his lips and whatever else she could manage to get her mouth on.

He hooked a finger down the front of her bra and pulled her against him, his sigh of triumph a magical sound. "Kiss me, lassie," he commanded, his hands cupping her bottom to urge her hips against his. "Make the first move, and I'll do the rest...this time." He ran his tongue across his teeth, his smile growing by the minute.

Meara giggled, relaxing into his embrace. He really was wonderful. He knew all the right things to say—and she was absolutely certain he knew all the right things to do.

She traced her fingers across his mouth, watching in fascination as his eyes darkened and his breath sped up. His cock swelled in his jeans and he wiggled her harder against him, the thrill of the contact sending a blaze of desire racing from between her legs—a need so intense, Meara could not suppress a whimper.

"Now we're making progress," he said in satisfaction. His fingers traced up her back to undo the hook of her bra before sliding the straps off her shoulders. "I'm still waiting for that kiss," he mouthed against her hair, one finger dipping beneath her bra to barely brush against her nipple. Meara felt it swell, begging for a harder touch.

He thunked his head back against the door, as if daring her to come and get him.

It was an unspoken offer Meara couldn't resist. Leaning deeper into his embrace, she rose on her tiptoes and gently touched his lips with hers. He opened his mouth instantly, eagerly allowing her to delve deeper, and Meara let the kiss grow stronger, teasing him with her tongue...only to cry out in stunned desire when Jamison took over.

He wrapped one hand around her waist, holding her steady while he drove his tongue deep into her mouth. Meara shuddered and her knees grew weak as he plundered the heat of her. He took his time, easing the pressure, gentling the kiss, giving her a second to catch her breath before his tongue speared once more between her lips.

Without warning, he picked her up and carried her to bed, pulling away just long enough to peel off her bra and unzip her jeans. He tugged them down her legs and tossed them onto the floor before doing the same with his own.

"So much for ceremony," Meara muttered, pleased when he smiled and jumped next to her on the bed.

"Do you need ceremony, sweet fairy princess?" He laid his hand on her stomach and she tried not to tremble. "You are as beautiful as I imagined."

Meara felt herself blush. "I have too many freckles."

"I happen to adore freckles." His hand roamed lower. "I don't need perfect...I just need you." His fingers slipped into her curls before sliding down her thigh. They closed around one knee and pulled her legs apart.

Meara shook when those fingers trailed up to nudge into her slit.

"Um...shouldn't we turn off the light or something?" Her voice sounded as breathless as she felt.

"I'd rather not," he replied, his fingers beginning to circle her clit.

Meara whimpered and bit her lip. Jamison chuckled and captured her eyes with his as he snugged one finger high into her cunt. She was wet, ready, the scent of her desire strong and heady in the air. Jamison's eyes burned as he pressed his finger deeper.

"Oh my G—" she started to cry, but Jamison stopped her with a shake of his head.

"Don't you dare say god," he warned, grinning wickedly. "Unless, of course, you are referring to me." He let his thumb rub her clit while she squirmed and bucked against his hand. "More?" he asked bending his head to lap at one nipple.

Meara fought back the urge to scream like Banshee as Jamison continued his magical seduction. When he clamped his lips around her nipple and sucked it into his mouth, the sensation that shot down her stomach was wild beyond imagining. His teeth bit the budded flesh, tightening to the point of almost pain, and Meara threaded her fingers in his hair, not certain whether she was drawing him nearer or pushing him away.

She cried out when he released the pressure, licking softly as if to soothe her now aching flesh. But he soon had a different torment in mind.

He sat up and took both her knees in his hands, spreading them wide across the bed until she had no way to hide from the heat of his eyes upon her. Then his hands moved to part her sex even more.

"Sweet, soft and ready for the taking," he murmured, rasping his thumb over her clit. Meara gasped and grabbed handfuls of the sheet.

"Relax, my little fairy. I promise you will not regret it."

"I don't know if I can," she replied. "I swear my toes are already curling up."

A chuckle rumbled deep in his throat. "Then I won't keep you waiting." He trailed his mouth down her stomach. "Very nice," he whispered before thrusting his tongue into the heat and wet of her sex.

Meara cried out and arched off the bed, but Jamison held her down as he tongued her hard again. Now his mouth nibbled at the sensitive pearl of her clit, slipping over and over her flesh until Meara grew weak with the bliss of it.

His thick finger drove high into her cunt, this added pleasure wringing another cry of longing from her throat. She had never known it could be like this...that her entire being could ache and burn with so much desire she thought she would melt from the heat of it.

When he pushed a second finger in with the first, the shock of the stretch caused Meara to gasp. Jamison stilled instantly, but did not pull his fingers free.

"It has been a long time." He moved up to look at her again. His face glowed with triumph and need. "Trust me," he said, bringing his mouth to hers.

He was gentle, letting Meara explore the taste of her on his tongue. For a long time he did not move the fingers he had buried in her cunt, allowing her to adjust to his touch. His thumb began to circle her clit, faster and faster as he built her need again. Meara's hips rose and ground against his hand, begging for him to give her release and let her fly into the paradise he offered.

At last he slipped his fingers free, only to plunge them into her once more. Meara cried out his name, her words swallowed by his kiss. Deeper and harder he took her with his hand, working the tight sheath of her cunt until Meara couldn't think, couldn't speak, the spark flaming deep inside her body to rise in wave after wave of release. She shook wildly in his arms, her body clenching tight around his fingers, needing more, wanting more, giving him everything he demanded.

"Ahhhhh, uhhhhhh, Jamison!" Meara screamed, unable to stop the words as she came. Every inch of her body begged him to continue his punishing touch. "Please," she whispered, her teeth digging into his shoulder. "Give me all of you."

Before her trembling had even stopped, he pulled a condom out of his pants pocket, slid it on and rolled on top of her, positioning the wide head of his cock at the entrance to her cunt.

"Look at me," he ordered. "See how much I need you."

His eyes were dark, the green of long forgotten forests. She was not frightened by the hunger. She longed for it as much as he, raking her nails along his back as he speared her slowly with his length. Inch by inch, he worked himself inside her, controlled and careful not to cause her any pain.

But Meara grew tired of his cautious coupling. She curled her legs around his hips and pulled him in as far as he would go.

Now it was Jamison's turn to cry out as he felt her sex clench tight around him. They fit together perfectly, as if she had been put in the world for no one else. He could feel the thick wall of her cunt contract, quivering as her body made room to accept him.

The last of his tenuous control slipped. He pulled out and drove hard into her again, reveling in the sound of her whimpers as she clung to him in desperate need. There was nothing that could stop him now.

His cock swelled and jerked inside her, his balls clenched tight against his body, and he swore his love to her over and over as the rush of release nearly broke him down. He had never been so satisfied in his life as he fell into her arms.

"Jamison," Meara whispered, her hips still wiggling beneath his. "I, um, oh hell, could we please do that again?"

Chapter Five

"Meareee!"

Meara rolled over and looked at the alarm clock. Nearly four a.m.—way too early to wake up. If she woke up she would think of Jamison. And if she thought of Jamison she would grow lonely and hot and needy. The ache was already beginning to build and he'd been working double shifts for two days straight.

"Meeeeeaaarrrreeeeee!"

This time she turned on the fan, hoping the noise would drown out the sound of the sniveling outside.

"MEEEEAAARRREEEEEEEE!"

This was bad, really bad. How was she supposed to sleep with all that racket going on? She pulled on her robe and stomped her way to the door. After turning on the porch light, Meara stared in utter disbelief at the large plastic wasp-catchers she'd stuck up on plant hooks just before she'd gone to bed. Although she'd been forced to make the holes larger, the end result had succeeded beyond her expectations.

Nearly a dozen trapped fairies jostled and pinched at each other in their struggle to be free, and several pieces of wing and fur stuck to the sides of the bubbles.

"Well, well, well," she said, opening the door and crossing her arms over her chest. "Lookey what I've got here."

"Meareeee," whined one, its face twisted into a pitiful expression. "Lets us outs. We don't likes it here." It screamed when another fairy clawed up its back to bare its teeth at Meara.

She watched them for several long moments, their pleas for freedom actually tugging at her heart. What was she supposed to do? Leave them trapped to die slow and horrible deaths, tearing each other apart in their desperation to escape? It was one thing to make them suffer horribly in her work...quite another to actually do it in real life.

"Will you go away and leave me alone?"

Their pinched faces glared back blankly. A fight started in one catcher as two of the more aggressive fae attacked a smaller one who was trying to lick some honey off the side of the ball. The sound of rending flesh was more than Meara could take. She twisted the plastic catchers open and ducked back into the house before they had time to fly free. Amazingly they did not scratch or claw at the door. After several minutes of silence, Meara grew curious. She opened the door a crack and snuck a peek outside. The fairies were nowhere to be seen, the only sign of their capture the tiny bits of iridescent dust that floated in the lamplight.

A single feather drifted down to land on Meara's porch, so badly mangled she couldn't even tell its color. Without thinking, she reached down to pick it up, shaking her head in disgust when she realized her intention.

Her plan had worked. They had gone and left her alone. Funny that she felt more abandoned than fulfilled. Stupid...silly...sad.

Meara clutched her robe tighter and stepped into the night. No lights flickered in the trees, no orbs glowed in her garden. It was dark and silent and no other thing was near. A crisp night breeze rose up from the ocean, bringing with it the faint sound of waves lapping against the shore. Drawn to watch the surf roll in, Meara slipped on a pair of old sneakers and made her way slowly to the edge of the cliffs.

A few clouds scudded across the moon's bright light and stars twinkled like jewels in the bowl of the sky. The surf sighed against the strip of beach, and Meara could see the bob of fairy orbs surrounding two glowing forms.

Intrigued, Meara moved closer, curious to see if some young lovers were having a hidden tryst near the water. High-pitched laughter was followed by a deeper male chuckle, and as she listened, Meara began to think she knew the secretive pair.

"Banshee? Lugh? That you?" Her voice carried far in the still of the night.

The laughter grew as the two forms floated up to hover in the air, holding hands and smiling in sheer delight. Banshee and Lugh acted like two teenagers in love as they waved happily.

"I see you managed to find each other," Meara said wistfully.

"She adores me." Lugh wrapped one huge arm around the fairy's tiny waist. "And I think she is more beautiful than any creature I have ever seen," he added, his eyes glowing.

"We can't thank you enough," Banshee gushed, blushing when Lugh stroked her cheek. "If you ever need a favor, just ask."

Meara smiled. "Someday I might take you up on that."

Lugh glanced worriedly across the dark expanse of ocean. "We have to go. I promised Banshee we'd watch the sun rise over Ireland, high in the clouds where no one else can find us." He wiggled his eyebrows and Banshee giggled before they sailed up and out of view.

The fairy lights followed them in an arc of color, leaving Meara alone again. She smiled, however, knowing Jamison would be off by late afternoon. And he'd promised to show her his place...starting with the bedroom.

ᏠᏡᏢ

The phone woke them before dawn had even broken. When Jamison answered his voice grew dim. "This isn't funny anymore." He slammed his cell-phone shut.

Meara smiled and swiped the bangs out of her eyes. "Whasa matter?"

Her sleepy gaze lulled him back to peace. With a sigh, he slid back in bed beside her and ran his fingers across her cheek. "Boring work stuff."

"Mmmm." She propped up on one elbow and the sheet slipped off her shoulders to catch on the soft swell of her breasts. "I like boring work stuff." She shook her head when she saw the way his eyes had fastened on the tightening nipples outlined by the sheet. "Nope. I need some coffee first."

She yawned and stretched, letting the sheet fall completely free.

He leaned in fast and sucked one of the dusky pearls into his mouth. His cock stood to attention when she stifled a whimpered moan.

"You are so bad," Meara scolded, running her fingers through his hair and pulling his mouth closer. "I like that in a man...after he makes me breakfast and coffee."

Jamison looked down at his swollen cock and sighed. "Are you really going to make me wait?"

Her laugh made him want to touch her even more, and when she threw off the covers and ran bare-bottomed to the kitchen, he followed, letting his cock lead the way. He'd feed her and woo her with his excellent morning brew...then he'd get to have his fun.

A few minutes later, Jamison poured coffee and sat next to Meara at the table. "Drink fast," he said, nudging an elbow into her side.

Meara laughed before sipping slowly at the steaming liquid. "Got anything that remotely resembles pop-tarts? Sugar, flour, butter?"

"I could make you some whole-wheat French toast."

"You've got to be kidding. I don't do whole wheat. No doughnuts?"

Jamison chuckled and stood. "You'll love it, I promise."

Meara snorted. "Tell me about what's bugging you at work."

Jamison watched her open the fridge. "Butter is in the little cubbyhole marked butter. Eggs in the egg holders."

"Good grief," he heard her mutter. "Do you have everything in here where it's supposed to be?"

"A place for everything and everything in its place. Too many years of military training."

"Uh huh." She stuck out her tongue as she plopped the butter on the counter.

He let his gaze darken. "Do that again," he ordered, one hand tangling in her hair to pull her face to his.

"After breakfast." Nonetheless, Meara touched her fingers to his mouth, the gesture compelling in its simplicity.

Jamison sighed and turned back to the toast.

"Work?" Meara prompted.

"You are as single-minded as a kid," he teased, breaking eggs into a glass bowl. But he really wanted to discuss his frustrations with someone. Someone who would take his side and then take him to bed to soothe his worried mind. "I've had three recent cases where evidence has gone missing. No evidence, no trial. The bastards walked off scot-free."

In spite of himself, he threw an egg across the room. It hit the wall and splattered in all directions. "Sorry," he said when Meara raised a delicate brow. "It's just...when I find out who's stealing from the files, I plan to put us both out of our misery." He flipped the French toast with way too much energy and growled when the piece landed in the sink.

"That one's yours." Meara curled her arms around his waist. "But are you sure it's a someone, and not a something?" She pointed out the kitchen window to where a group of fairies tugged insistently at the lock on Jamison's mailbox.

"Oh, hell."

"Yeah, you think you've got them under your thumb," Meara stated in an *I-told-you-so* voice, "but you can't control them anymore than I can...not twenty-four/seven."

Jamison pounded on the window. The twisted faces stared back at him in utter disregard. "Shit." He piled the hot bread on one plate and doused the entire lot with powdered sugar.

"Now you're talking." Meara licked her finger and stuck it in the fine white powder.

"Then why just my evidence?"

"You're their best friend?" She poured them both more coffee. "How do I know? They smell you?" She took a tentative bite of the French toast. "Mmm, not bad, but it needs a bit more sugar. She reached for the box but stopped in mid-grab, slapping a hand to her forehead. "Why didn't I think of this before? I have the perfect solution. A fairy catcher."

Jamison gave her a frown. "A fairy catcher. This is your perfect solution."

"Yep. I have two at home, and they work great. Only problem is, I don't know what to do with the miserable creatures once I've caught them. But the fairies can't resist if you put something sugary and sweet inside."

Jamison looked at her as though she had finally lost her mind. "What on earth are you talking about?"

Meara gave him a glance that said *oh-you-stupid-man* and started to explain. "I bought two wasp-catchers. I was going to see if they would catch fairies. Well they work—at least the one time I tried. I caught about a dozen...of course I had to let them back out again. Damn things look so pathetic trapped with their little noses and faces smooshed against the cage." She frowned. "I used up the last of my honey. Do you think they'd go for lime Jell-O?"

Jamison looked as if she were talking some foreign language. "How does this help me?"

"We put one in the evidence room. If fairies are responsible for the stuff being taken, they won't be able to resist."

Realization dawned slowly over Jamison's face. "And if we don't get any fairies, we'll know it's a someone and not a something."

"Duh." Meara tapped her knuckles lightly on his head. "Get it?"

"And, um, how do we plan on getting this fairy trap in the evidence room?"

Meara let her smile widen. "That's your problem. I can't be expected to think up everything."

෮෮෮

"I can't believe I let you talk me into this." Jamison stared at the blobs of green Jell-O dripping on the floor.

"Hold it still," Meara ordered, spooning in more of the sticky lime goo. "Almost done."

"Why do we need both?" Jamison sat one plastic orb on the table and picked up the other one. He'd never done anything so utterly ridiculous in his life, he thought, staring stupidly at the contraption. Two pieces of plastic screwed together to make a single ball, with a narrowing tube that opened into one side. The theory was that wasps, bees, and yes...even fairies...could crawl in, but the smaller opening inside prevented them from crawling out. The bait—in this case, lime Jell-O—was spread liberally inside to lure the creatures to their doom.

Except, of course, Meara insisted on setting them free, with a stern warning not to bother her again. Which, as far as Jamison could tell, worked about as well as ordering the grass not to grow.

"There." Meara smiled her satisfaction. "I'll go hang one up, and in about five minutes, we should catch at least four or five." The look in her eyes was almost maniacal as she carefully suspended one trap on a pole outside her door.

"Shhhh," she motioned him back inside, and they both peeked out of a window to watch the show begin.

She was right on the money, Jamison had to admit, as the fairies swarmed in by the dozen. They actually fought to be the first inside, the temptation of the sweet treat vastly overcoming their caution or control.

In minutes the catcher was full, with more tiny creatures still trying to get inside.

"Told ya." Meara's voice was triumphant. "The miserable things can't resist."

Jamison gave her an assessing glare. "You're taking this way too seriously. Should I be concerned?"

She laughed. "Maybe. But as long as I stick to fairies and not Hansels and Gretels, I think the world is safe. Are you ready?"

"Do I have a choice?" He frowned at plastic ball now swinging wildly back and forth, knowing, with a true and utter defeat, that he really had none at all.

Barely a half hour later, Meara pulled her car onto a side street behind the police station. She watched Jamison fling a handful of fairy dust high into the night sky—just in case any wandering fairies decided to get nosey—and followed him to the back door.

"This is crazy." He stopped dead in his tracks. "If we get caught, I'll be arrested...and so will you."

"If we don't do this," Meara replied, "the bad guys will never get caught. Sometimes you have to do the wrong thing to get the right result."

He stared at her for several long seconds. "I never thought of it like that before," he said, slowly shaking his head. "Not that I intend to go along with your twisted logic every time you ask me to."

Meara snorted. "What makes you think I'm ever gonna ask you to again?" She poked him in the ribs. "Shhhhh, we're almost there." She peeked in the window of the door, enjoying the subterfuge with an almost eager delight. She hadn't done anything this risky in her life. "Is that him?"

Jamison looked to where the new guard sat snoring in his chair. "The idiot's actually fallen asleep. This could be our lucky night. If we're caught, I'll just claim I was proving he was not doing his job. Come on." He took out his key and unlocked the door. It slid open soundlessly and they crept quietly down the hall.

The guard didn't move as they opened the evidence room door and hurried quickly inside. It was filled from floor to ceiling with metal shelves, each one stacked with perfectly matched brown boxes. Hundreds and hundreds of brown boxes.

"How on earth do you ever find anything in here?" Meara ran a finger along the edge of one shelf.

"Shhhhh." Jamison frowned. "That guard could wake up at any time."

Meara snorted. "Hardly."

She shut up anyway when he gave her a nasty glance. Huh, he would pay for that one later. She felt like poking him again just for fun.

"Where should we put this damned thing?" The scowl on his face was so serious, Meara giggled. When his lips thinned even more, she giggled again, clamping a hand over her own mouth to keep the laughter from spilling over. Tears streamed from her eyes as she tried desperately to remain silent despite the increasing humor of the whole situation.

She nodded to the corner. "Stick it over there," she whispered through her fingers.

Jamison took it out of the box and cursed when a glob of green Jell-O fell on his shoe. Meara thought she would die from the effort it took not to squeal in amusement.

"And now?" His mood had grown even darker.

"We...we...h-have t-to h-hide," Meara managed to choke out between chuckles. "Then you h-have t-to s-s-say...h-ere little fairies...h-h-here l-little—f-f—" She couldn't finish the sentence she was giggling so hard.

Jamison glowered and shoved her behind a metal rack, pressing his face close to hers. "So, you think this is funny?"

Meara nodded, still not trusting herself to speak. Then she saw a small gleam of mischief twinkle in his eyes.

"What was I supposed to say? Here little fairy...here little fairy fairy?" His mouth twitched up at one corner.

Then they heard the unmistakable sound of buzzing wings.

"I'll be damned," Jamison said. "This crazy scheme of yours might actually work."

Meara fought down the urge to scream *I-told-you-so* as they watched a trio of fairies hover over the catcher.

They seemed torn between temptations—eat the Jell-O or poke into the boxes. The Jell-O quickly won out. Like a bad cartoon show, they followed each other into the catcher, practically rolling in the sticky goo as they purred their satisfaction.

In seconds, Jamison had picked up the plastic ball and shoved it back into the box. The muted protests of the fairies barely floated on the air.

"Time to go," he said, opening the door. Over his shoulder, Meara could see the guard still asleep in his chair.

The box began to shake as the fairies realized their dilemma and tried to escape. Jamison held onto it for dear life as he followed Meara back to the outside door. But before he could get it open, the guard snorted and raised his head.

Chapter Six

Meara shoved Jamison into the closest doorway just as the guard opened his eyes. "Um...could you tell me how to get back to the front desk?" She twirled her hair, opened her eyes wide and gave the befuddled man her best Marilyn Monroe imitation, fighting the urge to grimace when he bought it tooth and nail.

"A pretty lady like you shouldn't be wandering back here alone." The guard stood and hiked his pants up around his substantial girth. "You could get into all kinds of trouble."

Meara attempted a sultry pout, wanting nothing more than to roll her eyes at the man's stupidity. "You're not gonna arrest me, are you?" When Jamison snorted, Meara coughed to cover the noise. "I was supposed to meet someone for dinner, but it seems he stood me up. Can you imagine that?"

The guard's smile grew. "The man must be a total fool," he said, stepping close and running a hand up Meara's arm.

She tried not to shudder as his sweaty palm scraped across her skin.

Just then, Jamison stepped back into the hallway. "There you are, my dear," he said, taking her other arm and pulling her away from the guard. "I've been looking all over for you."

The guard dropped his hand to his holster. "Who are you?"

"Jamison Murphy, Petty Officer First Class, United States Coast Guard Investigative Service."

"Got any ID?"

"Of course." Jamison handed the box to Meara. "Don't open this until we get outside," he admonished. "It's a birthday present." He pulled his badge from his pocket and showed it to the guard.

The guard frowned. "You're not allowed in here."

Jamison frowned back, and Meara could see he was gearing up for an argument. Men, why did they always feel the need to pull rank?

"Jimmy, baby," she whined, batting her lashes at him. "I'm hungry. You promised me a special dinner." She stamped her foot, making sure it landed on Jimmy-baby's toes.

He grunted, but was smart enough to take the hint. "You are so right, my darling. Dinner it is." He turned back to the guard. "Sorry to have bothered you, my man, we'll let you get back to your job." With a quick nod, he grabbed Meara's arm and practically hauled her down the hallway. He unlocked the door and let them out, heaving a huge sigh of relief when they were finally back in Meara's car.

"That was way too close. If that guard decides to write a report, I'll have a lot of explaining to do."

The box shook violently and the sound of shrieking fairies grew.

"We'd better not let them out here." Meara started her car and drove quickly to the quiet street her parents lived on. "Don't let them go until they've answered some questions." She turned on the inside light and watched Jamison pull the catcher out of the box. The trapped fairies blinked as their eyes adjusted.

"Jamseeee." A pretty sprite with rainbow wings smiled, showing a double row of teeth.

Jamison shook his finger at it. "Are you the ones who've been taking my evidence?"

They stared at him in complete non-comprehension.

"Have you been messing with Jamseee's things?" Meara added. "If you tell the truth, we'll let you out. If not...somehow I don't think you want to stay in there forever."

The sprite bared her fangs even more.

Meara shrugged and nodded to Jamison. "Okay, put them back in the box."

"Wait, wait, wait," begged one with sticky purple feathers. "We'll tell, we'll tell." It pulled off a piece of the sprite's wing, who turned and bit off a mouthful of its feathers.

"I'm listening." Jamison sat the catcher on his lap and folded his arms across his chest, looking for all the world like a disgruntled father scolding his wayward children.

Meara had never thought of Jamison as a father, but she realized he would be a good one—the perfect mix of discipline and fun. She imagined him laughing as he tossed their son or daughter in the air or smiling softly as he kissed one a sweet goodnight. She shook her head to clear the pictures from her mind. Wanting too much was never a good thing.

"Bad things in room," the third fairy offered, licking Jell-O off its foot. "Not for Jamseeeee."

Jamison gave Meara a puzzled glance. "Do you think they're talking about the drugs?"

"Drugs, drugs, drugs, drugs, drugs," the purple one sang. "Nots, nots, nots, nots, nots."

Meara had to chuckle. "Do you think that's the fairy version of just say no?"

"I hope not. How am I supposed to convince them to leave the stuff alone?"

Meara shook her finger at the fae. "If you take the drugs, Jamsee cannot catch the baddest guys."

"Baddest?" His voice was thick with amusement. "And I don't think we're going to start this Jamsee business."

Three pairs of fairy eyes grew round in surprise. Then, to Meara's utter astonishment, the trio put their heads together and whispered among themselves in some language she had never heard. When they looked at Meara and Jamison again, their expressions had changed completely.

"Done," said the purple-feathered fae. "Jamseee catches." The other two nodded their heads in agreement.

Jamison gave Meara an interested look. "Should we believe them?"

"I don't know. I've never heard them sound so serious. Do you think they really understand?"

"We does, we does," came the affirmative reply.

"Then off you go." Jamison unscrewed the plastic ball and let the fairies free before rolling down his window and watching them fly off into the night. "I guess that settles that."

He closed the window and put the box in the backseat before he pinned her with a sultry look.

"Take off your jeans," he said suddenly, his voice calm and in control.

Meara's wasn't. "Here?" She glanced around uneasily. "What if somebody sees?"

His laugh soothed her ears. "This from the woman who just broke into a police station and could have been arrested for stealing valuable evidence? Come on, Meara, getting arrested for public indecency is a much smaller offense." Jamison's look dared her to refuse. "Do it." He reached over and turned off the car light.

His eyes narrowed as Meara reached down to untie her shoes. She slipped them off and reached for the zipper of her jeans.

"Go on."

Her heart raced when she realized he was serious. Without another word, she did as he demanded and shivered when her bare legs met the cold. A flick of his wrist turned the car back on, and a welcome heat blew from the vent.

"Are the doors locked?"

Meara pushed the button and nodded.

"Good. Now take off your panties, lean back against the door and spread your legs."

She felt wanton stripping in the car, brazen and sexy and bold. She managed to get her panties off without too much difficulty, and leaned back against the door. Her bravado faltered, however, when she came to the next part of his demand. Raising her legs up onto the seat, she let her knees slowly fall apart.

Jamison wasn't satisfied. He hooked both hands behind her knees and pulled her hips toward him, pushing one leg back to the floor. When the chilly air hit her open sex, Meara shivered until he placed one hot hand on her mound. His fingers probed the hill of her clit, rasping and pinching the knot of flesh into wild and vibrant life.

"Tell me what you want. Should I make you come like this or do you want my fingers inside you?" Desire spiked high into her cunt, the blast shooting all the way to her breasts. His fingers stilled when she did not answer. "Talk to me." He made no move to continue.

Her heart was pounding so loud she thought surely he would hear it. "Both. I want both."

"Now we're getting somewhere." His fingers began to strum her again, easily working her arousal higher. Meara squirmed on the seat, nearly screaming in frustration when he refused to give her what she'd asked for. Her body was open, empty and waiting...needing him to fill her and take her over the edge.

She could feel the climax building—with each circle of his fingers her want built higher. Without shame she bucked her hips against his hand. "Damn it, Jamison I—ahhhhhhh." Her voice cried out in shocked surprise as Jamison finally took her with his hand.

Meara moaned when he drove his fingers inside her with one hard thrust. She cried his name when he wiggled even deeper, stroking the sensitive wall of her sex while his other hand worked at her now begging clit.

"Come for me," he told her, surging his fingers high again. And again. And again.

Meara couldn't have stopped even if she tried. Jamison stroked deep inside her in a way he hadn't done before. The teasing of his fingers against the thick bundle of nerves sent the madness racing from her toes. Her climax hit her hard and fast, the rush of pleasure climbing and climbing as her cunt clenched hard around his hand and her body shook uncontrollably.

He continued to thumb her clit as the waves of bliss subsided. When Meara's breathing slowed, she peeked at him out of one eye. "Come here and kiss me," he said, reaching for her hand. "And then take me home with you. I have other plans for us tonight."

ജ൏ഠ൙

Jamison sat on her couch, his shirt unbuttoned and his legs spread wide. He pointed to the floor in front of him. "Kneel."

Meara swallowed when she saw the look that crept into his eyes. She took a tentative step toward him, willing her legs not to falter.

"Now," he added without the slightest bit of humor. Meara wasn't certain whether she should be totally turned on or apprehensive by this new side of Jamison's personality.

Turned on won when he lowered the zipper of his jeans. She dropped to her knees before him, her gaze riveted to the swelling bulge between his thighs. His fist tangled in her hair, pulling her face toward his stomach. He smelled of sweat and male arousal, and Meara rubbed her cheek against his skin as if she could draw his scent into her.

He let out a sigh and leaned back into the couch, shoving his hips forward. His hand stayed threaded in her hair, keeping her close against his stomach. "Taste me, little fairy. I want to feel your lips around me."

Desire hit heavy again between Meara's thighs. The ache already tingled in her sex, an urgent need to please him in any way he demanded.

Timeless magic surrounded them in the night. Was he the hero who had rescued her from danger, now awaiting his reward in the hot kiss of her mouth? She would repay him in full for his bravery and daring, listening to him cry her name as she brought him to sweet release.

Wind howled as it swept in from the sea, whistling through the cracks in her small cottage, creating an atmosphere that reeked of myth and legend.

As her hands slid up his thighs, Meara admired the feel of well-used muscle, strong and thick beneath the tight denim. Jamison sighed again, the sound mingling with the wind-song and the faint crash of waves upon the shore. She felt wanton and bold, like a woman who knew all the secrets of love and intended to share them with the man who held her heart. Trailing her face down his stomach, she let her hands move to cup his cock. This time his sigh grew into a moan as he arched up to press himself against her. Meara fingered his zipper all the way down and pulled his jeans apart to set his swollen length free.

"Take them off," he ordered, lifting his hips.

Meara did as he demanded, her eyes widening in admiration as she slid the pants to the floor. He raised his feet to let her peel the jeans off completely. This time she let her mouth travel up his leg, splaying her fingers over his hips.

His hand tugged in her hair, tilting her face back until her eyes met his. "You are the fairest of them all," he whispered, running a thumb over her bottom lip. "Tell me you love me, Meara, that you know we belong together."

She wanted to say the words, she really did, and he made it sound so easy to believe as he whispered his truth for her to hear. Instead, she smiled and sucked his thumb into her mouth, rolling her tongue over his skin until his eyes slid shut and he growled his need.

She let her teeth scrape against his chest as she moved her mouth down his flat stomach. His erection pressed between her breasts and she cupped them together with her hands, encasing him between the soft mounds of flesh.

"Please don't stop," he said. The words came out like a plea.

Meara had no intention of stopping as she took the velvet length of him in her hands. She rolled his cock between her palms, loving the way his skin slid so soft and supple over hers. She stroked him faster, his groans like music in her ears as the wind blew wilder outside in the night.

But she needed more. She needed to taste the strength of him, run her mouth over his flesh until he both begged her to stop and begged her to continue. At last she wrapped her lips around the tip of his cock, letting the heat of him slide into her mouth inch by delicious inch. He jerked as she sucked him in. His thighs quivered on the couch and Meara could feel him fight to keep from thrusting too hard against her.

She withdrew her mouth slowly, listening to him swallow back his cry of frustration. Her own body burned with a rising fever, her cunt aching to feel the weight of him pushing deep inside. It was a joyous pain, one she would never care to give up. She sucked him faster and faster, matching his rhythm as his hips rose to meet her mouth. The taste of him dripped on her tongue, tangy and thick and perfect man.

She glanced up to see his head thrown back against the couch, the muscles in his neck taut as he struggled to keep control. She let a hand reach down to squeeze his balls before she grew even bolder, licking her finger to nudge it up into the crease of his ass.

To her absolute surprise he bent one knee and placed his foot on the couch, giving her greater access to explore the tight ring of muscle.

"Fair warning," he whispered through gritted teeth. "Whatever you do to me, I plan to return in full and greater measure."

A thrill of fear and expectation raced up Meara's spine. Did she dare? Was she ready to take their discovery further? Already her tiny entrance screamed in need, asking for things she'd never dreamed of. The thought of him reaching deep into her ass drove her desire to a pitch she had never known before.

Throwing all caution to the wind, she wiggled her finger deep between Jamison's cheeks, piercing the ring of muscle while he cried out her name. When he growled, she pulled her finger out and sank it deep into him again. He clenched both hands around her shoulders, pulling her mouth hard onto his cock as she continued to drive her finger into the opening of his ass.

Every muscle in his body tensed and she felt his balls curl up into the root of his cock. He screamed, a low and guttural sound as the length of him stiffened even more and he came with a rush in her mouth.

Meara held onto him as he jerked his hips beneath her, swallowing the seed he jutted down her throat. His growls died slowly and his breathing became more steady. Meara slipped her lips away and laid her head down on his thigh.

"Look at me," he finally commanded.

Meara found herself suddenly shy as she remembered his earlier admonition. Full and greater measure he had promised...she began to anticipate just what that meant. Very slowly she lifted her eyes to his. They were the darkest green she had ever seen, almost black in the candle light.

"You know what I am going to say," he warned her, a terrible smile tugging at his lips. "Now it's your turn to pay."

Meara felt the blood heat up her cheeks. Damn, she hadn't planned to blush. She'd planned to act as if she'd done this every day of her life. But Jamison knew better. She'd told him as much in the beginning. And the feral look on his face made her want to run away and lock herself in her room.

"Come here, my precious," he hissed, crooking his finger at her. "My turn to play."

Meara shivered in need and hesitation. Did he plan what she thought he planned? "Um...I, uh...what are you going to do?"

Her nervousness must have shown in her voice, for his eyes softened and an easier smile tilted up one corner of his mouth. "Nothing you don't want me to...but you already made it clear you wanted to. Do you have a vibrator?"

Meara swallowed. "The batteries are dead."

"Doesn't matter, go get it anyway. You don't really want me to wait...do you?" The hint of threat in his voice was enough to spur her to delicious dread. "If you don't have any lubrication, we'll need some olive oil. Got any?"

"In the kitchen," she whispered, her throat closing around the words. "The cabinet over the sink."

He chuckled, a rich and heady sound. "You have three minutes to get your toy and meet me back here." He pulled her face up to his and kissed her gently on the mouth. "Say no now," he stated.

Her legs were shaking so bad she didn't know how she would stand. "What if I don't like it?" The catch in her voice was obvious.

The truth in his was just as plain. "Then we stop and move on to other pleasures." He bent close and bit the lobe of her ear. The sting was enough to make Meara whimper as a new thrill of longing raced across her flesh. "Two minutes," he whispered.

Meara swallowed and stood, somehow managing to make it to her bedroom without stumbling. She could hear Jamison whistle as he rummaged in her kitchen, and she wanted to shout at him to stop, give her more time to decide...but all the while she was digging through her drawers, searching for the thing he'd demanded.

She actually squeaked when she heard him come into the bedroom. "I can't find it," she admitted, clasping her hands together. Then she froze when she saw the new look on his face.

He stood rigid in the doorway, a piece of paper crumpled in his hand. "When were you going to tell me about this?" One clenched fist held up the letter for her to see. "You must have thought it was some great joke to hear me tell you how much I love you while all the time you were packing to leave."

Meara felt her hackles rise at his unfounded accusation. "That's not fair, and you know it. We only met a few days ago. Do you really expect me to change my life based on some sexual fling?" She wanted to bite back the words as soon as they'd left her mouth. The need to run to him and beg his forgiveness set her teeth on edge. She gritted back the emotion—Meara Magee never begged for anything...at least not until she'd met Jamison.

But his face had already paled beneath his tan and the hurt in his eyes was unmistakable—so was the resolve that turned their green to black. "You are right," he bit out. "What could I possibly have been thinking?" He let the letter slip to the floor before striding back into the living room.

Meara fought with herself as she listened to him put on his jeans and shoes. Wasn't it easier to end things now? Let him go and get on with his life while she got on with hers?

No. No it wasn't. She ran to catch him, to beg him to come back, but she was too late. The furious sound of his motorcycle engine ripped through the air, growing fainter and fainter as he raced out of her life.

ೞೲೞಓ

The storm rolled in just after noon the next day. By dusk it had grown to near gale force, the wind and rain slicing through the air like glass. Meara paced her small living room, growing more and more worried as she watched the weather outside. Lightning streaked from the clouds to crash wildly into the water and thunder rattled the windows.

She'd tried to call Jamison all day, but if he was home, he'd refused to answer.

In desperation, she decided to call him at work. The gruff voice of the Chief Petty Officer only added to her despair. Jamison had gone out on assignment just after dawn. They'd lost contact with his boat several hours ago. If they heard anything they would let her know, but it was too dangerous to send anyone to search for him when they had no clue where to look in the still growing storm.

Jamison was out there somewhere, lost, alone, his radio long dead and no one coming to his aid.

Meara looked to where the lighthouse once stood on the bluff and thought of all the women who had waited through the years for their men to return from the sea. No welcoming glow lit up the night; no beam of light shone to guide her sailor home.

A sharp knock on her door had Meara running to open it, only to freeze in panic when she saw Banshee's dripping form.

"No." Meara backed away. "No. Not now. Go away, I don't want you here!"

She tried to slam the door shut, but Banshee's icy hand closed over hers.

"He is not mine yet," she said, her voice barely quivering. "But he will be soon if you don't do something."

"Me?" Meara's throat wanted to close around the word. "What can I do? You promised me a favor...this is what I want. Find some way to save him!"

Banshee shook her head, true sorrow shadowing her eyes. "We are forbidden to interfere. It has always been so. Meara, if he goes...if he does die, I promise I will see him safely across. It is all I can do." Tears spilled from her eyes as she floated slowly into the sky, her hair and dress trailing like tatters behind her.

Meara wanted to scream, cry, anything to release the harsh emotions rushing through her. She could feel the frenzied energy of the storm. It pulled her toward it, urging her to leave the safety of shelter and journey into its beckoning grip.

She didn't even bother to put on a coat as she followed the call of the elements. Drawn by an ageless need, Meara bent her head and trudged through the mud and muck until she stood on the bare outcrop of land, hoping for any sign of Jamison at all. She knew she was crazy, knew and did not care.

The sea-spray stung her eyes and skin, but she refused to cower from the blast as she paced back and forth, her hair whipping around her like a shroud, her body shaking from the numbing cold.

She couldn't see a thing. The world was dark, bleak, not even the smallest hint that Jamison was near. And yet she swore she could feel him call her across the distance; saw the stubborn look on his face as he struggled to reach her side. They were the same, he had told her, and Meara knew it was true. He was her other half, her soul. Without him, she would shatter. Without him, she would never be whole.

A light bounced along the ground beside her. Meara frowned at the bedraggled fairy who grinned at her through the rain. What on earth would possess it to follow her out into this mess?

On another day she would have cursed it into oblivion, but now she found a comfort in its pulsing light, as if at least one friend had come to keep her company.

She was startled to see another join the first, their contrary natures seeming to take a gleeful delight in taunting the elemental powers. They soared above the water, skimming the sand as they came racing toward Meara's perch on the bluff. And then, to her utter astonishment, hundreds of them descended upon her, talking and laughing as they tangled her hair and picked at her clothes.

Too preoccupied to swat them away, Meara turned again to the ocean, offering pleas for Jamison's safety to every power she knew. Still the fairies continued to flock around her, their combined light so bright she was forced to shield her eyes.

In a flash of understanding, Meara finally saw their game for what it was, the feisty fae's way of helping her cause.

They glowed with the power of a thousand candles, untouched by the wind and rain, their lights shining strong and clear and bright. If Jamison was anywhere close, he would surely see and be guided home. She smiled at them for the first time in her life and stood proud to be among them as they swarmed gaily in the storm.

Jamison struggled to keep his boat afloat. He'd chased the drug runners way too far in his determination to discover where they kept their stash. But he'd found them, the bastards. He knew exactly where they were hiding, and he'd managed to call in the co-ordinates right before his radio went dead. Now he was trying to make it home before his boat was slammed onto the rocks that littered the coast, and he was lost at sea as so many of his ancestors had been before.

He thought he saw Banshee streaking through the rain-drenched night, her wails of warning drowned out by the shriek of the wind and the pounding of the surf. In a perverse way it comforted him to know she was there, that if worse came to worse, someone familiar would ferry him over to the other side. But he had no intention of dying...not now...not tonight.

Meara was still in her cottage by the sea and he had to see her one last time, even if he had to call the very gods themselves to aid him in his quest. He couldn't let his angry words be the last thing said between them.

He grinned fiercely as he fought the raging sea, battling her fury as men had done for ages. "Do your best," he shouted through the gale. "You haven't beaten me yet!" Forcing his numbing hands to keep the wheel steady, he plowed on through the churning waters.

But the elements were winning. Waves splashed over the sides of the boat, filling the hull and weighing her down. He couldn't reach the pump. If he left the wheel he would crash on the rocks.

Banshee swept closer, the look on her face both terrifying and soothing. Shit, he thought, I'm not gonna make it. Damn it all anyway, he still had things to do.

He heard the boat grind and felt it lurch as it scraped across a hidden rock. More water poured in and she listed to one side. Banshee dropped to hover behind him, nodding her head toward a far and distant spot. Jamison followed her glance.

An arc of rainbow colored fire swept to the heavens, radiating a glow that could not be missed. It twisted and writhed in the mist and clouds, but remained a constant beacon, giving him hope that land might be near. In a last ditch effort, Jamison guided his sluggish boat in the direction of the glow. It would be a long shot at best, but given the odds, he didn't have a choice. League by agonizing league, he struggled to make it through.

He hit another rock as the water grew shallow. This time his boat had had enough. With a groan of regret, her bow went down and she sank without another sound. Jamison screamed his frustration as the icy water closed around him. Even with the life jacket he was too far out—he couldn't keep warm long enough to make the swim to shore.

He choked on a mouthful of ocean that forced its way down his throat. His fury knew no bounds. Another wave pushed him under again, holding him below for what seemed like hours. He couldn't breathe, couldn't find the surface. Could feel nothing as the cold set in.

Fuck.

A deathly pale hand reached down for him to grab; Banshee was determined to do her job. He hesitated, torn between coming to terms with his situation, and the need to see his beloved Meara one last time.

Banshee had no such reservations. She curled her fingers in a death grip around his and hauled him from the water. "Not one word," she whispered in his ear as she carried him the last of the way and dumped him on the shore. He could have sworn he actually saw her smile as she vanished like a wisp of smoke.

He laughed in celebration as the fairies swooped to surround him. He didn't care that they poked fingers up his nose or yanked out fistfuls of his hair. He was alive. Period.

"Jamison Murphy," he heard Meara call as she raced to meet him on the shore. "I swear, if you ever scare me like this again, I'll kill you myself and spare Banshee the trouble."

Her face was as beautiful as he remembered, even with mascara dripping down her cheeks and her skin turning blue from the cold. "Maybe Nevada wouldn't be such a bad place to live," he answered, letting his eyes snap shut.

"I've changed my mind," he heard her say as he passed out in her arms.

ಐ೮ಐ೮ೈ

"What in the world?" Jamison stared in fascination at the bits of cloth, string and plastic Meara had strung across the yard. Wind-chimes and pieces of colored glass hung from every tree and bush, spinning and tinkling in the breeze blown from the sea.

Fairies swarmed among the chaos, flitting from one new toy to the next like children the day after Christmas.

Meara smiled wickedly. "That should keep them occupied for quite some time. When they get tired of those—" she pointed to a huge stack of boxes sitting in the kitchen, "—I have plenty more to tempt them with."

Jamison grinned and pulled her tight against him. "Do you have something tucked away that you could use to tempt me?" He rubbed his morning stubble against her neck, causing her to shriek delightedly. He had just gotten her back into bed when they heard the baby laughing.

"Your turn," Meara said, snuggling under the covers. "Bring her in...she might go back to sleep."

"Fat chance," he muttered, pushing open the nursery door. Their new daughter, Brianna, lay staring out the window, babbling excitedly at the fairy preening itself on the outside of the glass.

"Your mother is not going to like this," Jamison said, picking her up and holding her close. "So, let's not tell her for a while, hmmm? A long, long while."

About the Author

To learn more about Gia Dawn, please visit www.giadawn.com. Send an email to Gia at info@giadawn.com or join her Yahoo! group to join in the fun with other readers as well as Gia Dawn! http://groups.yahoo.com/group/giadawn.

Look for these titles

Now Available

Lord Demon's Delight
Lady Strumpet

Heart of the Sea

Sela Carsen

Megan —
Hope you enjoy
the story & the
writing ride!
Sela

Dedication

Without fail, to my family, whose patience knows no bounds.

To Angela James, who, despite her protestations to the contrary, is a Nice Editor.

To Dayna Hart, who held my hand while I speed-wrote the first draft.

To the Crit Wits, who put up with my inconsistencies.

To the Romance Divas, whose humor and knowledge help me grow as a writer and a person.

Prologue

"You will find all you need in the sea."

Ronan Burbank raised an eyebrow. Then he smiled at the old woman with the thick Scottish accent who had obviously crashed his party. He extricated his hand from hers.

"Thank you very much, ma'am. I'm sure I will." As the guards escorted her out, he gestured to his head of security. "Make sure you take her through the kitchen first. I'll see if Harry can't look in on her for a moment before you take her home." The poor woman looked a little blue around the lips. Probably needed her medicine.

Harry was actually Dr. Harold Kilhausen, noted cardiologist and head of staff at Providence General. The doctor was an avid sailor in the little spare time he had and crewed on the best yacht racing team that Burbank Industries sponsored. This party was not just the annual fête, but also a celebration of their latest win.

Ronan enjoyed celebrating success. It felt good to bring everyone to his home. Burbanks had lived here off the south coast of Rhode Island for over a hundred years, building one of the massive mansions that were synonymous with turn of the century wealth. Ronan loved every stick and brick of the place where he'd grown up.

This little portion of the coastline boasted an impressive cliff and the view never failed to soothe him. The old woman had accosted him as he stood alone on his balcony, enjoying a quick moment of quiet overlooking the ocean before wading back into the social fray. Now, as he prepared to return to his guests, he thought he heard a faint splash. He glanced out to sea again, scanning the water for a disturbance. When he saw nothing, he went back to the party.

Chapter One

It was cold! Meriel hated being cold and it was always fricking freezing in the North Atlantic, even in late April. She longed for home down in Tennessee and tried to remember what a summer's night felt like. It was no use. Even under layers of blubber and fur, she was still human and still cold.

Seven years had passed since she'd gone to the Burbank company party and fallen into the waters of Block Island Sound in Rhode Island. She should have died. There had even been days early on when she wished she had. But nope. Not her. She was cursed.

No, seriously.

Cursed.

Meriel Byrne had turned into a Selkie.

Seven years ago, she'd thought impressing her boss was important. Since then, she'd learned otherwise. Now, finding fish was important. Staying away from seal-eating killer whales was important. Fending off the damn real seals who wanted to mate with her was important!

"Back off, fur face!" she barked at an importunate male. "I am not your girlfriend du jour. A) We're in open water, not the rookery, B) it's not mating season, and C) just yuck. Call me politically incorrect, but I don't think I can go for the whole interspecies thing."

She grumbled to herself as she dove away from him. If she'd known how attractive she was as a Selkie, she wouldn't have worried so much about shaving her legs when she was human.

A lone halibut, separated from its school, swam past her. Lunch time. In a burst of speed, she chomped down on it and swallowed.

If she ever regained her human form, Meriel swore she would never, ever eat sushi again.

But she had no time to waste, even for lunch. Nose pointed south, she swam for the small, historic village of Misquapaug.

Twisted it might be, but she couldn't help herself. Every year, she had this urge to return to the place where the curse had changed her. And why not? It wasn't as if she had anything pressing on her calendar. Just a lot of fishing.

At the edge of the sound, she made her way around the inlet to an immense, turn of the century mansion. The house was even more impressive for perching at the top of a lone cliff. She'd been there once. It belonged to Ronan Burbank, heir to Burbank Industries, where she'd been low man on the totem pole in the finance department.

Meriel sighed gustily. She'd had a massive crush on the man. At the company party, she'd been trying so hard to impress him, she stabbed her stiletto heel into the soft, sandy earth, then tripped and fell off the cliff.

It was such an idiotic way to die. Except she hadn't died. When Meriel hit the water, a curse she hadn't even known existed kicked into action and she turned into a Selkie. It had taken her months to learn to make her new body work for her, but after such a long time, she was as agile in the water as any born seal.

She bobbed in the surf, wondering if Ronan lived up in that big house now with a perfect wife and perfect children. Someday, she'd stop coming here and hurting for things she couldn't have. But someday wasn't today.

A lone sailboat floating in the active waters caught her eye. The choppy sea frothed at the tip of every wave and a particularly vigorous gust of wind sent the blue and silver sail jibing wildly around the mast. That was wrong. Whatever lackbrain was crewing that craft needed to get his rear in gear or he'd sink it.

The boat tipped hard and she realized why no one was at the helm. The solitary sailor was lying at the bottom in a haphazard array of limbs, either unconscious or dead. Meriel dove under the waves and shot toward the sleek little racing yacht, praying she'd be in time.

She was almost there when the boat heeled over in the wake of a high wave and dumped its human cargo into the unforgiving sea. The cold must have revived the man enough for him to panic. Meriel darted over to him and grabbed his collar in her teeth, pulling until they broke the surface. The buoyancy of the water didn't do nearly enough to counter the effect of the wind and tide. She struggled landward.

"Idiot," she said between clenched teeth. There was blood in the water from his head wound and the taint of it washed into her mouth. She wanted to gag, but then she'd lose her hold on him.

"If you can't sail, you shouldn't be on the water." She growled at him as she lugged his weight. The boathouse at the end of the Burbank dock became visible through the spray.

"Finally. Hey, moron. I know you're passed out, but if you can hear me, you need to get up to the house. This is the Burbank place and they'll take care of you."

The man burbled, but it might have been the water rushing by. They reached the beach and Meriel nudged the man onto the sand, but he didn't move away from the rising waves.

"Come on, mister. Get out of the water." She smacked him with a flipper, but he didn't move.

"Great. Just great." Meriel hated going on land. All the grace granted her by the sea fled when she touched the sand, but she didn't have a choice. She hauled herself up on her flippers, then snagged the guy's collar again and yanked him higher onto the beach. He didn't move.

"You'd better not be dead. I better not have just dragged my two hundred fifty pounds of blubbery ass onto land for no reason." Panic crept into her voice and belied her words. He couldn't be dead. Meriel didn't do death. Even being a Selkie was better than being dead.

She flipped him over and finally saw the face of the man she'd saved.

"Ronan?"

All the silly, immature feelings she'd once had for him came rushing back like the tide and vanished again as quickly. Now was not the time. He needed help and there was no one else around. She couldn't even give him CPR in her current shape.

"Help me!" she cried out to the wild sea. "It isn't fair! You can't take him the way you took me!"

Except the sea could do anything it pleased. Magic of a kind she never dreamed about on land was the stuff of ordinary life under the waves. And it was magic that she desperately needed now.

A sound reached her. The song of the finfolk—the magical beings of the water—pierced her ears and the spray of the surf carried enchantment. A single wave reached out and touched her flipper, leaving something behind.

In the sea, it didn't take much time for metal to corrode or become a resting place for other creatures, but the silver brooch that washed up on the shore glittered as if newly made. Another piece of ocean magic. The metal was twisted and hammered into a complicated design that looked Celtic, or perhaps Norse. The edges of the brooch were a series of complex knots surrounding a stylized seal. The seal was curved around a jewel so dark she thought it was black onyx. A ray of fading sunlight touched the surface and she realized the gem was a blue sapphire, its color so deep she could almost drown in it. She picked up the talisman with her teeth and laid it on Ronan's too-still chest.

"Please." Meriel put all her heart into the prayer. "Oh please, let this work. Whatever curse I'm under, please don't let it touch him, too. Mercy, I beg you."

"Mercy granted. For this." The voice she heard was a chorus of sound. The gentle trill of a country creek, the roar of the ocean as it crashed violently against immovable rock. The swift rush of an icy river down a frozen mountain. Even the light bubbling of hidden hot springs that warmed the earth from beneath.

"Make no mistake, descendant of Constance Byrne. Saving his life has entwined his destiny with your own."

She gasped in horror. She wouldn't wish her life on anyone, but what was done was done. She couldn't have let him drown.

Finally, Ronan coughed and gurgled, a pint or so of Block Island Sound leaving his lungs and soaking into the sand. He rolled to his side, sucked in huge draughts of air and coughed up more water.

"Thank God! You didn't die." She kept up a chant of gratitude as he coughed harder. The amulet slipped off his chest and he opened his eyes.

Meriel heard a yell and a form appeared over the dunes. A man, waving and shouting at her. The last thing she wanted was for strangers to discover her, so she hauled herself behind a hillock of rock and sea grass. The man came down and shook Ronan's shoulder.

"Mr. Burbank," he said, his Down East accent thick as winter fog. "Are you all right?"

"What the hell?" Ronan's voice was rough and harsh with the abuse it had taken. He rubbed his face on his sleeve.

"What happened?" asked the man.

Ronan sat up, his fingers closing around the brooch. He shook off the other man's hand.

"Did you see anyone?"

"Might have. Thought I saw a woman standing over you."

"A woman? I thought it was... Never mind."

"Nice piece of jewelry you've got there, Mr. Burbank. Where'd that come from?"

Ronan looked at the silver in his hand and shrugged. His voice was slurred when he said, "I don't know. It was just there."

The older man looked around. Eerily, his focus seemed to settle right on the place where she hid and she crouched farther into the sand. *Idiot*, she chastised herself. *Why didn't you go back into the water?*

"Where's your boat, Mr. Burbank?"

Ronan lifted his chin. "Out there. On the bottom." He drew up his knees and stared out at the sea. For a while, the man sat with him, occasionally casting glances over to the rocks where Meriel hid. The sky darkened with sunset and storm. The man left. Ronan stayed on the beach, unmoving, shoulders slumped.

From her hiding place, she waited, shivering. Time had been unkind to Ronan. The man she thought could never rumple was now shabby in spirit. It showed in the sorry slouch of his posture, in the hair too long even for fashionable carelessness, in the rough bristle that coated his face. What could have happened since she last saw him to batter him so badly?

Chapter Two

Ronan finally stopped watching the sea when the first splatters of rain hit him. He might have a death wish, but he'd rather it was quick instead of something horrible like lingering pneumonia, so he rose. The brooch fell out of his hand, but he ignored it, consigning it back to the tide.

Steep steps cut out of the sand and reinforced with wood led Ronan to his home, where he let himself into the kitchen. He walked through the darkness to his bedroom and sat on the edge of his mattress, not caring that he was still soaking wet.

He tried to buck himself up. Burbanks had weathered the storms of bad markets and bad seas for generations. Burbanks didn't give up. Burbanks didn't commit suicide, although over the years a few tragic accidents had occurred with suspicious timing. But really, what else had he been thinking, going out on the little racing yacht as drunk as he'd been? He wanted to die.

Until that seal caught him. Ronan peeled off his sopping shirt to examine the frayed collar. Teeth marks and rips...and a faint stain of blood. He felt his head gingerly, burrowing through the grime of salt and sand, until he encountered the lump. He checked his fingers. The wound had stopped bleeding, but it explained the hallucination.

Because seals don't talk. And even if they do, they don't have Southern accents.

God, he was tired. He looked around the room that had become his haven and his jail.

Seven years ago everything had been beautiful. He'd had wealth, a thriving shipping company and an unsullied reputation. Now, his family was gone and his friends had abandoned him. Even the ones who believed in his innocence no longer came by.

He felt dirty just thinking about it, so he stripped down the rest of the way and turned on the shower. Ronan stood under the hot stream without moving for a long time before he finally reached for the shampoo.

After the girl died, it was like the Spanish Inquisition showed up. Totally unexpected. Between the police, the IRS, and the paparazzi that disguised themselves as legitimate media, the Burbank name became modern slang for "murdering loser". His company started hemorrhaging money until he had to sell it off, piece by piece, while it was still worth something.

Thank God for the boats. He'd stanched the flow in time to save one tiny portion of his business. The little workshop where he and his team built racing yachts was the only thing he lived for now. And the only way he'd been able to save it was by gutting the house to pay for it. Pieces of furniture, works of art he'd grown up with and taken for granted were sold away until the home he'd loved all his life became nothing more than a shell. He couldn't even bear to live in it anymore, so he moved into the groundskeeper's cottage.

And how pathetic was that? He'd been Emory Charles Ronan Burbank IV, goddammit. Now he was nothing.

He stepped out of the shower and dried off on the way to bed where he dropped the towel on the floor. Then he crawled into bed—the clock radio said it was two thirty in the morning—and listened to the storm beat against the shore line.

What had that seal said? "Thank God you didn't die." Well. Bully for him. A seal was glad he lived.

෫෮෫෮

Meriel waited until all was silent. She must have dozed a little because when she looked again, Ronan was gone. She didn't know what had happened to him but it was past time she got out of there. Maybe if she left, went back to the sea and never came back, whatever fate she'd bound him up in would leave him be.

The amulet glittered dully for an instant in the little moonlight available. Meriel picked it up again very carefully. This belonged to the sea and she was determined to give it back. But as she hauled herself back down the beach toward the surf, a sleek head rose from the water.

"Iona!" Meriel was so surprised to see her friend and mentor she dropped the brooch. "You startled me. What are you doing in Rhode Island?"

"Waiting to see if you do something foolish," said the old seal. Iona's accent was so deeply Scottish that even after seven years, it still took Meriel time to translate it into something understandable.

"Too late. I already did my foolish deed for the day. It looks like I saved the wrong man and now I've bound up his life in my curse." Meriel took another determined heave forward, but Iona blocked her way.

"It may not be as bad as it seems."

"Or—based on the way my luck seems to run—it could be worse. I'm voting for worse, so I'm going to leave now. Get the heck out of Dodge. Go find a nice sunny beach somewhere and boil in my own blubber."

"Sounds nice. Except for the boiling in blubber part."

Meriel tried to feint a dodge to Iona's right, but the Selkie wasn't fooled.

"What's going on, Iona? Why won't you let me back down to the water?"

"You can't come back, child. This is your chance."

"For what? To break the curse? Or to take Ronan down with me?"

"A chance to triumph over evil."

"I don't want to triumph over evil, Iona." Meriel sighed. "I mean, I do want to triumph over evil...in a broad philosophical sense, but me? Personally? I just want to survive."

"Then consider this a matter of survival. You must stay on land to ride the wave that fate has sent you."

"Enough with the maritime metaphors, Iona."

"You want plain speaking, then? I'll give it to you. You're not meant to be this way, Meriel Byrne. Cursed or not, the life of a Selkie is not for you. You must try to find a way out of it and you carry before you the thing that will begin the change. Take it with you. When dawn touches the land, you'll have until the next sunrise to take back the life you're meant to live."

Iona turned her head in the boneless way of seals to look over the horizon. "The sun is rising now, child. Blessings of the sea follow you." She slipped back into the water as the first pale finger of dawn reached the sand.

Alone on the beach, Meriel dropped the amulet and tried to run, but she didn't make it to the sea. In that second, the sun rose over the horizon and time stopped. Magic happened. Agony ripped through her.

She would have screamed, but the enchantment trapped her vocal cords between forms. Another spasm caught her and squeezed until she thought her bones would break. Helpless, voiceless, she could only thrash against the pain until it eased. Finally, the last of the seizures faded and she lay on the sand, exhausted and beaten. Human.

ಔಙಔಚಚ

Morning light battered him as unmercifully as the sea. His mouth tasted like fish guts. Ronan rolled out of bed naked and rooted around on the floor for a semi-clean pair of jeans.

Coffee. He needed coffee.

He'd learned his way around the kitchen enough in the last few years to make a decent cup of caffeine and a bowl of cereal. He leaned against the counter and crunched away on his Chocolate Frosted Sugar Bombs as he waited for the coffee pot to gurgle its last. The storm had cleared away the murk of the last few days and the bay sparkled with light, glistening off a scrap of blue and silver fabric as it tumbled up the beach with the tide.

Ronan put his cereal down with a thump, uncaring when it sloshed over the side.

The sail. He hadn't dreamed it. That meant...

He tore down the steps to the boathouse.

The boat was gone. Gone! That meant he really had been stupid enough yesterday to go sailing out into that storm so drunk he could hardly stand up—much less crew the dinghy. The words that spewed from his lips would have made a merchant marine whistle in appreciation.

Snatches of memory came back. The sail had swung wildly above him, clipping the side of his head hard enough to knock him into the bottom of the boat. From his vantage point, he remembered smiling grimly as he watched the storm play hell with sky and unending sea before the cold arms of the ocean claimed him.

The frigid dunking combined with the crack on the skull must have sent him into shock. But he remembered...a seal. A seal had hauled him by the collar out of the sea. And it had talked to him. Yelled at him. Dragged him onto the beach and thanked God for him.

He picked up the swatch of sailcloth and found another lump of shimmering silver fabric nearby. Only when he shook it out, it wasn't fabric. It was fur.

"What the..."

A woman rose to her knees from behind a hummock of sand.

"What are you doing with my skin?" she asked.

Ronan stared. He wasn't touching her skin. Which, from twelve feet away, appeared exceptionally fine. Pale and smooth with not a freckle or tan line to mar it. Although, now that he noticed it, it did have a very slight gray tinge and her lips were blue with cold. Also, he noticed she was naked.

"Your what?"

"My skin, Ronan. What are you doing with it? I need it back."

"Lady, I don't know what you're talking about." Her voice sounded so familiar. Shock knocked him raw. That was the seal's voice.

"What are you?" he asked, his voice cracking a bit.

"I'm a Selkie," she said in the drawl he remembered. His whole body jerked and wrenched sore muscles.

"What. The hell. Is a Selkie?" He rubbed a palm against the side of his temple where a tiny, evil smithy pounded on the anvil of his skull. His throat felt like someone had pried his jaw open and sandblasted it.

"I'm a seal-person and don't you take that tone with me. This is all your fault."

He was talking to a naked-woman-slash-seal-person who blamed him for her existence. Proof positive he'd finally gone round the bend. Ronan wondered if Dr. Kilhausen would still talk to him long enough to find him a bed in a decent mental institution or if he should wander down Main Street chattering to himself until he got arrested.

"Where are your clothes?"

She made a disgusted sound, like he hadn't been listening or something. He'd been listening. He just... This was too weird.

"Not clothes. Skin. I. Need. My. Skin." She spoke as if he was a particularly slow-witted child.

"I. Don't. Have. Your. Skin," he returned, then shook his head. "This isn't happening. I'm either still drunk or this is the world's worst hangover."

"Hangover? So you really were drunk yesterday." She stood up and stumbled toward him. Wow. Nice ti— She shoved him back. "I should have let you drown."

"Whoa, whoa, lady—or whatever you are." He tripped and landed on his butt on the hard sand. The fur thing didn't cushion his fall much.

"What happened to you, Ronan? Why did you do something so stupid? Are you trying to kill yourself?"

"What if I am?" he roared back at her. "Why do you care? What business is it of yours if I live or die?"

"I care, Ronan Burbank! I don't know why, but I do."

Ronan slumped. "Don't. It's not worth it."

"Looks like someone forgot their Prozac today." She cocked a hip, swaying a bit, totally at ease with her nudity. But he had the feeling that if he put one hand wrong with her, she'd bite it off.

He snorted. She grunted, an animal sound at odds with her human voice.

"How do you know my name, anyway?" He didn't want to be curious about her, but he couldn't help it. She was the only thing that had piqued his interest in a very long time.

"I know a lot about you, Ronan. Or I did seven years ago."

"Seven years. What day is it?"

"Like I know exactly. Hello? Seal person. It's not as if I'm wearing a watch here." She waved a bare arm at him. "I do know that it must be around April twenty-fifth."

"How do you know that?"

"It's the day I became a Selkie. Every year around this time, I make my way back here to see if anything has changed. This time, something changed."

"How?"

"I saved your sorry ass." She made a huge, wild gesture with her arms. "And now the sea or fate or God...or something...has decided that you and I are in this curse together."

"Lady, I'm not in anything with you. You've got a curse, you deal with it yourself." Excellent news. He wasn't insane. She was.

"Gee. My hero. I think your silver armor needs some polishing up." She crossed her arms and succeeded in drawing his attention back to a really, really great set of breasts. Her complexion was so fine, he could see the delicate blue tracing of veins under the skin.

"Why don't you wait right there and I'll call the men in white coats."

"I'm not crazy, you drunk jerk. I'm cursed."

"You think you're cursed. What did you do?" She had to get off his property because this conversation was starting to get to him. He'd finally gotten used to the numbness and grief and he didn't need anyone shaking up his life anymore.

"I didn't do anything. Great-great-great-Granny Byrne did something and I'm paying for it."

"Byrne? Did you say Byrne?" He knew that name. It was imprinted on his brain. Branded there, with all the accompanying agony. In all this time, it hadn't healed.

"Yes. I'm Meriel Byrne."

A red wash of rage swamped Ronan's mind. He was going to kill her. With his bare hands, he'd strangle her. Drown her.

He rushed at her, hands clenched into fists. All semblance of civilization was gone and he didn't care that she was a woman, smaller and slighter than he. She stumbled away from him, back to the surf. He splashed into the water after her, screaming a litany of foul language. Ronan caught her in a tackle and they both went down. She swerved and twisted—a wild bronc at sea—but he clung to her, wrath compelling him to ride this tide until it was over.

A heavy wave caught them and tossed them high up onto the beach.

"Get off me, you maniac! What is wrong with you?" Meriel Byrne, who'd ruined his life by dying, slid out of his grip like an eel, but he caught her ankle. She kicked hard and clocked him on the jaw, snapping his head back and earning her release.

"You took it from me," he screamed, wild in his grief. "You took everything from me!" The words were the last of his strength and he sat in the sand, elbows on his knees.

That damn skin must have been following him, because when he reached down, it was right there. Ronan rubbed his thumb over it compulsively, smoothing the thick, glossy pelt. Tears he hadn't shed for months now poured out of his eyes, burning like acid. They landed on the silver skin and rolled off into the sand where they were swallowed up.

He was pathetic. He might have lost everything that ever mattered to him, but it didn't mean he could cry. So Ronan willed back the tears and stared resolutely out at the ocean until he could breathe again.

Chapter Three

"You asshole. You tried to kill me."

Meriel reached down and slapped him. She'd never hit anyone before in her life and she was surprised to find that it didn't help. She didn't feel any better and now her hand hurt.

He didn't even move. Something was very wrong here. Had he completely lost his grip on reality?

"Give me back my skin, Ronan."

"No."

"Give it back."

He didn't answer her and she ground her heels into the sand in frustration.

"Fine, then. I'll take it." Meriel bent to retrieve the corner of her pelt that was visible under his knee, but he reached out, quick as thought, to latch onto her ankle.

"Let go of me, or I'll kick you again."

"No."

"You have a serious vocabulary problem. Try this: 'Yes, Meriel. I'd love to give you back your skin. Then you can change back into a Selkie and get the hell away from me'."

His jaw clenched and she noticed that it was swollen and red. "What happens if I keep it?"

Meriel's mouth dropped open. "You can't keep it. It isn't yours."

"Answer the question. I think I deserve at least that much."

"Deserve? You tried to drown me, which in retrospect is kind of funny, since I'm a Selkie." She finished on a yell, but he didn't respond.

"You took away seven years of my life, Miss Byrne. You owe me."

"I don't know what you're talking about and I owe you nothing. You owe me my skin, which you're sitting on."

"If this is what I think it is, then there's something bigger going on here. I don't think I can hand it back and go on as if nothing happened."

Meriel ground her teeth together. "You can't keep it. Don't you get it? This could be very dangerous and you shouldn't get involved."

"It's too late for that." He'd become curt over the years. She remembered a smiling, expansive man, not this shaggy grump.

"Please, Ronan." She shivered. "I'm freezing."

"You're naked."

Meriel looked down. So she was. Naked and... "I hate being cold." She hugged herself, trying to hide the pertinent bits, although it was a little late for that.

"What happens if I keep your skin?"

"Excuse me?"

"You heard me." He never looked at her. Just kept staring out at the ocean.

"I...I'm not going to tell you." They were on dangerous ground here.

"If I keep the skin, you have to stay on land, don't you?"

Damn. "Where did you hear that?"

"I do occasionally read fiction, Miss Byrne. I read Irish mythology in grade school."

"Geek," she said derisively. "And I...I'm not sure exactly how it'll work for me. I'm a cursed Selkie, not a born one." Meriel rubbed her arms rapidly to try to build up some heat. "I'm cold, Ronan. I don't have anything to wear and I'm hungry. Not to mention, I saved your life yesterday. Help me and I'll tell you."

"Tell me and I'll help you."

"What are you, eight? What will people say when they discover my frozen, dead body on your beach?"

He looked down at her with eyes as cold as Arctic ice. "That it's about goddamn time."

ꞵꙅꙅꙅ

He left her. With her pelt and a ratty piece of what used to be his sail, Ronan walked up the sand steps and disappeared. Meriel tried to follow him, but without anger and adrenaline propelling her forward, muscles long unused were no longer up to the task. She took two steps before she fell to her knees.

Meriel stared at her legs in furious horror. Her limbs were strong enough, but the mechanics of putting one foot in front of the other had somehow become a little foggy. She thought of yelling for help, but she wasn't sure if Ronan would come back for her. And even if he did, she wasn't sure her pride was up to his frigid attitude.

She went up on her hands and knees. The brooch she had dropped earlier winked in the sunlight just beyond her reach.

"Ocean magic, my ass," she muttered. "If you're so special, why don't you help me walk?" She stretched out until she snagged the circle with her fingertips. Nothing. No help.

She had to walk. She couldn't drag herself across the beach because she'd lost her protective layers of thick fur.

"Fine. No walking. How about clothes, at least? Magic's no good if I freeze to death first." Meriel swore she could hear the waves laugh at her.

"Oh, that's great. No clothes." She waved her arms dismissively. "No, really. It's okay. It's fiiiiine." If the ocean had been a man, he'd have known enough to back away from her in this mood. "I don't need your help. You just go right on sitting there. I can do it on my own."

She held the brooch in her hand and pushed herself up. Each tiny rock felt like glass digging into her flesh. On the way, she stumbled and faltered, but she walked. She tripped once and had to dig a viciously pointy pebble out of her knee, grinding her teeth against the sting. Several scrapes later, she made it up the stairs.

With the massive mansion before her, other concerns pushed themselves forward—she was starving. Meriel's stomach growled as she tried to remember when she'd last eaten. That halibut. Its memory rolled around in her empty stomach. She'd been too exhausted and sick to eat that morning before Ronan showed up and ruined her life. Again.

So maybe technically he hadn't ruined it the first time. But how dare he accuse her of doing the same to him? There was one good way to solve all her problems, so Meriel walked up to the closest door of the immense home and started banging on it.

"Open up, Burbank. We need to talk."

"There's no one there." His voice came from off to the side, behind a hedge. She walked around a corner, trailing a hand along the side of the house for balance, to find him lounging in the doorway of a small cottage. He stood straight when he saw her and frowned.

"Go away." He stepped in and closed the door.

She marched over and put her mouth to the frame. "I can't. You've got my skin. Now open up."

His face appeared abruptly in the glass. "No." And he walked away.

That tore it for Meriel. Trying to kill her was one thing. Being rude was completely another. She unleashed a frenzy of pounding on the wood.

"Emory Charles Ronan Burbank IV, if you don't open this door right this second I am going to pitch a fit so loud your grandbabies will be born with it ringing in their ears!"

The echo of her yell died out and silence assaulted her. Her screeching had even made the birds go quiet in the trees. She slumped against the doorjamb.

"Where did you say you were from again?" The door opened unexpectedly and she yelped like a puppy.

"Tennessee."

"It figures."

"What's that supposed to mean? I'm freezing here, Burbank."

Ronan reached out to steady her with one hand when she stumbled and the heat of his palm on her skin burned her.

"Jesus, you're an ice cube." He reached behind the door to retrieve an enormous towel and tossed it at her. "You're still naked, Byrne. Cover up."

She glared at him so hard he ought to have splintered into a thousand pieces, but it only gave her a headache. She took the towel and wrapped it around her shoulders. It was scratchy, threadbare in places, and it smelled a little fishy, but it helped ease the worst of the cold. Her stomach growled again.

He lifted an eyebrow and smirked, but didn't say anything. So that's how he wanted to play. By his expression, he wasn't going to feed her unless she asked and she wouldn't ask if he had the last steak on earth.

"Fine." Meriel shook her hair back. "I'll go into town and get something to eat."

"You don't have any money," he said, his lips tilted up obnoxiously.

"Money's not going to be an issue. Anyway, I'm sure someone will buy me a meal." And she opened the towel up to flash him. His eyes widened and his jaw clenched so hard she thought she heard his teeth grind. Kind of cute, really. But she was a little surprised at her own actions. Where had her modesty gone?

Oh yeah. Seven years as a nudist seal.

Ronan grabbed her arm and hauled her in the house. "You are not going into town to proposition some tourist. They'll pick you up for solicitation."

"Whatever, Ronan. I'm still hungry." His jaw set again and she smiled at him. "And naked under the towel." She let it slip just a bit off one shoulder.

"Witch."

"No. *Halichoerus grypus*." He looked at her blankly. "Gray seal." Ronan turned and stalked away from her, offering a surprisingly nice view of taut muscles moving under his jeans. With no shirt on, his back was beautiful. Tanned and smooth, a symphony of muscular control.

Meriel stomped her feet hard on the sand mat to get rid of her gooey, girly thoughts and stepped in. The blinds and curtains were all drawn, leaving the house in dismal shadow despite the bright sun. A haphazard array of shabby furniture littered the floor. Nothing in the little house spoke of wealth or privilege, or even comfort.

"Ronan?" she called, the sound falling dead.

Footsteps pounded on the naked wood floors. "Get dressed."

He threw a pile of clothes at her. A wrinkled blue polo shirt and jeans worn almost white smacked her in the face. Meriel tucked the towel under her armpits to keep it from falling while she sorted out her new wardrobe. He stood, obviously waiting for her to make the comment that was on the tip of her tongue, but she swallowed it and smiled sweetly instead.

"Thank you, Ronan."

He grunted at her and headed through another set of doors. She followed him.

The tiny kitchen was clean, aside from what appeared to be this morning's breakfast congealing in a puddle of milk in the sink. The coffee pot was still full and hot.

"What are you looking at?" he demanded. "I said, get dressed."

She placed a hand to her brow—a precarious move because she had only a tenuous grip on both the towel and the fresh clothing—and slathered on her thickest Southern accent.

"I do declare, your gentlemanly ways will make me swoon." Her normal voice returned as she stood straight. "Where's the bathroom?"

He brushed by her on his way out of the kitchen and she followed, expecting him to point her to a powder room in the hall, but the door he opened surprised her.

The stripped simplicity of its furnishings couldn't detract from the beauty of the room. Green sprigged wallpaper and a plain white bed frame left it fresh and lovely despite a thick layer of dust. He stood in the doorway and pointed inside.

"There's a shared bathroom there."

Meriel had to slide past him to step into the room, leaving a scant few inches between them. His bare torso, muscled and rough, radiated heat, anger and bitterness.

She paused, confused. "Ronan, I don't—"

"Then don't." He cut her off. "Get some clothes on and come back to the kitchen." He closed the door when he left.

Chapter Four

He had a Selkie in his house.

A Selkie who didn't seem to have any problem with nudity. It had been way too long since he'd gotten laid and suddenly sex was at the front of his mind. With a Selkie. That wasn't bestiality, was it?

Nah. She was cursed, not born. She was human. Oh baby, was she human. She had exactly the kind of body he liked. Little and curvy in all the right places. Not board straight and not Barbie silicone. She was also a natural brunette. Cuffs and collars definitely matched. He stared down at the cutting board and couldn't remember what he was supposed to be doing.

"Can I help?" Her voice startled him out of his reverie and instead of slicing the tomato in front of him, he cut into his finger.

She rushed over and grabbed it before he could put it in his mouth. "Don't do that. Here." She grabbed a paper towel and pressed it tightly to the wound. She'd brushed her teeth and washed her face, the familiar scents going straight to his head. "Let me look at it."

"Haven't you done enough?" he said. His shirt swallowed her. She'd pinned a heavy, dark brooch on her shoulder. It tickled his memory, but he dismissed it. There were more interesting things to see. The two buttons she'd left open on the shirt would have been modest from a foot or two away, but standing as they were, the vee offered a clear line of sight down her cleavage. Her unbound cleavage.

Ronan pulled away from her and went to the sink, aching from the cut and the sudden hard-on.

"You go wash that out and put a bandage on it. I'll slice the tomatoes." He nodded, too tired to fight for the moment.

He went into the bathroom and found a bandage in the medicine cabinet. His finger throbbed in time with his dick, but he ignored it. Ronan glanced into the mirror when he was done and actually looked at himself for the first time in years. Jesus. It was a wonder he hadn't scared her to death. He needed a shave. And a haircut. And some Visine. His eyes were so red from both his hangover and his seawater dunking that they glowed demonically.

He reached for the shaving cream, but drew back his hand. Was he seriously considering shaving for this woman? Hell no. He narrowed his eyes at his reflection and ran a hand over his chin. The stubble really didn't suit him. He'd tried a beard before, but it grew in patchy. He should shave anyway. So the guys at the shop wouldn't tease him about his crap beard.

But not for a woman. Besides, she wouldn't notice. She didn't even like him. And he didn't like her. He splashed his face with water and started rubbing on the shaving foam.

When he got back, Ronan watched as she assembled sandwiches out of the few things he had in the fridge. She scraped up the last of the mayonnaise and, without turning around, asked, "Where's your list?"

"My what?"

"Your grocery list. You're out of..." Meriel finally looked over at him and her next word was garbled. Ronan's face felt naked, like he'd scraped off a layer of armor with his stubble. He also felt like an idiot and had to make a conscious effort not to cover his cheeks while she stared at him. After another moment, she blinked and took a deep breath.

"You're out of mayo. I was going to write it on the list so next time you go shopping, you don't forget."

He shaved for this? His temper snapped. "How can you do this? How can you make sandwiches after everything you did to me?"

"I didn't do anything to you, Ronan." She slapped a sandwich down on the plate. "I don't know what happened here, but let me tell you what happened to me. I fell off a damned cliff. Off. A. Cliff. The only cliff on the southern tip of Rhode Island, in fact. Why can't you live on the beach like everyone else?" Meriel paced the galley kitchen, picking up the sandwich fixings and putting them away. Bread into the breadbox. Tomatoes into a bowl on the counter.

"I hit the water and I nearly drowned. I was a breath away from death, Ronan. This life I have is a blessing given to me by a curse, so I don't know if I should be grateful or miserable. But I'll tell you what. If you're what it's like to be miserable, I'll take gratitude."

Pickles, roast beef and cheese in the fridge.

"When I woke up, I wasn't even human anymore. I was a seal. There is no possible way to explain that to you. Iona, another Selkie, taught me everything I needed to know about surviving in the ocean, but she can't help me with the curse I live under." She put the lettuce into the crisper and slammed the refrigerator door. A bottle of milk inside the fridge rattled ominously, but didn't crash.

"The ocean gave me this brooch to save you and told me it was magic. Because of it, because of you, I can be human for a day. Iona told me to use this time to figure out how to break the curse, but now you've gone and screwed me over yet again."

"Me? What did I do?" Ronan rose to tower over her. Everything was out of control and he needed to win at something. Even if it was just being bigger.

"I saved your hide and in return you took mine, you jerk!" She didn't back down from him, even when he stood an inch away with her hard nipples brushing his chest. The arousal that hadn't completely died down sprang back to life. He grabbed her arms and pulled her flush against him.

"That's right. Hate me. Hate me as much as I hate you." Ronan's gaze roamed her face, watching her blush suddenly, feeling the shudder that racked her body. She didn't pull away.

"I...I don't hate you, Ronan." Her soft breath warmed his jaw, whispered in his ear.

"I don't hate you, either." He kissed her. He had to. If he didn't kiss her, his head would explode. Or some other part of him. And she was so sweet. Even under the toothpaste, she tasted of the wild sea—of sights he'd never seen and places he'd never go. Not without her to guide him.

Ronan delved deeper, groaning when she opened to him, when her tongue rolled against his, softening the kiss that had begun too harshly. He let go the grip of his hands and wrapped his arms around her shoulders, holding her close, pulling her up to his height. She came willingly. Her fingers fluttered over his shoulders, wound into his hair.

His palms slid down her slender back until he filled his hands with her ass and lifted her so he could grind himself into the niche of her thighs. A gasp of shock left her, but he smothered it with his mouth.

Ronan nipped lightly at her and paused to gauge her reaction. She opened her eyes and smiled wickedly, her mouth wet and glistening, before she swooped back in and sucked his bottom lip into her mouth, returning the nip.

Perfect. Because what was pleasure without pain to remind them of the heights?

Ronan tugged at her legs until Meriel wrapped herself around his hips, then he walked them to the kitchen counter. Now she had the freedom to touch him and she indulged herself. His chest wasn't completely smooth, but had a sprinkling of dark hair that made a perfect shadowy triangle in the center. She spread her hands over it until she felt his nipples with her little fingers. Nipples. God, she wanted his hands on her breasts so badly she actually whined in eagerness.

He got the hint and pulled at her shirt until he finally touched her skin. She arched into him and hissed in a breath at the heated contact. His palms were rough and calloused, not what she expected of a business man, but she didn't care to pursue that rabbit trail. Not while his strong fingers stroked her spine, spanned her waist, slid up to the valley between her breasts. Teasing her with his touch while she squirmed for it.

Meriel tore her mouth away from his and put her plea into her eyes. He knew what she wanted. She could read it in his feral grin. But he asked anyway.

"Tell me, Selkie. Tell me what you want." His fingertips danced up her sides, almost touching her aching flesh, but then skittering away.

She whimpered. He put his hands around her waist, cupping the swell of her ribcage. "Tell me, Meriel."

Two could play this game, she thought, understanding his ploy for dominance. But she didn't have a submissive personality, so she retaliated. She dragged her hands down his back, fingernails leaving a light trail, and he shuddered hard, his eyes dilating with pleasure. When she reached the waistband of his jeans, she kept going until she slipped her hands into his back pockets and squeezed. He flexed, his jaw set as hard as the erection he rocked against her, and she grinned at him.

"Touch me, Ronan."

And he did. He put his hands under her tender, aching breasts and lifted, pressing them together. He flicked her nipples with his thumbs and she choked back her cry of pleasure.

"Don't hold back. Scream for me." He put his mouth over hers again and swallowed her next sob. Over and over, he caressed her, tracing each inch of skin, pulling and tugging at her nipples until they were swollen and hard enough to cut glass.

He pulled the shirt over her head in one smooth tug, and the press of breast to chest made her moan. They had passed coherent speech long ago and it took her a moment to understand when he muttered, "Need you," in a voice harsh with desire.

Not smart. Meriel knew that. Screw smart. She needed him, too.

"Yes." She nodded against his neck, reaching down to pop open the button on his jeans. He did the same to her, lifting her to yank them out from under her bottom. Their pants landed in a heap with her shirt. He hadn't provided underwear and she'd already realized that he was going commando, so nothing impeded them when he stepped between her thighs again. Nothing.

Meriel's eyes went wide.

"Condom," she squeaked against his mouth.

"Clean," he mumbled, pulling her hips to the bare edge of the counter.

"Me, too." The head of his penis, broad and smooth, slid up and down the wetness that seeped from her body, readying them both for his entry. Muscles long denied ached as her brain flickered.

"Pregnant," she moaned. That made him pull back. He dropped his forehead to her shoulder.

"Shit." They were both breathing hard, and every time they inhaled, his chest hair abraded her nipples. "Not on the pill?"

"I've been a seal for seven years, Ronan. It hasn't been an issue." He had the strength to chuckle and she was grateful for the sound. Carefully, he rearranged himself before pulling her into a tight hug. He felt so good, solid and warm, snuggled up against her. Her breathing slowed as sanity returned.

"You haven't had sex in seven years?"

"Please don't remind me right now." She wanted him so much her whole body thrummed as if she'd walked into an electric fence.

"I still want you." His voice rumbled through her and her skin absorbed the vibration.

"I know." There was more she wanted to say, but now that the heat had dimmed, she couldn't push herself past her sudden shyness to do it.

"You want me?" Ronan's face was carefully neutral when she looked at him. Too neutral. This was a man whose emotions had been boiling over the rim a few minutes ago, so she wasn't fooled. And it was a little late for her to be bashful. She was sitting naked on a kitchen counter, for Pete's sake.

"Yes, I do. But..."

"Yeah. I know." He stepped back and the cold that had vanished when he held her in his arms returned. Ronan bent down to grab his jeans and her shirt and, although she knew they had done the right thing by stopping, the sight of his trim, rangy form made her body clench.

He handed her the shirt, but stopped her with a hand on her breast, cupping the weight of her.

"We'll do this, Meriel. We'll finish this soon."

She nodded, trembling at his touch, before he turned away to tug his pants on.

"I have to get to work," he said, facing the sunny window. He couldn't look at her. She'd finally put the shirt on, but now that he knew, intimately, what lay under it, his control danced at the end of a thin thread.

"At Burbank? How long does it take to get to the city at this hour?"

"There is no Burbank Industries anymore, Mer." He shortened her name automatically, liking the way it felt on his tongue. "I had to sell it off, piece by piece. The only thing left is the boat yard, and it's in hock up to the mainsail."

Ronan looked down at his fingers. He hadn't had a manicure in years and he didn't miss them. He'd earned each callus, each nick and scrape, and he was proud of the history on his hands now.

Meriel hopped off the counter and slid her jeans—his jeans—up her hips. He'd started to calm down, but his body hardened again as he recalled the path his hands had traced there. She had great legs. Muscled and firm. He shook his head.

The touch of her fingers on his arm startled him. "You build racing boats now?"

119

Ronan couldn't trust his voice, so he nodded shortly.

"Do you like it?"

He shrugged. Like. Not like. It's what he did now.

"Are you good at it?" He glanced around and she had a shrewd smirk on her face. Ronan barked out a laugh. She'd hit the right button. He pushed himself to be good at everything. He hated to fail, or even worse, be only mediocre at what he tried.

"Think you know me, do you?"

"Not really, Ronan." She sighed and turned on the tap to wash her hands. She had such graceful fingers, long and slender. They hadn't eaten their sandwiches, so she wrapped them in plastic wrap. "You want to take this with you?"

He nodded, watching with growing curiosity. She did things that needed to be done. She didn't ask, she didn't wait. Meriel was a lot like him in some ways. She found lunch-sized paper bags in a cupboard and tossed in a baggie full of chips and the last apple from the crisper.

"That ought to hold you." He stood out of her way as she wiped down the counters, pausing at the spot where she'd been sitting a short while ago.

"So you'll be staying, then?" he asked.

Meriel nodded. "You have my skin. I'm bound to you until you return it to me."

Her skin? That's what this housewifely industriousness was about? Ronan's body went cold with betrayal. He grabbed her arm and swung her around, but his anger clashed with shock when she flinched away. He might be furious, but she was afraid. Of him.

"Don't do that, Meriel. I'm not going to hurt you."

"Then let go." He did, opening his hand abruptly. It sickened him that she thought him capable of harming her. Then he remembered the episode on the beach and realized that she was right.

"God, Mer. I'm sorry. I...I have to go."

She nodded, her face closed, and he missed her. Missed her smile, missed her response to him. "Hey, if you need to go out, there's a bike in the garage."

Meriel nodded again and opened her mouth to say something, then hesitated before she finally spoke. "I may do some grocery shopping."

Immediately, he pulled out his wallet and all his cash. All fifty-two dollars of it. He'd put himself on a pay schedule like everyone else in the shop and that was what he had left until Friday.

"Keep it, Ronan. I told you before, money's not a problem."

"Not a problem? Money's the only problem I've got."

"I doubt that. But it's one of the odd-ball benefits of being a Selkie. All the treasures of the sea are mine for the asking. Nothing useful like clothes when I ask for them, or granting me freedom from this curse, but I can have all of these I want." She opened her palm and where there had been nothing but smooth skin a moment ago, now half a dozen Spanish doubloons glittered dully, caked with the patina of centuries and the residue of the ocean.

She dropped them onto the counter. One fell off and landed with a solid thunk before rolling under the edge of the cabinet. Meriel searched for some paper to make a grocery list.

"You mean, you ask for it and gold shows up in your hand?"

She nodded absently, testing a pen on the back of an envelope. "Sometimes it's jewels. They don't do me much good in the middle of the ocean, but I like the sapphires."

"You like the sapphires." She said it so casually. Not greedy, not expecting anything. Just a fact. "You're dangerous, woman." He glared at her sideways, even though she ignored him. "Or is this a test? You want to trade those for your skin?"

She sighed and put down the pen. "No, it's not a test, Ronan. If I thought I could buy you off with a few moldy gold coins, I'd have done it already. I only want to know if you're picky about your brand of mayonnaise."

"I don't care, Meriel. Buy whatever's on sale."

"Oh, I can't do that. If you've got a favorite, then nothing else tastes right." She sounded dead serious, too. As if mayonnaise were the most important thing on earth right now.

"Buy whatever you want, Mer. Hell, buy the whole damn store if you want to. Do you have any idea how much those coins are worth?"

She stared at the greenish lump of gold on the white counter, then shrugged. "No."

"I thought you were an accounting geek."

"I crunched numbers, Ronan. I didn't deal in gold or antiquities. What kind of soda do you like?"

"I'm not going anywhere. It's not safe to leave you alone." Ronan grabbed the phone off the counter and called the yard. His foreman answered.

"Ayuh."

"Devon, it's Ronan. Something's come up and I can't come in."

There was a long pause before Devon spoke. "Gray seals in the harbor."

"Beg pardon?" What the hell? What did that have do with anything? He had a gray seal sitting at his kitchen table, so he didn't think anything else should surprise him.

"They only come once a year. Usually one. Sometimes two."

"Oh-kay."

"There was one in the harbor that day seven years ago. Waiting."

This time it was Ronan's turn for silence. Devon knew about the Selkies. He'd never figured the taciturn old man for a believer in myths. But then, he hadn't believed in them, either.

"Devon, what day is today?"

"April twenty-fifth. She only wants one thing from you. Don't fall in love with her. And don't come in to work." And he hung up, leaving a dial tone ringing in Ronan's ear.

Chapter Five

That was the most Devon Murphy had said to him in twenty years. Hell, it was probably more than Devon had said to his wife in twenty years. Ronan hung up the phone and turned to Meriel.

"He believes," he said.

"In what? In Selkies?"

He nodded, still reeling. There was a lot to take in this morning. But at least his hangover was gone.

"That's not as big a surprise as you might think, Ronan. A lot of people who make their living at sea believe things that ordinary people don't understand. From what I hear, the folks in Orkney don't even blink when one of us goes on land."

"Haven't you been on land before?"

Meriel shook her head as she poured coffee for them both.

"Part of the curse, I guess. I can't shapeshift when I want because I'm condemned to stay a Selkie. Somehow, saving you shorted out part of the spell. This amulet showed up when I asked the sea not to take your life, and I think it was the catalyst for me becoming human again. Even if it is just for a day." She sat with the mug cradled in her hands, breathing in the steam. "I didn't realize I missed coffee until I walked into the kitchen earlier and smelled it."

This woman was messing with his brain, because it didn't even faze him anymore when she talked about curses and magic from the ocean. From across the table, he watched her enjoy the cup. She was a shiverer, he realized. The things that turned her on made her whole body shimmy. He couldn't wait to see what happened when she came.

He shifted uncomfortably in his seat. The constant recurrence of his erection getting caught in his jeans was going to put a permanent crimp in his dick.

"What else did he say?" She interrupted his wayward thoughts.

"He said you were only after one thing, and I shouldn't fall in love with you."

"You shouldn't what?" she spluttered, using a napkin to wipe up the spills.

He waved away her question. He wasn't going to fall in love with her in a day, so it didn't need to be part of the discussion.

"I don't get how he knows all this stuff. He's never said a word about Selkies before. And he knew about you. Knew what happened the day you...you know."

Her brows knit together. "That's odd. I've never heard of another Selkie around here."

"What, you know every Selkie alive?"

"Hey, it's a small community." Meriel jabbed playfully at his arm. "I haven't met all of them, but word gets around."

"I knew it. A bunch of gossiping seals. What do you do when you get together? Toss beach balls around and slap your flippers together?"

She laughed and he smiled. The happy sound felt foreign and strange in this house and he drank it in, thirsty for joy.

"Not even close. I spent the last several years with Iona, learning the seas, eating more raw fish than a sushi chef on a busman's holiday, running from killer whales and freezing my butt off shuttling around the top of Great Britain."

"So being a Selkie isn't all it's cracked up to be?"

"Not even close. It might not be so bad if I'd been born a Selkie, but as a cursed one, it's not that much fun."

"Tell me more about this curse."

"I'd love to, really, but I have to say that sitting at the kitchen table isn't helping me figure out how to break this curse. And even if I can't figure it out, it's not how I want to spend my time as a human."

"You want to do something? Go out somewhere?"

"That sounds perfect." She stood and took her coffee to the sink. "Something that involves walking. I find I really miss walking. And I could use the practice."

"We can go down to the boatyards from here along the beach. Not too many people."

"Great. Do you have any shoes I can borrow?"

"There might be a pair of flip-flops in my room. It's a mess, but you can look."

Meriel opened the door to a cave. A dark, funky smelling cave. He might keep his kitchen clean, but it didn't look like he was so picky about his room.

It wouldn't hurt to air it out a little, so she pulled up the shade, wincing again when the sudden burst of light illuminated the true extent of the mess, and cracked the window.

A pile of clothes she hoped were clean tumbled out when she opened the closet doors, but a quick search didn't reveal any shoes. Where else could they be?

Meriel dropped to her knees and thrust an arm under the bed, knocking out various bits of clothing, discarded paper, a few carnivorous-looking dust bunnies and one expensive brown Italian leather wingtip—nearly gray with dust. She moved around to another end and continued the search. The other wingtip appeared, equally in need of a shine, before her hand encountered something soft and silky.

A tingle of magic traveled up her arm.

Her skin.

She could leave now. Get away from him before he realized how much control he could wield over her. Forget about breaking the curse and go back to the ocean.

It wasn't really as bad as she'd painted it. Not really. Well, aside from the cold part. And the killer whale part. And the raw fish part.

No. She knew where it was now. She could leave any time she wanted. And it would be nice to walk on the beach for a little while before she went back to the open seas. With no clues to work with, Meriel didn't hold out much hope for breaking the curse. Better to enjoy the time she had left and let the future take care of itself. She tucked the fur back under the bed.

"I don't want treasures," she said to the listening air, "but I could really use a pair of shoes." She opened her hand to find a pair of dripping mesh water shoes dangling from her fingertips. They were even in her size. "You know, you've got a really twisted sense of humor." She slid the shoes on before she went to find Ronan.

They walked down the sandy steps to the small beach where she'd brought him yesterday evening.

"It's been less than a day since I dragged you out of the water. How's your head?"

"Fine. There's barely even a bump anymore. So tell me about this curse."

"You've got a one-track mind, Ronan."

"I prefer to call it focused."

"I'm sure." Meriel sighed. "I don't want to talk about my curse right now. Can you tell me what I've missed? What happened to Burbank Industries?"

It was his turn to sigh.

"You went over the cliff at the party and the whole damn world fell apart. Naturally, we called the police and they ended up discovering that someone had been siphoning money off the corporation and cooking the books."

Meriel gasped. "Who was it?"

"Evan Murtaugh. He was using your terminal so he could pin the blame on the new girl if he ever got discovered."

"VP of Finance? That lying weasel. I never liked him. He always tried to look down my shirt."

Ronan glanced over and the light in his eyes turned hot. "I can't blame him for that."

"Men." It was so wrong to be flattered, but a thrill went through her anyway. "What happened then?"

"Murtaugh had his hands in deeper than we could have imagined. By the time we got the accounts straightened out, several of his sections were already bankrupt. After that, it was like quicksand. Everything around them got sucked down, too."

"I still don't understand how it could have been such a complete disaster. I mean, Burbank's was so diversified."

"It was the name that went to hell, Mer. Anything that had my name on it became suspect and deals started turning to dust in my hands." He looked down and shoved those hands into his pockets.

Meriel pulled him to a stop. "That doesn't make sense, Ronan. Something else happened."

Ronan turned to stare out at the sea. Yeah, something else had happened. Before they discovered the real culprit, the spotlight had turned on him. Every detail of his life had been laid bare to the courts—and to the press.

Someone found a sticky pad on the allegedly dead girl's desk with her name scribbled on it as "Mrs. Meriel Burbank", and a firestorm of speculation exploded. They'd been secret lovers. They were planning to run off to Brazil, or the Bermuda Triangle, or somewhere equally absurd. But in true tabloid form, the media speculated that something had happened between the doomed lovers and they fought. Ronan was even accused of shoving her off the cliff himself. Thankfully, there was no proof, not even a body, so no charges were brought.

Too late. He was already convicted in the eyes of the press and the public and after a while, even the few friends he had left began to distance themselves. That was the unkindest cut of all.

He told her. All of it. Even the parts that made his chest ache, though he kept the ache to himself.

"I don't know what to say, Ronan. I'm so sorry." She fought her way through his stiff stance, burrowing her arms under his and holding tight. Her lush little body gave off a blast of warmth and he took his hands out of his pockets. Slowly, he touched her. Put his hands on her shoulders and embraced her.

"No wonder you wanted to kill me."

"Meriel, I'm so sorry about that. I never meant to hurt you."

"It's all right, Ronan. I forgive you. And I'm sorry about my part in it. If I hadn't had that crush on you—written that stupid note—it might not have been so bad."

"Don't worry about it. It's over." The note meant nothing. He hadn't even known her then. But for what he'd done to her on the beach, he didn't deserve her forgiveness—and treasured it all the more. Ronan dropped a kiss on the top of her head and turned her back down the beach toward the boatyard.

"Come on. You still have to tell me your story. And I want you to meet Devon."

He tucked her hand firmly into his as they walked.

"I already told you a little bit of it. It's to do with great-great-Granny Byrne. A Selkie named Murchadha—"

"Who?"

"Murchadha. That's the old name. They're something else now, but I forget what." She pronounced the unusual word with a distinctly Celtish lilt, as if she'd learned to say it only one way—murkaya—pursing her lips, rolling over the r, with the accent on the first syllable. It didn't sound like any name he'd ever heard before.

"Anyway, he fell in love with her back in Ireland and gave her his skin, but she loved her husband and didn't know the magnitude of the gift she'd received. She left for America and took the skin with her. When Murchadha realized he'd been abandoned, he cursed her. Any child of her line would become a Selkie forever the moment they touched the sea. There's a way to get out of it, but everyone seems to have forgotten. Tough to break a curse when you don't know the way out."

Their fifteen minute walk took over an hour while Meriel wandered and played all over the beach. Things he took for granted, things he never even saw as he trudged to work each day, caught her eye.

"I've never really been to the beach before, Ronan," she said, breathless from playing chase with the tide. The sun made the silver medallion pinned to her shirt gleam almost as brightly as her dark hair. "I mean, going to that party at your house was the first time I'd been so close to the ocean and we know how that turned out."

"I've lived here all my life," he said. "I can't imagine not being near the water."

"It was just as hard for me to imagine not being around mountains and hills. Tennessee is beautiful, but so is this. I can see why people never want to leave."

They finally reached town and walked along the docks until they reached the boatyard.

"'Winner Take All Racing'. I like it."

Pride and an old bitterness warred in his blood at her words. Bitterness that he couldn't put his name up there if he wanted any business, but this time pride won. The race wasn't over yet for him.

He poked his head in the door and discovered silence.

"Anyone here?"

No answer, which was unusual. Devon practically lived at the yard. Not that it mattered. They were a little ahead of their deadline for the Sonar racing keelboat they were working on, so if he wanted to take some time off, it was no big deal.

He took her down to the boathouse to see the almost-finished boat, but there was no one there, either. "Looks like we're all alone." Ronan pulled aside the tarp that covered the gleaming little yacht. "Meriel, meet the *Sea Bright*."

"Oh my gosh, Ronan. She's beautiful." Meriel touched the boat reverently, rubbing her fingers over the sleek hull as it rocked on the water.

Fierce joy rushed through him as he watched her admire his work. At odds with the hopelessness of the night before, he realized that though he might have lost a lot, he'd also gained some things. He was proud of the work he did. As president of Burbank, Inc., he'd always been able to look at the company he inherited objectively, filtered through market analysis and stock figures.

But Winner Take All was personal. He had his hand in each product. Each boat bore his blood and sweat, his frustration, his pride and, at last, his joy.

"Thanks. She's the second we've built for these clients, and they won a cup at the Bay Haven Regatta with the first one. It looks good for marketing."

"Always thinking of the big picture," she teased. "But she truly is wonderful. Do you do the building yourself?"

"I'm only one part of the team here. We all have a hand in design and we all get in there with the tools and the grit." He showed her around the rest of the shop, pointing out different aspects of the design. When they walked past the *Sea Bright* again on their way out, Meriel paused.

She touched his hands, turning them over in her palms, tracing the rough spots. "These are good hands, Ronan. Strong, capable hands." She brought them to her face and he stroked her cheek with his thumbs. "I'm proud of you and I'm glad I was there to save you."

"I didn't think I was glad yesterday, but I am now." He bent down to kiss the smile from her lips. He'd forever relate the clean tang of the ocean with the wild flavor of her mouth.

She responded eagerly again, throwing herself into the kiss. Without hesitation, he pushed his hands under her shirt to touch the smooth skin of her back.

"Still want you," he whispered into her mouth, opening his eyes to see the flush of her cheeks.

She nodded, wordless, but her stomach chose that moment to growl loudly. They burst into laughter and it felt good. As if some dam inside him had broken at last.

"Let's get some dinner," he said. "You want sushi?"

"You think you're pretty funny, don't you?" She tickled his side and he twisted away from her.

"I'll have to work on my crabby hermit routine, I guess."

They left the building and Ronan locked up before he took her hand and walked with her up the pier.

Chapter Six

Toab's Market provided sustenance in the form of spaghetti, sausage, a jar of pasta sauce and a bottle of red wine. The loaf of warm fresh bread didn't quite make it back to the house as they tore off chunks and nibbled while they walked along the empty shore.

Misquapaug wasn't a popular tourist spot. The town had business to attend to and travelers soon discovered that unless they were fishing or visiting family, there wasn't much in the way of luxury amenities. Block Island, across the sound, catered to vacationers, but Misquapaug had no time to waste on such frivolity.

"Mrs. Toab likes you," Meriel said, watching the sky change hue over the water.

"She's about the only person in town who likes me. Everyone else thinks I murdered you. They wouldn't throw me a rope if I was drowning."

She punched him on the shoulder. "Hey, I didn't throw you a rope, either, buddy."

"That's right, you didn't." Ronan stopped. "Have I thanked you for that? For saving me?" His dark eyes were serious as he stared down at her. She was here for a day. Dawn to dawn. And in the space of a few hours, she'd lost her heart.

Stupid Selkie.

"Come on," he said, grabbing her hand and dragging her behind him.

"What? Wait. Where are we going?" She'd hoped for another kiss, not the Bataan Death March. Soon, however, they arrived at a familiar patch of beach. Sandy steps rose in front of them and Meriel tilted her head back to see the bulk of the Burbank mansion.

It was an impressive place, built at the turn of the twentieth century, and uniquely American, unlike the Roman, French and English revivals that influenced other mansions of the time. A Yankee clapboard house on a gigantic scale, it towered over the cliff in simple splendor.

"Ronan?" He led her into the mansion. They entered through a huge kitchen and he opened the refrigerator to deposit dinner fixings inside. He'd have kept going, but she went back to the fridge to take the wine out and set it on the countertop.

"Red wine likes room temperature."

"Mer, it's a six dollar bottle. With a screw-top."

"So? It might surprise you. Haven't you learned by now that appearances can be deceiving?" She grinned at him and he shook his head.

"Got any more clichés you'd like to spring on me?" He took her hand again and set off through the rest of the house.

"Money can't buy happiness."

"True, but poverty sucks."

"Beauty is only skin deep."

"That's disgusting, considering I know where your skin is."

"Ok, yeah. That's gross." It was covered in dust bunnies. She hoped they wouldn't itch when she had to put it back on.

Ronan Burbank was a determined man, she realized as they crossed room after room, each one devoid of furniture and decoration. The stark simplicity, however, emphasized the true grandeur of the home. This place didn't depend on decoration for its beauty. It had beauty built into its bones. Like its owner. Ronan was as stripped down as his house, but his inner strength was undimmed. Right now, he had one goal in mind and didn't intend to deviate from his course. He was so focused, he wasn't even answering her. She was curious enough to let him keep going. For a while, at least.

Finally, he brought her into a dim hallway, illuminated only by what little sun could reach into the shadows. Before he could open the door, however, she stopped him with a hand on his arm.

"Here's one. Better to have loved and lost than never to have loved at all."

He looked down at her, his face indistinct in the darkness.

"We'll see about that."

Ronan opened the massive oak door with an appropriately eerie creak. They stepped into the black.

"Stay right there for a sec." He left her standing in what could only be called stygian darkness, but that was a little too close for comfort, considering her already otherworldly circumstances. The prickly fingers of self-inflicted terror crept up her neck as his footsteps abruptly disappeared.

A metallic jingle sounded from far ahead of her, then light. Ronan drew back the heavy velvet curtains and thick motes of dust danced in the sudden sunlight. They were in the library.

But not any library. It was the kind she'd read about in Gothic novels. Floor to ceiling shelves crammed with leather bound tomes, odds and ends of natural history, and a few rows of paperback novels. There was even a rolling ladder attached to a brass rail at the top so readers could climb up to reach books on the highest shelves. A bibliophile's dream come true.

Meriel drew in a deep, wondering breath and choked on the dust.

Ronan pounded her on the back until she held up a hand in surrender. "I'm fine. But this...this is amazing." Meriel straightened and walked to a shelf to run her fingers over the spines.

"It's pretty impressive, but a lot of it's for show. There are six sets of *The Rise and Fall of the Roman Empire*, all in different covers. My great-grandfather thought they looked important." His eyebrow quirked, letting her in on the cynical joke, and she laughed. She had to. The library that looked like a fantasy really was one.

But not entirely. She could tell that people had used it. Her eyes were drawn to the paperbacks and she discovered title after title by Georgette Heyer.

"My aunt." Ronan's voice came over her shoulder. "I mean, Georgette Heyer wasn't my aunt, but my aunt loved those books. Said they made her happy."

"I've read a few," Meriel answered. "They made me happy, too."

"I tried one, and it was kind of fun, but, you know, a guy reading romances." He looked sheepish at his admission.

"Which one did you read?"

"I can't remember the title. I remember she shot the hero. That was cool."

Meriel laughed again. The room absorbed the sound as though hungry for it. Every time she laughed, it felt as though some oppression lifted.

"So if we're not in the library to admire your aunt's collection of Regency romances, why are we here?"

"You."

"What about me?"

"Your curse. We can't play all day, Meriel." He looked so serious, his dark eyes focused on her.

"We haven't played all day. We fought until lunch time."

"And other things."

She felt her face flush. Yeah. Other things. Things she'd much rather be doing now than scouring through a library for the solution to a curse that was mostly forgotten.

His hands, big and rough and warm, gripped her shoulders. "Hey, if it doesn't work, at least this way you can say you tried. And if it does work..." He tipped her chin up with a finger and his gaze heated. "Wouldn't you like to stay and do...other things for a while longer?"

Ronan's head dipped to hers and stopped a heartbeat away. Her choice. She closed the gap in surrender. He tasted good. Like home, but not her old home. A home she dreamed of. The tang of toothpaste had faded and all that was left was Ronan. Rich, like dark chocolate and red wine. Under her fingers, his hair curled and clung like silken ties, binding her heart to his.

He wrapped his arms around her and she leaned on his strength, soaking it in because she needed it. Needed to feel his hard body against hers.

"Ouch!" Her cry was muffled against his mouth and he let go abruptly.

Meriel rubbed at her breast—not exactly ladylike, but darn it, something had poked her in the boob. The jeweled amulet from the ocean had nicked her. What a metaphor. Stabbed by magic.

She took the brooch off and laid it on the table.

"What is that thing, anyway?" Ronan bent down to examine it. He touched it and then jerked his finger away with a hiss.

"What happened?"

"It shocked me." He brought his finger up to his mouth and sucked on it for a moment. "Like I touched a live fuse. Not a bad shock, but it got me." He looked at the brooch in disgust. "Maybe it doesn't like me."

"I don't know if it likes you or not, but it saved your life." In the stillness of the abandoned house, the aquatic song rushed again in her ears.

"What?"

"When I hauled you out of the water, you weren't breathing. It wasn't fair."

"Fair?"

"I mean, it's bad enough that I'm already cursed. But watching someone die in the water where I changed seemed infinitely more awful than I could handle. So I called on the ocean to save you. The amulet washed up on shore. I laid it on your chest and mercy was granted, but at a price. The magic said that your destiny was now tangled in mine. Then you came back."

It sounded ridiculous when she put it into words. Ronan's eyebrow was back up, too.

"Don't look at me like that. Like you don't believe me. I'm a Selkie, for crying out loud. And you're here. Not dead."

Ronan pulled a chair out from the table and sat down backwards, resting his arms on the ornate back. Meriel sat as well, precisely, knees together, ankles crossed. She needed to get this right so he would believe her.

"Ronan, there's a world under the water you can't imagine. Deeper than humans can understand. After seven years, after all I've seen, I still don't understand it. If I live forever, I never will."

She touched the amulet, tracing her finger around the wrought seal—stark and fantastic.

"I didn't even believe this existed."

"What is it?"

"This is the Heart of the Sea."

The Heart of the Sea. A fairy tale. A myth. But a powerful one. The name resonated in Ronan's head with the buzz of truth.

"It can't be."

Meriel looked at him sideways.

"What do you mean, it can't be? Do you know what it is?"

"The Heart of the Sea. It's just a story. It doesn't really exist."

She opened her mouth, but he stood up, cutting her off. Where was it? Ronan tried to remember. He'd been about ten years old. Grounded again for God knew what reason, so he decided to check out the library. It couldn't be any more boring than his room.

He walked to the door and turned around, surveying the room, trying to see from a child's eyes. It had been up high, which was part of the attraction. Something about the cover had sparkled, catching his eye. There was gold leaf on the spine, but now everything was coated with a thick layer of dust.

Ronan climbed the ladder and shoved off, the way he had back then. But he was heavier now and the rail was spotty with rust, so he only creaked over a few inches.

"Meriel, can you give me a hand? Just push. I know what I'm looking for."

She looked up at him for a moment, no doubt questioning his sanity, but she pushed. She trusted that he'd find it. She trusted him. He pulled along the rail until he was there. Right there. The spine wasn't perfectly aligned with the other books and it stuck out a little. *Tales of the Cold Sea.*

"Found it." He climbed back down the ladder, and took Meriel's chin in his free hand. "Thanks, Mer." He kissed her quickly and her eyes widened, so he smiled and kissed her again. Slowly. With his eyes open, watching her watch him until her lids fluttered shut. He shouldn't get distracted. There was no time for it, but he couldn't help himself.

Her lips were cool against his, her cheek smooth under his hand. The scent of the sea went straight to his head and he wanted to kiss her in the water, float next to her, touch her wet, bare skin and feel her slide against him.

She was pressed to his side and he nudged his thigh between hers, needing to feel her response the way he had earlier. She took his invitation and purred as she rubbed against him, layers of denim in their way. A whimper of frustration left her—God, he loved listening to the sounds she made. The book slipped from his hands and landed on the floor with a sharp smack.

The sound startled her out of his arms and they both laughed.

"Maybe we should work on this," he said as he bent to retrieve the book.

She cleared her throat and pushed her dark hair behind her ears as she opened the pages and began to read. She'd brushed it before they left the house, but playing on the beach had whipped it into a carefree style, individual strands set free to catch the sun. Layers of color shot through the brown and he watched gold and red intermingle.

Ronan knew the woman in front of him wasn't model gorgeous. She was better. She was real. And until dawn, she was his. The idea nearly made him grab her and take her right there on the table. So tempting to step back between her legs, strip her naked and indulge himself between those beautiful thighs until the sun broke the sky again.

Shit. *Eight times four is thirty-six. The United States has won twenty-eight of thirty-two America's Cup yacht races. The Block Island Race was established in 1946 and George David's ninety-foot boat,* Rambler, *took top honors there this year.* Ronan's breath slowed as he cited statistics. If he lost control now, Meriel would be gone at dawn. But if they could find the answer to her curse, she could stay.

In a way, he felt responsible for what had happened. If she hadn't come to work for him, she never would have come to the company party, never would have come near that cliff. If not for him, she would never have been forced to live out a curse that wasn't her fault at all.

A low gasp drew his attention.

"Ronan? I think I found it."

The illustration on the front page of the story was an almost perfect replica of the brooch on the table.

The story told of the Viking ocean god, Aegir, who loved his wife, Ran, so much that he wished to travel to the depths of his domain to bring back the most perfect jewel in existence. However, even Aegir, with all his power, could not swim as

142

deeply as he needed to find the jewel, so he asked a Selkie to help him. In return, the sons of Ivaldi, dwarves and master craftsmen, molded the setting in honor of the seal-folk.

"Okay, so what does that say about the power of the jewel?" he asked when they finished reading.

Meriel groaned and laid her head on her arms. "I have no idea."

"So we're not any further along than when we started." Maybe this hadn't been such a good idea. He wanted to help her, not make this puzzle more difficult.

"There's got to be something there, but it's not on the surface. Maybe it's like analyzing literature back in high school. A deeper meaning, some symbolism that we're not seeing."

"Mer. I sucked at analyzing literature." He did remember that Mr. Connor had always worn his pants hiked way up above his waist, but that wasn't very helpful right now.

"Well, I didn't. I was good at it. It's like those puzzles where you have to focus your eyes just right to see the picture. We need to adjust the way we're looking at it."

Ronan rose to his feet and stretched. "Let's bring the book back to the house so we can think and eat at the same time."

"Multi-tasking. You're a man of many talents, Ronan." She smiled at him and he stared. She fit. Here, in this house he loved so much. Sitting in the library with dust on her cheek and the sun in her hair. He wished he could give her what she needed. The very least he could do was feed her. He held out his hand.

"Come on, Meriel. Let's go home."

Chapter Seven

They ended up with a decent meal, considering that Meriel hadn't cooked in a while. Ronan had learned a few things about making do for himself, and they bumped hips in the kitchen. They ate playing footsie under the table with their sandy toes, her body growing tense with anticipation.

"I'll wash, you dry," he said and Meriel nodded. She cleared the table while he filled the sink with soapy water. She tried to keep her mind on the story they'd read, but she couldn't concentrate. She had nothing, although that wasn't quite true.

She had the rest of the night with him.

Twice while they worked, she opened her mouth to say something. Anything. But then her mind blanked out. She couldn't think of anything that didn't sound lame or desperate.

Finally, she put away the last dish. The towel in her hands was damp and she folded it. Then folded it again. The edges had to be just so. Because if they were perfect then he wouldn't notice how nervous she was, right?

It was odd. She'd never been a particularly sexual person before she changed. She'd had boyfriends, some more serious than others. She'd even indulged in a fling or two. And this...this was a fling, right? Just sex?

She didn't really know him, he didn't know her. Though that wasn't true anymore. She knew more about the real Ronan

144

Burbank now than she had learned after weeks of moon-eyed day-dreaming and mild obsession. And he was the only person now who understood what had happened to her. What she'd become.

This wasn't as simple as she wanted it to be. But the dish towel had perfectly square corners.

Ronan took it from her, opened it, undoing all her work, and laid it out over the dish rack. She couldn't look at him, so he tucked a finger under her chin.

"We don't have to do this, Meriel. We can wait."

She shook her head, tears starting. "We can't wait, Ronan. The curse is impossible to break. I go back to the sea at dawn to be a Selkie forever. And I want this. I want you. But I also want time. The one thing I can't have."

"Then we'll make the best of the time we have."

The kiss in the kitchen was followed by a kiss in the living room. They kissed again in the hall and stumbled through the door to his room.

"We're changing the sheets first," she said. At least it smelled better than it had that morning. He eyed the rumpled bed and the chaos on the floor.

"Fast. We're changing the sheets fast." He went back out to grab a set from the linen closet in the hall. She shoved the piles of clothes into one towering mountain in the corner and stripped the bed with a yank. The magic of her skin under the bed called out to her, but she ignored it.

Hurriedly, they tucked the fitted sheet on the bed, tossed the top sheet over and stuffed pillows into fresh cases.

"I'm not making hospital corners for you, woman."

"What? Not interested in doing the job right?" she teased, seeing the tension in his body. Somehow, it made her feel better that she wasn't the only one running on nerves tonight.

He dropped his pillow onto the mattress and crossed around the bed in two strides. "Oh, I plan to do one job right tonight," he growled. She shivered at the sensual promise in his words.

"Want to see you," Ronan said. Meriel stood pliable in front of him as he slowly drew the shirt over her head. The nubby texture of the cotton shirt, smooth a moment before, now felt like burlap, scraping at her senses until she was free. The weight of moonlight on her skin was all she could bear as she returned the favor for him.

She took base advantage of his beautiful flesh as he removed his clothing. His skin under her lips was hot and smooth as she kissed her way around his body. Meriel reached up on tiptoe to press a soft kiss at the nape of his neck, following the trail down to the rise of his tight, muscled ass.

She straightened and pressed her breasts into his back while she reached around to tweak his hard nipples. She loved being in this position herself, loved the power of a man enveloping her from behind, but had never experienced it like this. She hummed, a throaty sound that they passed between them.

His hands took their own path, reaching back to pull her thighs closer to his, running his fingers up the cleft between them.

Meriel sucked in a breath as he discovered the wetness that had been seeping from her for the past hour in anticipation of this moment.

His head bowed with a groan and she pressed her brow to his spine.

Ronan turned abruptly. "I'm going to try to take this as slowly as I can, Mer. I'll try."

"At least we can start that way." Slow...fast...she knew there would come a point where all she would want was him inside her.

He walked her to the bed and watched as she lay back. This had always been a difficult moment for her. Like this, with him standing over her, she was vulnerable, open. His gaze burned where it touched, but slowly she tensed. When they touched body to body, he couldn't see her flaws, but they were all on display while he watched her.

In a moment, he looked away and bent to retrieve his jeans, digging in the back pocket. He held up the packets like golden coins. "Buried treasure," he said, tossing a handful of condoms onto the bedside table.

"Where did you get them?"

"They've been in the bathroom. But earlier I was so obsessed I couldn't think straight."

"Obsessed, huh?"

"Muddled. Lust-crazed." Each phrase was punctuated by kisses. Along her neck where he tongued the flesh under her ear, which made her shudder. Down to the sensitive spot at the top of her shoulder. Ronan bit oh-so-gently and she cried out. "Out of my head with wanting you." He whispered the last words to her collar bone as he lazily kissed his way down her chest.

Meriel dug her heels into the mattress and arched up, trying to reach his mouth with her breasts, but he was inexorable in his determination to make her wait.

He didn't even touch them, but let his fingers drift around her belly, drawing circles around her navel until finally, he held the weight of her breasts in his hands. She'd been wound up for

147

hours since the abrupt end of their kitchen session. The sensation of his body on hers now made her desperate for more and she breathed out one word.

"Ronan."

The sound of his name actually sparkled in his ears as he heard her softly moan. A few more of those pleading words and he'd be plunging into her, past coherent thought.

Her breasts were a feast and he gorged himself, finding the difference in flavor and texture from one nipple to the other, from the skin at the top of the sloping mounds to the flesh underneath. But as he tasted, another sense was aroused.

Her scent rose from beneath him, cool and fresh. Ronan kissed his way down her body to find its source, pleased when she opened for him. He'd always preferred women who expected the best from their lovers. He enjoyed the challenge of living up to their expectations.

The soft, short hair around her pubis shifted back from his touch, leaving him with bare skin, sweet lips that already shone with moisture.

He kissed it away, listening to the sound of hungry approval she made. Ronan parted her outer lips with his hand, revealing the treasure beneath, the silken flesh, the hardening bead at the top. He breathed her in.

Each lick, each suckle, each probing touch of his tongue and fingers wound her tighter and tighter. Her hands were in his hair, on his face, her smooth, strong thighs tensed around him and still he pushed her, concentrated on finding the places that made her shiver until finally she exploded beneath him. Meriel cried out, her body shaking in time with the pulses of the orgasm that coursed through her, the climax he could feel run under her skin as he changed his focus. Ronan soothed her now with kisses on her smooth belly, two fingers buried inside her body until she breathed again.

Meriel turned away, breaking his hold, and buried her face in a pillow. Ronan climbed up to lay next to her, dismayed to find her shoulders shaking. She was crying. He'd seen her laughing, angry, and afraid, but these tears were beyond his understanding.

"Mer," he said, sliding an arm under her. She threw herself onto his chest, sobbing even more wildly, and there was nothing he could do but hold her until the storm passed. Not that he was complaining. Meriel was a perfect armful. Soft and feminine, graceful and earthy. She was a woman of wonderful contrasts and he wondered if he'd get the chance to learn more of them. Slowly, the sobs ebbed.

"I'm sorry," she whispered.

"Did I hurt you, Meriel? Did I do something wrong?"

"God no, Ronan. I was just...overwhelmed. I've never—"

"Never what?" Because if he'd hurt her in some way, he wanted to know so he never did it again.

"I've never flown that high before." Her words were so quiet, he had to strain to hear. "It was amazing. Absolutely amazing."

As her tears dried, one of her slender hands began to move across his chest and abs. He tried to concentrate on her face, on her voice, but it was damn distracting.

Finally, he simply let himself be distracted and leaned back into the pillows, allowing her free rein. Her body temperature was lower than his and the slight contrast of her cold fingers on his hot skin left a trail of buzzing sensation wherever she touched.

Boldly, she circled her hand around the base of his erection and used her palm to slide skin over nerve endings until liquid leaked from the tip and dripped over her fingers.

Ronan reached for a condom. "I've been ready for hours, Mer. I can't wait much longer."

She let him tear it open, but then took matters into her own hands, pressing a tender kiss to the head of his shaft before she rolled the rubber over his aching cock. Even those light touches felt like lightning bolts to his system.

"Then let's not wait anymore," she said, spreading her legs to straddle him. With his hands on her hips, he watched her face as she sank down to swallow him in one agonizingly slow move.

He wasn't a talker and neither was she, but she was vocal. Her moans fed his and the occasional "More" or "Harder" or "Oh yes" were the only words that punctuated the silence of the room along with the soft, wet, sliding sounds of their lovemaking.

They moved. He was harder than ever as he rose above her, sliding in and out of her body, her legs wrapped around him, their tongues mimicking the movement of their hips.

They shifted again. On his knees, he skimmed a hand down the smooth skin of her back, reaching under her to cup her breast. Ronan moved his hands under her shoulders, bringing her back to his chest, pulling her down onto his cock, pushing himself deeper than he'd ever gone. The gasps and groans were almost constant now as her pitch wound ever higher. Meriel began to curl in on herself and at the first silken contraction of her womb around him, he let himself go, pounding into her, shouting out her name over and over in his climax while she keened and sobbed again, twisting as the waves of her peak slammed her against him.

Meriel slumped forward and he grasped at her desperately, needing her body against his as their breath heaved in tandem. Her fingers fluttered over the arm he held around her waist and the words that tumbled from her lips were in no language he had ever heard.

Exhaustion hit him hard and he lowered her to the bed, watching as she curled up into a ball. Her eyes were still open when he returned from cleaning up, but she was covered by a blanket now.

"Your skin."

She nodded.

"You knew where it was the whole time."

"It's not like you hid it very well, Ronan." She smiled and lifted a corner, inviting him in. Cautiously, he slid his body behind hers, bending up his knees so they fit together like spoons. He put his arm around her waist and pulled her closer. Her hair floated into his face and he freed himself with a smile.

The fur settled over them. The warmth and the evenness of Meriel's breathing lulled him to sleep.

Chapter Eight

Wrapped in the arms of her lover, under a blanket of magic, Meriel woke. Someone was calling her name. Iona? What was she doing on land?

Meriel pressed a kiss to the tips of the bristles on Ronan's cheek and slid out of bed. She pulled her discarded blue polo shirt on over her nudity and crept out the door. A storm brewed over the ocean and the wind whistled around the edges of the house.

"Iona?" she called. "What's wrong? It's not close to dawn yet, is it?"

"No," said a harsh male voice from the shadows. Iona stumbled forward, propelled by a shove from behind. The Selkie was old and her skin was wrinkled and gray with the cold. Meriel reached out for her, but rough hands grabbed her. Their captor, having what he wanted, pushed Iona away from them. The old woman didn't even have time to cry out before she fell. The sound of her head hitting a paving stone made Meriel's stomach churn with dread. A strong hand over her mouth prevented her from calling for help.

"We've got you now, Byrne. You've had your day in the sun, but now it's time to end this." He held her close, his arm a steel band around her waist, cutting off her air. She knew that voice.

She'd heard it before somewhere, but she was too scared to think it through.

"What do you want?" Meriel asked. Terror and breathlessness kept her voice low.

"We want you to finish this curse. We've waited more than two centuries for a Byrne to touch water. We won't give you up after only seven years."

"What do you mean, finish the curse? I couldn't find a way out of it. I'm going back to the sea at dawn. I know that already." She looked over at her friend, but in the dark, she couldn't tell if Iona was breathing or not.

"You think that's it? You think the curse is that you only get to come on land once in a while?" He laughed and the sound made her feel filthy, as if she'd lain in rotten kelp. "You're as stupid as your granny. No, this is a curse for all time. You ruined us. Left us on land, alone, until we died, dry as a husk and bitter as the Dead Sea. No, we're after despair and grief. We're after seeing that you feel our pain."

"We?" Who was he talking about? And how did he know so much about the curse? "Who are you?"

"The name changed, but the curse lives on." The crazy man's voice was a discordant sing-song in a thick Yankee seaboard accent. The accent. She knew that accent.

"Murphy. Devon Murphy. You're Ronan's friend."

He snorted. "Spoiled rich boy. Trust fund baby. One little scandal and he spends the next seven years whining and moaning about how they took everything away from him." He dragged her down the sandy steps to the beach. Meriel tried to trip him. She'd rather be dead of a broken neck than let this man take her, but he just picked her up and carried her, pinning her legs so she couldn't kick. A dead-looking hummock of fur lay on the sand. Iona's skin.

Meriel swallowed hard. "Don't you talk about him that way, jackass." She pounded his back, but he ignored her.

"He thinks his family was strong. My ancestor is in my blood, in my head. Murchadha passed long ago, but his children were all raised on the bitterness of his life. And now that we've got you, Byrne, we mean to make you pay."

A sturdy motorboat was tied to the boathouse and he pushed her in. The last thing she saw was his huge fist swinging toward her head. The last thing she heard was the motor firing.

ഇരൂര്

Ronan woke to the smell of fish. He opened his eyes to the unwelcome sight of a naked, wrinkled, saggy old woman.

"Gah!"

"Gah, yourself, Ronan Burbank. Get up and bring Meriel's skin with you."

"What?"

"Get up. Devon Murphy has Meriel and he's planning to kill her."

The mere mention of danger to his woman galvanized him and he leapt out of bed. Unfortunately, he forgot he was naked, too, and cupped himself, trying to avoid the old woman's knowing gaze.

"It's a pity I'm not a few dozen years younger or I might have come on land for that, myself."

"Umm, thanks? Turn around, lady."

She sighed and turned as he yanked on his jeans and shoved his feet into deck shoes. He pulled a shirt over his head and grabbed Meriel's sealskin. It still held her scent—their scent. When he picked it up, something tumbled out and thunked on the floor at his feet. Ronan bent to pick it up. The brooch lay heavy and cold in his hand.

"She left it here?"

"It was pinned to her shirt. Must have fallen off." He shoved it in his pocket. Then Ronan pulled the only decent shirt he owned off a hanger and handed it to his guest. "Please. Now what happened?"

The old lady didn't waste any words as she buttoned the shirt and followed him down to the dock. "He's a descendant of Murchadha and he knows the rest of the curse. That means he knows how to break it, too. Careless of the Byrnes to have forgotten it over all these years."

Shit. The motorboat was gone from the boathouse. He'd wrecked the dinghy yesterday—was it only a day ago?

"Come on. We can go out on the *Sea Bright*," he said to the lady, and settled in for a run to the boatyard. When they got there, Ronan charged the door, knowing he'd locked it. He bounced off with a new bruise.

"Calm yourself," the old woman said. A sealskin was draped over her arm. It must have been her own, mottled with white spots. Meriel's was purest silver.

As he watched, the old lady's hands glowed. Silver and blue-green light played over her fingers for a moment before she opened them, showing him the key.

"Who are you?" he asked as he unlocked the door and started flinging off the dock lines that bound the boat.

"My name is Iona and we've met before. I told you this would happen then."

The keelboat's hull rocked in the waves as he pulled open the massive doors that led straight out to Block Island Sound. He had no idea what she was talking about and he didn't care. Only one thing mattered.

"Are you in or out?" he asked.

"I'm in," the old lady said as she climbed nimbly aboard. Ronan pushed the *Sea Bright* off from the dock and set about running up the rigging.

The squall beckoned them closer, lightning dancing along the water as wind filled the spinnaker. The sleek little boat shot forward.

"You're the old woman from the party," he shouted over the noise of the wind and storm. Ronan remembered her now as he brought the mainsail around to take advantage of the whipping storm. "You said I'd find all I needed in the sea and then you disappeared. You knew all this would happen."

"I was right then and I'm right now when I tell you that your true love will die if we don't get to her in time. Now sail!"

True love? How did you fall in love with someone in a day? He didn't deny it. He couldn't. Maybe it was only the beginning, only a seed of love, but it was there. Enough to let him know that if he saved Meriel, it would grow into something strong and true.

The line in his hands nearly jerked him over the side when a vicious gust hit. It had been a long time since he'd had the time to crew a racing yacht. In truth, he was a better builder than sailor. But now it was time to face facts, do what he had to do, and concentrate on the task at hand.

Devon Murphy was a madman. And an unattractive madman, at that. When he cackled to himself, he sounded like an old bag lady and his lips peeled back from huge yellow horse teeth. Then there was the smell—a scent of rotting fish and decay.

Meriel's entire head boomed in tandem with the throb of the motor as it chugged mightily against the storm.

"Have you lost your mind?" she yelled at him.

"Hee hee," he screeched. "Murchadha will have his vengeance."

"Murchadha was a juvenile bastard who blamed the wrong person for his stupid decision. He knew Granny Byrne was married to a man she loved, but he thought he was so damned special he could change her." Meriel scrambled to her knees. "I hope you and your entire screw-loose family rot in hell for this!"

"You're going to die, and your true love is going to die, and Murchadha will rest in peace and finally get the hell out of my head." He really was nuts. He thought a dead Selkie was talking to him. She'd have felt sorry for him if he wasn't trying to kill her.

"My true love? You mean Ronan?" Was this the ocean's prophecy coming true? That Ronan's fate was bound in hers—even if it killed them both? Surely the curse couldn't ask so much of her. Meriel realized she needed to deflect the psycho's attention back to her.

"He doesn't love me, he barely knows me. And I want you to keep him out of this curse. It's got nothing to do with him."

"It's too late for that now. Too late since the moment you called on the sea to save him. You love him already and that's the truth of it. That's the curse of it. Any child of the Byrne line will become a Selkie forever if it touches the sea."

"Yeah, yeah. I know that part already."

"But you didn't know about the loophole. The one that gave you the ability to become human for a day. You saved a man and in return, you were given a day of humanity. It gave you hope, though you knew you had to return to the sea by dawn or die, right?"

Meriel closed her eyes against the truth. She had hoped. And she had loved. "Right."

"You need your skin. Without it, you can't swim well enough to survive in the water."

"Again, I know this part." Now she was starting to get annoyed. He was enjoying her misery way too much.

"But when you shifted and found your true love, that's when the clock started. You never had a chance."

"Could this be any more complicated? Your ancestor must have had a lot of time on his hands to make this up."

"Shut up, faithless whore," he screamed at her, spittle flying.

"Ew." She made a show of wiping her face, though she couldn't tell his spit from the splashes of water that drenched her.

"The same sea that saved your true love will kill him now. Ronan will die trying to save you tonight. He'll sacrifice his own life for yours." Murphy leaned close and she swore she could see hell-fire burning in his eyes. "And you'll live forever as a Selkie then. Unable to shift ever again, knowing that your love is what killed him."

The urge to weep in terror and hopelessness was strong. They were far out to sea and with the squall blowing around them, she didn't know in which direction they'd fled. She could dive over the side, but she knew she'd never make it back to shore as a human.

Without her skin, she couldn't shift back. And without her... Meriel grabbed at her shirt, looking for the amulet pinned there, but it was gone. Oh no. It must have fallen off, but when? In the bedroom? Or on that torturous trip to the boat? Worse, what if it had gone overboard, back to the ocean it came from?

A brief, quiet hole in the storm made one thing clear.

"No more gas," Murphy shrieked as his manic glee turned to fury. A large wave lifted the little boat and slapped it back down into a trough. Meriel watched as it finally dawned on her kidnapper that she and Ronan weren't the only ones who might die that night.

"Do something," he demanded, twisting the starter in vain.

"Gee whiz, what do you think I should do?" She knew it wasn't smart to taunt a nutcase, but what the hell, right? What else could he do to her? So she lifted her brow and mocked both her tormentor and the raging sea.

"Help. Help," she said in her most deadpan voice. Meriel settled back into the corner and crossed her arms. "There. I did something."

He grabbed a wrench and raised it to wallop her when another wave crashed over the stern and flooded the cockpit. Enemies became teammates for the frantic minutes it took to scoop out the water.

"It's almost dawn," Murphy said as they panted in tandem. "You're going to die now."

"You'll die with me, you miserable piece of lobster shit." Inspiration struck her as something became clear. "And if I die without my true love, the curse dies with me. Bet Murchadha will be real impressed with you when you meet him in hell."

The crazy man blanched at her words and she was almost cruel enough to laugh at him.

Then she heard her name. It should have been impossible over the wind and crashing thunder, but there it was.

"Meriel, wait!"

The *Sea Bright*'s sail cut through the gale. It was an extraordinary feat of sailing to have made it this far through the storm, Her pride knew no bounds. He really was good at everything he did.

But her euphoria was followed by bowel-loosening fear. Oh God, no. He couldn't be here. She couldn't let him die. She waved at him, frantic for him to go back to shore and safety.

"Go back, Ronan! Go back!" Murphy's hand at her back was so cold it burned. His mad laugh rang in her ears as he shoved her over the side.

Meriel twisted, tripping over a loose line in the bottom of the boat and she grabbed at him, at anything. He looked surprised when her hand closed on his shirt. She was too far over the edge to recover and, hauling Murphy with her, they fell into the cold embrace of the sea.

Looking up at the roiling sky from two feet down was like peering into a different world. Under the water, it was calm, serene and dark. Peaceful.

Meriel pulled herself up and broke the surface right before a wave swept over her head. Salt water flooded her mouth and nose and she choked, clawing for air. Ronan swam toward her and she grabbed for him.

"Here," he yelled, dropping something over her head. As soon as it touched her skin, the magic shot through her. The transformation back to seal was as painful as the change to human had been and she struggled weakly back to the air when it was over, searching for Ronan's beloved face above the waves.

She saw him, but only for a moment before he slipped under.

"No!" Meriel swam out, but lost him in the darkness under the water. Lightning above her illuminated a pale arm sinking down and she dove for him.

This was worse, infinitely worse than saving him had been the first time. It felt as if something was pulling against her, dragging him into the depths.

She looked down to see Murphy's mad eyes staring up at her. He wasn't even fighting to get back to the surface. Meriel realized he was already dead, his fingers locked around Ronan's legs.

Oh God. She couldn't pull them both to the surface, but if she let go of Ronan, he'd die before she could get Murphy free of him.

The curse was winning. Ronan was sacrificing his life for her, and she would live all the rest of her days alone at sea. She hadn't realized a heart could actually break, until hers shattered in her chest.

Ronan reached out and rested both his hands on her face. One hand was clasped around something—a glimmer of silver— the brooch.

"I love you," he mouthed. A trail of bubbles left his lips and he arched in pain as his lungs filled with water.

Ronan Burbank died smiling at her.

Chapter Nine

The weight was gone. Murphy's hand had finally unclenched and he sank like hell-born brimstone as Ronan's body rose with her to the surface.

The fast-moving storm had swept over them while she fought and lost the battle for Ronan's life under the sea. Now, as she raised his face above the waves, stars peeked out of the thin clouds racing past in the sky.

The *Sea Bright* was still floating, but her mast was snapped in half, the mainsail trailing in her lazy wake. A sleek gray head popped up next to her.

"Help me get him in the boat, Iona." Her friend blinked and a trail of water that looked like tears dripped down her cheeks. Meriel wondered if there was a matching trail on her own face.

Other heads appeared, bobbing along the surface. Selkies from all over the area had come, called by magic...called by love. The words that left her mouth sounded even and calm.

"Can you help me get him back to port? Back to his people? He built a fine boat and it would be a shame to let it go to waste out here." And the *Sea Bright* was a fine boat. She'd carried him through the storm and it was fitting that this great vessel bear him home again.

"Aren't you going with him, Meriel?" Iona asked.

"I'll help guide the boat." She'd fall apart later. On her own. In the quiet depths of the ocean where no one could hear her scream her grief to heaven.

"No," the older Selkie said. "You're going back with him."

Meriel laughed, though it made the broken pieces of her heart pierce her so she bled. "I'd like to see that tabloid headline. 'Seal haunts bay, mourning dead man'. I don't think so. I never want to be around humans again. Look what I did, Iona. The curse came true because of every stupid mistake I ever made and a good man—a great man—died for it."

"I didn't take you for a coward, miss."

Meriel gasped. The last thing she expected from her friend and mentor was cruelty.

"What makes you think a curse can have any effect on true love?"

"I don't understand."

"That's because you weren't born magic. That's what we are, Meriel. We're magic. Magic from the hands of God Himself. And what is God?"

"God is love," Meriel answered. Some Sunday school lessons stuck forever.

"And love always, always triumphs over evil. Though it may occasionally take quite some time." The other Selkies clustered around Iona and Meriel and their sad eyes spoke of shared tragedy. She could feel the charge of destiny in the water.

"A curse cannot stand in the way of true love," Iona repeated. "Do you want to remain a Selkie forever?"

"No," Meriel barked immediately, then paused. "No offense." A chuckle went through the gathering.

"None taken. Do you love Emory Charles Ronan Burbank IV?"

Meriel answered more carefully this time. "He's only part of the man I am coming to love. I love Ronan Burbank. A boat builder. A good, strong man."

Iona smiled and touched Meriel with a flipper. "Then go to him."

This time, the change wasn't painful. Music—the creek's trill, the ocean's roar, the river's rush, the spring's bubble— lifted her out of the water. A silver, blue-green light flowed out of the water upward, into, and around her. Her feet touched the water and she sank back into its embrace. A weight was gently lifted away and then the light receded. So simple. Except she forgot to tread water and was promptly dunked under a small, lapping wave.

Meriel came back up coughing, laughing and crying at the same time as her friends, her ocean-bound family, laughed with her. She swam to the side of the boat and hauled herself up and over. She looked down over the edge to find Iona holding something in her teeth. It was her skin, and when she touched it, she realized it still held the tingle of magic. She pulled her arm back.

"It won't hurt you," Iona said through her teeth. Meriel took the pelt and discovered that it held something besides magic.

"Don't drop them," warned the Selkie as Meriel peeked inside. The dark blue glitter of a hundred sapphires threw the weak light of dawn back at her.

"Find a place for the stones and then lie down with your love. Use the magic that's left in the pelt to bring him back to you."

"Thank you," she said to her friend as she realized that the boat was moving. Sleek, round heads in every shade of brown and gray bobbed through the water as they propelled the craft landward.

Meriel found a covered tin pail in the tiny hold and dumped the stones in there before she settled in next to Ronan's still form. He was so cold.

"This will work. It has to work because I love you." She kissed him and cuddled closer, draping his arms around her body. His fist was still closed around the amulet and she kissed his fingers. Meriel pulled the silvery fur over them both and fell into a deep sleep.

"Wake up, sleepyhead," said Ronan. He cradled Meriel's body against his own for a moment before he looked around. The *Sea Bright* was a mess, but they were back in the sound. Docked at the marina on Block Island, in fact.

And there were the harbor police bearing down on them to prove it. Frank Harmon had always wanted to be a cop, but didn't want to go too far from Misquapaug to do it, so he was content with doing guard duty at the marina. He wasn't bright, but he was diligent.

"Did you actually take this dinghy out in that storm, last night, Mr. Burbank?"

"Looks like it, Frank."

"Why would you do something so crazy? And how'd you get back with no mast?"

Meriel stirred against him and he wanted to be the first thing she saw, the first voice she heard, so Ronan bent back down to her as her eyes fluttered open.

"Good morning. I love you." He watched as she came fully awake, as she remembered things he had no memory of, things he wasn't sure he ever wanted to know about.

Meriel threw her arms around him, dislodging the fur that covered her naked body.

Frank gawked and Ronan wanted to rip his eyeballs out, but he reached for the skin instead, tucking it firmly around her.

"We're going to have to do something about you walking around naked in front of strange men," he muttered, but she wasn't listening.

Meriel scrambled to her feet and looked out over the bay, searching for something. He looked with her until they found it—a hundred dark heads bobbing at the mouth of the harbor. Gray seals barked, dove and leapt through the air.

"Thank you," she yelled, waving to them as her hold on the pelt slipped dangerously. "I love you!" One leaped higher than the rest before they all turned and swam away, back out to the open sea.

"Do you think we'll see them again?" she asked, leaning back against him. She felt so right, so warm and alive, and he held her tightly.

"I wouldn't bet against it." Ronan knew they had a fair bit of work ahead of them, getting Meriel back to civilization, learning more about each other. But he always had his eye on the future. Iona was a lovely name for a little girl.

About the Author

To learn more about Sela Carsen, please visit http://www.selacarsen.com. Send an email to her at selacarsen@gmail.com or comment on her blog.

Look for these titles

Now Available

Not Quite Dead

Wildish Things

Carolan Ivey

Dedication

For Mom and Dad. You did everything right.

Acknowledgements

Kemberlee Shortland. For generously lending her insights about Ireland. And for literally saving my life in Killarney.

Dr. Raymond Horwood. For my new hips, and my new life. You rock.

Prologue

The Hag turned over onto her pendulous belly in order to warm her craggy back under the near-midsummer sun.

Earlier in the day a pesky bulldozer had approached one of her favorite wells, but she had taken care of that problem with no more effort than it took to sneeze. One well-aimed glob of snot had glommed up the machine's engine and sent its muttering human driver in search of a tow truck. Her work was done for the day.

Yet she found she could not relax and soak up the Irish sun in peace. Her breasts were turgid with unspent sexual energy, her legs restless and rubbing against unsatisfying stone. It had been too long since she'd had a man. Centuries. Of old, few were strong enough to withstand her appetite for more than a few minutes. These days, even the few who remembered her name spoke it timidly.

Bollixless creatures, these new men were.

She heard a noise overhead. Head turned to the side, pillowed on a mountain, she opened an eye to peer at one of the silver-winged beasts and its snow-white vapor trail. These days, few people scratched her back with their traveling feet, muttering prayers for safe passage in hopes the Hag would let them pass unharmed. Oh no, it was all smooth wheels and shiny wings. People with things plugged into their ears so they couldn't hear themselves think, much less hear the cry of a bird, the splash of a salmon in the river, or the very heartbeat of the land as the seasons turned.

Her sounds.

Something about the silver object flying overhead tickled the Hag's attention. She rolled to her back, cracked open the other eye, watery gaze following its path. She expanded her nostrils and took a sniff. Overhead, the silver bird hit what the pilots thought was a random air pocket. Below, the Hag closed her eyes and sorted through the scents in her nose.

Ah. She smiled and stretched. A woman rode that bird, one who was ready. A wildish thing. She may not yet know it, but soon she would understand. Like the Hag, all she needed was a man. One strong enough to fulfill her every desire without cracking under the onslaught of a woman's true power.

The Hag shook her mossy hair out of her rheumy eyes, opened her full lips, and called.

Satisfied that events would now unfold as they should, the Hag spread her bare arms and legs wide to the sun.

And awaited her pleasure.

Chapter One

"You mean...she's not coming?"

Beith gripped the telephone receiver and cast a quick glance over her shoulder at the bustling mezzanine of the Dublin airport. The din of mingled languages and accents, rattling luggage trolleys, fussing children and the PA system's unintelligible reports assaulted her ears. Unfamiliar scents drifted from the food court. Signs in several languages pointed in all directions, adding to her sense of disorientation. She turned back to the wall, plugged the other ear with one finger and tried not to remember the dinginess of the ladies room she'd just vacated.

I will not panic.

"Say again?"

"I'm sorry, Beith. I tried to get a hold of you before you left Cleveland. Kemberlee had an appendicitis attack and had to have surgery. She won't be able to make the trip." Kem's brother's voice sounded tired and genuinely regretful. Beith closed her eyes and breathed slowly. Belatedly she remembered the slightly sick feeling which had settled in her stomach as she'd boarded the plane and stayed there the entire flight. The same feeling that had sat heavy on her stomach the day of her accident more than a year before.

"She's going to be okay, isn't she? What hospital is she in? I'll call her as soon as..."

"She'll be fine. It burst so she'll be in for a couple days, so I'd wait to call her at home. But I promised her you wouldn't be stranded."

Beith glanced at her watch, still set on Eastern Daylight Time, and twisted her head this way and that to look for the Aer Lingus ticket counter. Then she remembered it wasn't on this level. She sighed. "Tell her not to worry, Patrick. I'm catching the first flight back to the States as soon as I can arrange it. I'll fly to New York and help her out for a few days."

"No way! You've been planning this for too long. And seeing as how it's your first big commission since—"

Beith interrupted, determined not to let him go there. "Be reasonable, Patrick. Kem was going to be my guide—" She swallowed a sudden lump in her throat.

"This from a woman who summitted Rainier? Since when do you need a tour guide?"

Patrick was clearly trying to make light of the situation, but the words stung nonetheless.

"That was when I had two good legs, Patrick. You know that. These days I need a little help from my friends."

Patrick's voice gentled. "That's what I'm trying to tell you, sweetheart. I've contacted an old friend to arrange for a guide and personal assistant for the trip. We used to work together some years ago. Someone should have met you when you got off the plane, holding a sign with your name on it. You can't have missed it. O'Neill said the guide would be tall and red-haired."

She vaguely remembered a long queue of people beyond the immigration checkpoint, holding signs of various shapes and sizes with names scrawled on them. Expecting that Kemberlee's plane would have landed first, Beith had been too busy searching the crowd for her friend's round, freckled face to notice.

Though now, as she thought about it, her eyes had snagged briefly on one man who stood a bit taller than the rest, broad shouldered and slim-hipped, his thick, dark russet hair pulled back and tied behind his head.

She'd ignored the electricity shooting down her spine when his sea-green eyes had caught hers. His brows had lifted as if asking a silent question and his mouth had widened into a smile that had nearly caused her to trip over her own feet. She'd given him a brief, shy smile in return before looking beyond him for Kem.

Now, a clear picture of his high-cheekboned face sprang back into her mind, and that inkling of foreboding nudged in the pit of her belly.

"Patrick. Listen carefully. It is just plain foolish for me to be over here alone with no idea what I'm doing or where I'm going. And...and you know darned well it could even be dangerous."

Patrick's chuckle on the other end of the line did nothing to dispel her trepidation. "You'll be fine. Trust me, I'm a doctor."

"As if that's supposed to reassure me. Patrick—"

"O'Neill will take good care of you."

"Patrick—"

"You're not weaseling out of this, Beith. This commission is the chance you've been waiting for to get back in the groove."

"Patrick!"

"Grow some balls, woman!"

In spite of herself, Beith laughed. "I'm *coming home*."

On the other end of the line, she heard Patrick sigh. "You'll regret it, honey."

"Maybe. But it's the smartest thing to do at this point." She squared her shoulders and hitched her carry-on a little higher. She had yet to claim her luggage, and wondered how she was going to handle the huge suitcase along with the bag on her shoulder, weighed down with a camera and several lenses. She wasn't supposed to lift even this much weight, much less a suitcase. Without any Irish money, how could she even tip a porter? She'd have to find an information booth somewhere.

Fatigue dragged at her limbs.

"At least look around so your guide knows not to wait for you," Patrick put in.

She nodded. "That would be the polite thing to do, though I don't see how I'll find anyone in this crowd, sign or no sign."

She felt a light tap on her shoulder. "Miss?"

She waved a hand and threw over her shoulder, "I'll be off in a second. What did you say, Patrick?"

"...about six feet," Patrick was finishing. "A little tall for the Irish, but it's the Viking blood coming out."

"Can I have a *name*, please, Paddy? I'll have them paged." Her question was met with nothing but static. She sighed in exasperation. Patrick and his mobile phones, she thought disgustedly. You'd think a respected surgeon like him could afford a decent one.

The tap on her shoulder again. "Miss Molloy..."

She turned, sagged back, bumping into the wall and dropping the telephone receiver. The same tall man she'd noticed in the queue now towered over her, much too close for comfort. And what a curious discomfort it was. The fine muscles in her fingers twitched, and she clenched them to stop from reaching to touch his hand, which had shot out to steady her. His palm burned hot even through the long-sleeved knit top she'd worn to ward off the airplane's chill.

She looked up past the collar of his dark green shirt into the face of a Viking. The heaviness in her stomach grew while at the same time her knees turned directly to water.

Up close, her artist's eye automatically absorbed details she'd missed before. His long, strong jaw was lightly stubbled with a day or so's growth of beard, his nose nothing remarkable and looking like it had been broken at least once in his life. His lips, turned down slightly in concern, not too full or too thin, but something about their shape told her woman's instinct he had the ability to drive a woman to distraction with words, or crazy in bed. Whatever the lady would prefer. But it was the eyes that took her breath. Shadowed with fatigue, which told her he'd not had enough sleep the night before; deep sea-green, framed by just enough lines to reassure her he laughed often, contrasted by faint worry lines between his brows that deepened as he regarded her.

His gaze dropped to her mouth, and she stiffened her back, raised her chin and let him look. The thread-thin scar on her lower lip and chin was the only one she couldn't hide among the many on her body. If nothing else, she viewed this little piece of furrowed flesh as her insurance policy against anyone planning to hit on her.

Time seemed to slow as she watched the parade of expressions march across the man's face. Interest. Surprise. Confusion. Compassion. It was the last one that had her clenching her teeth against the emotion in her chest. Then he smiled and all tension diffused rapidly to flush her body with unexpected warmth.

Oddly, time seemed to stretch, and the airport sounds around her faded to an eerie silence in her ears. Except for his voice.

"Are you all right, miss?" He had a voice to match the rest of him. Masculine but not overly deep, with a native accent that made even those five simple words sound like music.

It took her a second to realize she was staring at him, mouth hanging open, surging hormones tightening her lower belly into a knot. The mezzanine noises resumed, almost as if someone had restarted a slow tape recorder. She shook herself and straightened away from the wall. His hands slid down her arms before he stepped back. She saw his eyes widen, then quickly narrow, and his nostrils flare before a pleasant mask slipped over his face, lit by an amazingly sexy half-smile.

"Yes, of course. You just startled me. I guess I'm through with this, now," she said ruefully as she bent to pick up the phone receiver. Too late she realized the angle of her left leg was wrong, and her hip joint clicked and slid in a rude warning. Stifling a curse, she dropped her carry-on and quickly straightened. She fought a wave of dizzy panic, even though the joint had reseated itself. *Dummy. The last thing you need is to land in a hospital in a foreign country. Pay attention, Beith!*

The man's head tilted as if regarding her for the first time. "Jesus, woman. You're pale as a ghost." His hand was back on her arm, offering support as he gently took the phone from her hand and hung it up for her. "Patrick told me you might be needing an assistant."

Travel-frazzled nerves prickled. "I don't need an assistant to hang up a phone," she muttered. Then she blinked him. "How do you know me?"

He grinned as he picked up her carry-on and guided her a few steps away from the phone so someone else could use it. She walked gingerly, and she didn't miss the way his eyes flicked down to her legs and back. She saw the question there, maybe a trace of surprise and confusion. She set her jaw and forced herself to walk with more confidence. After all, Patrick had assured her she had no reason to fear simple walking. Eventually, she'd even be able to return to some fairly long-distance hiking. Just not the heavy-duty backpacking she'd been accustomed to. She pushed aside the twinge of regret that curled in her chest.

She reached for her carry-on but the man swung it over his shoulder, out of her reach. Irritation flashed through her, but the man was already talking.

"T'rough the picture he faxed over. Still, I wasn't sure until I overheard you yelling at him on the phone."

She relaxed, but only a little. "I was not yelling, and you must be the gentleman he arranged for me while I'm here." She realized how those words sounded, and felt her cheeks turn as hot as the palm that supported her elbow. Normally she was as exacting with her words as she was with her brush strokes. She thought she heard him chuckle, but she couldn't be sure as she took a breath and blundered on. "Paddy didn't tell me your name, though, before his mobile phone died. I think he said it was...O'Neill? I don't think I caught your first name."

She looked up and thought she saw something shift in his eyes, but then it was gone.

"Indeed. Kellan O'Neill at your service for the next t'ree weeks, miss." His eyes met hers, sparkling with more than a bit of the devil. His thumb lightly caressed the crease in her elbow, and she felt her knees start to go again. "You can be callin' me Kel, if you like."

Oh, no, this would not do at *all.*

She cleared her throat. "I'm Beith Molloy. It's nice to meet you and I'm glad you're here. I'm going to need some help transferring my luggage to whatever flight I can find to go home." She hated that phrase, "need some help", but she choked it out anyway. She was going to have to get used to saying it, she realized bitterly.

His dark eyebrow lifted. "Oh, no. Patrick's instructions were very specific. Under no circumstances am I to allow you to...how did he say it? Chicken out?" He picked up the pace and tucked her hand into his elbow, a gesture that might have seemed courtly if she didn't feel as if she were being towed behind a motor boat. Why was he in such a hurry?

Beith laughed in spite of herself. "That's very sweet of him, but really, I should go home."

"...and somet'in' about not letting you be *shouldin'* on yourself," Kel put in without missing a beat.

Beith allowed herself a smile. "Ah, yes, that sounds like Patrick. My mind is made up, I'm afraid. It isn't fair to ask you to give up three weeks of your life on such short notice. I'm sure you can't take that much time away from your regular job just to show me around." She glanced up at him again but he wasn't looking at her.

He shrugged affably. "I'm free for a while. It won't be any trouble, I assure you."

"Oh, I, uh, I see," she stammered, realizing he might not have another job.

He lifted a dark auburn eyebrow with obvious amusement. "Do you, now?"

She felt a knot begin to form between her eyebrows, and a dull throb at the base of her neck. She decided to shut up before she said anything else embarrassing or insulting. Inside her stomach, the need to get back on the plane for home warred with the intriguing idea of spending three weeks photographing and sketching endangered Irish wildlife in the company of a native.

Kel led her around clumps of people and careening trolleys. "We'd better be on our way, then," he said, sounding much too cheerful for Beith's travel-weary ears. "City traffic is no place to be at any hour, and we have a bit of a drive ahead of us." He steered her toward the stairs, then, glancing down at her legs again, changed course toward a lift.

Something told her that her life had just changed course as well, but suddenly she was too dog-tired to fight it.

"Patrick sent you our, um, my itinerary?"

The pause was infinitesimal. "That he did," he said. "You'll be seeing the best little tern nesting sites in Europe."

The lift doors whooshed shut, and she found herself enclosed in a small space with Kellan O'Neill. His scent drifted over her, a pleasing combination of freshly showered man and what she imagined Irish turf must smell like. Clean and earthy. She opened her mouth but shut it again, sensing she would only babble if she broke the silence. And one thing she never did was babble.

She glanced up at the numbers changing at the top of the door and felt a warm prickle begin at the back of her neck and travel down... Oh, dear. Was he looking at her? Was that warm feeling at the small of her back his hand, hovering just above her skin? For a brief second a series of images flashed through her mind. Her turning into Kel's arms. Kel dropping her carry-on, hitting the lift's hold button and proceeding to press her up against the wall. His muscular arms lifting her off the floor, his broad shoulders sheltering her, one hand cradling her head while the other...

...would never happen. *Could* never happen. Beith took a deep breath and tried to get hold of herself, hoping he wouldn't notice the light sheen of perspiration which had broken out on her forehead. She closed her eyes and fought a wave of dizziness. Damn those pain meds she'd taken before her flight had taken off from Cleveland.

What was wrong with her? Kel O'Neill was a complete stranger. She'd never been given to wild, hormone-driven flings with anyone. She wasn't about to start. Especially now. She had a demanding career and had always kept herself in complete control, reminding herself of what was really important.

That accident must have shattered more than her bones.

She shifted on her feet, but he seemed perfectly comfortable with the silence between them, as if he tracked her thoughts and had no desire to interrupt them. Well, damn it, *she* had to interrupt them. She forced herself to think of the scars, and cold reality quickly reasserted itself.

As soon as I get that suitcase, I'm booking a flight home. Then I'll pop a Flexaril and wake up back in Cleveland as if this had never happened.

He made no comment about the size of her suitcase as he pulled it off the carousel, but the way he handled it easily with one hand while holding her carry-on with the other made her flush all over again. Fanning herself with the scraps of her plane ticket, she looked around and spied a bureau de change and touched his arm. She snatched her hand away as he turned, flapping it nervously toward the counter. "Isn't that where I get cash?"

"No." He took her arm more firmly and steered her down a corridor. "You'll be gettin' a better exchange rate at the ATM down here." He paused and studied her, that smile growing a little wider. "So you're stayin', then?"

Her heart thumped hard two or three times. *Grow some balls, woman.* The words to tell him "no" were poised on her tongue. To tell him, "No thanks, but here's a little something for your trouble." She wondered if he'd be insulted, and inwardly winced at what his expression might look like when she pressed the cash into his hand. Well, there was no help for it. She blew out a breath, opened her mouth.

What came out was, "For now. Chances are I can't get a flight out until tomorrow, anyway." She snapped her mouth shut. *No more Flexaril for me.*

His grin widened and she went a little light-headed at its power. She attributed it to jet lag and the meds. As he turned to pull the retractable handle from her suitcase, she thought he heard him mutter, "*That's long enough.*"

"Excuse me?"

"I said the ATM's over here," he said without missing a beat.

"Oh," she said, then concentrated on rooting through her purse for her credit card and tucking her passport away. As she got her money, she sensed him standing protectively behind her, shielding her transaction from prying eyes.

"You won't need a great deal to start out with," he commented. "Should you decide to stay on, that is."

She glanced over her shoulder. His back was to her, and he spoke quietly to her over his shoulder. *If you decide...* "Oh, but what if..." She glanced at him to find him giving her another patient half-smile.

"This isn't quite a t'ird world country, Miss Molloy. Most every town has a machine now. And you won't be wanting to flash a lot of cash for any unscrupulous types you might be comin' across."

Like you?

His scent drifted to her nose again. A strong energy hummed just under her skin, a rush of electricity, here and gone in an instant.

"Oh, um, you're right, of course..." Feeling her face flush, she turned and punched in smaller numbers.

She was in Ireland, at long last. Jet lagged and tired, but here. A place she had seen only in pictures and films, and just those had made her artist's soul itch to be here, surrounded by that extraordinary light and that vivid color, sketching and photographing to her heart's content. Beith Molloy, famed "Mistress of Light", the rare combination of critically acclaimed talent and marketing sensation, would give her millions of fans something new for their collections of art prints, rugs, wallpaper, blankets and throw pillows. And a good chunk of the proceeds would go to help save the bird she was here to study and paint.

Now that her feet were on Irish ground, a larger and larger part of her was clamoring to stay, to not turn tail and run home to the studio which had become her only world for the past year.

She turned to follow the tall man through the airport, presumably to a car. Kemberlee had reserved a rental, but Beith had no idea where to find the darned thing, much less how to drive it. She frowned at this thought process. The old Beith would have been racing Kem for the driver's seat.

She glanced over at the Aer Lingus ticket counter, which was already mobbed with people trying to get a flight out. Any flight at all. The harried manager waved his arms and called out to the irate crowd that it would be at least two days. Two days. Weariness washed over her.

I don't have to make a decision right this minute, she reasoned. *I can just as easily call from a hotel...*

Okay. So, she'd made a decision. Sort of. For now, she would stay.

A sudden wave of panic hit her, so strong she stopped dead in her tracks, one hand pressed over her heart. Kel kept walking and she resisted the urge to grab onto the back of his shirt and use it for a lifeline.

As if sensing she was no longer behind him, he halted and turned in a slow circle, his sea-green eyes searching for her. He singled her out finally, and she waited for the flash of irritation that was sure to follow. Honestly, freaking out in the middle of the Dublin airport. This was not the old Beith at all. This was the post-shattered-bones Beith. The afraid-of-everything Beith.

She didn't like this Beith.

Kel's eyes softened in what she could swear was compassion, and one side of his mouth lifted in that half-smile. He held one big hand out to her.

Damn it, she needed this chance to rebuild her career. Her life. Her self. *Grow some balls, woman!* Paddy had barked at her.

"Are you ready, Miss Molloy?" O'Neill's voice, though quiet, carried through the din around them as if borne on some bit of magic.

Her eyes stung, and she told herself it was the jet lag, the fatigue, the mild pain meds she'd taken. Not trusting herself to speak, she nodded jerkily, stepped forward and took Kel's hand.

Chapter Two

"I'm telling you, the girl must have left the airport on her own."

"But she said she was catching the next flight home," said Patrick. "Are you sure—"

Declan O'Neill held tight to his patience. "I checked the outgoing flights—what there were of them. There's a baggage handler strike going on. She wasn't on any of them. I also checked the car hires, taxi services and local hotels. Nothing. She either left on foot or with someone else."

Dead silence on the other end of the line. Then, "I think you'd better talk to Kemberlee."

Declan winced. "I don't think that's a good—"

"Is this Declan O'Neill? You'd better start talking to me." Despite having just had abdominal surgery, Kemberlee Shea's voice cracked over the phone line like a whip.

He blew out a slow breath and did his best to sound calm and reasonable. Fat lot of good that would do him—he almost expected the woman's clawed hand to come at him through the receiver at any moment.

"As I was telling your brother, the woman I assigned to be her guide called to tell me she was delayed. By the time I got to the airport to collect Miss Molloy, she was gone." Even as he spoke, he scanned the baggage area, hoping to find some trace of the woman who resembled the faxed photograph tucked in his pocket. That blonde head of hair should stand out like the silver flash of a salmon's belly in a dark lough, but nothing stood out among the sea of red, brown and black-haired heads.

"Think carefully, Mr. O'Neill. I'm aware that you're one of Patrick's, well, friends from his past. Is there anyone from your...well, before...who might still have it in for you? Is there a possibility—"

"No. That part of my life is over. As it is for your brother. You know that."

"I do know that. In my drug-induced state, that's why I let Patrick..."

Declan heard a solid smack and Patrick's muttered "Ouch!"

"...call you in the first place. Because you'd know someone who could show her the island like a tour guide pro and keep her safe."

"The only one over here who knows about my past is my wife and my—oh, sweet Jesus." Declan walked carefully over to the nearest bench and sat down. He let the mobile phone drop to his side and took a moment to rub his suddenly throbbing temples. Fury pounded through him, spiced with a healthy dose of annoyance. "That little bastard," he muttered. When he trusted himself to speak again, he picked up the phone. In the background, he heard Patrick telling his sister to calm down

"Get your hands off me, Paddy. You may have three more college degrees than me, but I'm still bigger and meaner. Declan!"

"Kemberlee, it's all right. I think I know what's going on. My brother was in the office with me when Patrick's call and fax came in. He must have overheard our conversation." In his mind, he replayed the scene now. His brother, fresh from assignment providing security for an ambassador's trip to a politically sensitive African country, walking over and casually retrieving the faxed photo and other documents and handing them over with barely a glance, then returning to sprawl in the nearest chair. Or had it been a glance? With this brother, one could never tell. Despite his laid-back demeanor, the boy had a keen mind and a photographic memory. Traits that had kept him alive in some very, very bad situations.

He heard Kem take a deep breath, then a short scuffle and suddenly Patrick was back on the phone.

"Which brother, Declan? Tell me it wasn't Kel."

Declan sighed. "Okay, I'll tell you it wasn't Kel, if that's what you want to hear."

"Shit."

"Well, you said you wanted her to have the adventure of a lifetime," Declan said lamely. "She's certain to have it, now."

Patrick groaned. "Yeah, but I'd also like her to live through it!"

荒荐荒荓

Kellan was within minutes of pulling this caper off.

Beith Molloy bore little resemblance to the fuzzy faxed photo he'd glimpsed in Declan's office last night. The same one Declan had snatched out of his hand and into a concealing file. As if his big brother didn't trust him around a beautiful woman.

He'd known if he wanted to meet her, he'd have to take matters into his own hands. Luckily he'd gotten enough of a look at her flight schedule to know when she would arrive in Dublin. The hard part had been acting completely uninterested while his mind had churned with plans to whisk her out from under Declan's very nose.

She was thinner than in the photographs he'd looked up an hour later on the Internet, the last of which had been taken two years ago. Those had showed a woman with the solid, long lines of an athlete, skin glowing with health as she put herself in more than a few challenging positions in order to hunt her artistic quarry.

The woman before him now had a carry-on almost bigger than she was. Her hair was darker, her skin still creamy but with a translucent quality, as if she'd been cooped up indoors too long. He'd pictured a tall, willowy American blonde, but he hadn't been disappointed by this woman who barely reached his chin, travel-rumpled hair twisted up behind her head and held in place by what looked like chopsticks.

His first prickle of conscience had come when she'd looked up at him, fearlessly displaying her scarred mouth.

As if she knew it would scare him off.

But something in those chocolate-brown eyes... The challenge in them had softened to complete trust as she'd accepted his story without question. He'd completely forgotten about her mouth once the eyes had softened. Where had she been living that she'd willingly walk off with a stranger without demanding so much as an ID card? In a cave?

Then she'd bent to pick up the dropped telephone, and she'd straightened with a face so gray he'd come close to calling a halt to plans he was still working on even as he guided her out of the terminal. His doubts faded as he surreptitiously glanced at her out of the corner of his eye and saw she walked with a sure, even step. Must have been a cramp from the long flight. The way her faded jeans hugged her hips and outlined her long thighs had him picturing the way she'd look completely bare, on a bed, sweating as he drove her crazy.

Outside on the sidewalk, he stopped and pretended to adjust his load of baggage, using those few precious seconds to scan the area. Good. No sign of Declan.

Fionna had slipped him Beith's itinerary; the first thing he'd noticed was that it wouldn't take Beith anywhere near the prime nesting grounds of the endangered bird she was seeking in order to fulfill a commissioned art work. He'd take her to the places she needed to be in order to complete her contract.

Along the way, he planned to enjoy her company, tease her, make her laugh and smile, and, if things went as he planned, she'd be inviting him into her bed before the trip was over. Preferably *long* before it was over.

In the few hours he'd pulled this plan together, he'd managed to do some homework on Beith Molloy. Despite her diminutive size, she had been known to trek far into back-country wilderness to capture on canvas rare glimpses of wildlife or a single, endangered flower. There had been a relationship, but that had ended about a year before, at which time she seemed to have dropped off the face of the earth. Key to his research was that Beith Molloy was a woman with a ferocious focus on her career, with neither the time nor the inclination to settle down.

That was just fine with Kellan. He wasn't interested in forming permanent ties, either. But a little summer fling would be good for both of them. He was certain of it.

Declan would have snorted at Kellan's apparent lack of logic. But Kel prided himself on his ability to read people. He'd known, from one glance at her picture, that she would be open to any adventure he saw fit to entice her with. He'd always followed his instincts, and though they'd sometimes led him into trouble, they'd also led him out again, free and clear. Every time. This time would be no different.

He detected a slight shiver in the arm he'd tucked into his. He'd felt the coolness of her flesh from the first time he'd touched her, and attributed it to the jet's air conditioning. The Dublin morning was damp. He was comfortable in his long-sleeved, button-down shirt. But for a foreigner it took some adjustment. She continued to follow him willingly down the row of compact cars, approaching his vehicle. He let a smile widen his lips.

She was going to love this. He was sure of it.

"Have you a jacket?" He kept his tone casual as he tipped her suitcase to stand on its end and let her carry-on slide to the ground.

"In my suitcase. Why?"

He watched her face as her eyes centered on his vehicle, and waited for it to break into a smile.

Instead, it went curiously blank. She swallowed audibly.

"Is this...is this your, um, vehicle?"

Kel gazed fondly at his pride and joy. A midnight-blue-and-silver Harley-Davidson Softtail.

"Indeed it is. She's beautiful, isn't she?"

He thought he heard Beith make a noise, but he was busy glancing at his watch, and caught a shiny red flash out of the corner of his eye.

Right on time. *Don't squeal the tires, Fionna.*

The boxy Honda van pulled up strategically between them and anyone who might be in the terminal looking for them.

Fionna unfolded out of the car, all six feet of her, vivid red hair tucked up under a battered baseball cap. She slid open the side door, then turned to smile warmly at Beith. Like all people

191

exposed to Fionna's smile, Beith smiled back, partially if not thoroughly disarmed. Kel had always thought Fionna possessed more than a bit of Fae blood in her veins.

"Offloading?" said Fionna cheerfully.

"A bit," he replied, swinging Beith's suitcase into the opening and unceremoniously unzipping it.

"What are you doing?" Beith squeaked.

Fionna and Kel stood staring into her suitcase, momentarily stunned.

"She has no clothes," murmured Fionna.

"Yes, I do," protested Beith. "Everything's in there. Lots of thin layers. I know the drill. There's just a few other things on top."

"A few other things?" Kel began lifting bubble-wrapped parcels out of the suitcase. Through the wrap he recognized thick sketch pads, colored pencils, and...heaven help them...an easel?

"I'm an artist," said Beith, apparently reading his expression. "These are the tools of my trade."

"Well," said Kel cheerfully. "There's nothing for it—they'll have to go."

"What?"

"They won't fit in the bike's panniers. Besides, if you're going home tomorrow, you don't need all this, now, do you? Fionna will keep it all for you until you're ready to go. And," he shrugged offhandedly, "if you decide to stay, there's nothing here we can't purchase on the road. If you need it."

Beith looked up into his eyes, and Kel met her gaze squarely, hoping not a trace of urgency showed. He could see in the dark circles under her eyes that all she wanted was to find a bed and sleep. He felt a prickle of remorse when she shifted her gaze to the car.

"I'd almost rather leave my clothes behind than my art supplies," she said absently.

The word "Brilliant!" was on the edge of his tongue, but he managed to hold onto it.

"Why don't we just trade vehicles?" suggested Beith. "If you don't mind, of course, Fionna. Then, if I end up staying, I'll have everything I need."

Um...

Fionna didn't miss a beat. "I'd be happy to, but me cousin needs it for his pizza delivery route." She reached out and touched Beith's arm, and that Fae magic did its work.

Kel watched in growing fascination as Beith took another long look at his Harley, lifted her chin and squared her shoulders. "All right. I'll just need my camera, and..." She reached between Fionna and Kel, grabbed a sketchpad and a package of pencils, then turned away to unzip her carry-on. If possible, she looked even paler.

Kel didn't miss the look of interest Fionna gave Beith. He mentally rolled his eyes. *Here it comes.*

Fionna lapsed casually into Irish, keeping her voice cheerful as she pulled what little clothing there was out of the suitcase and handed it to Beith to tuck into one of the panniers.

"I dreamed of the Hag last night, Kellan."

"Did you now?"

"You're taking her to the Burren?"

"Of course. She's to go to the prime little tern nesting sites." He snorted. "Whoever set up her itinerary hadn't any idea what they were on about. I know where the best ones are."

"Just be careful. The Hag is restless, which doesn't bode well for a man like you. Whatever you think this woman needs..." She hitched her chin toward Beith.

"Oh, I fully intend to give her what she needs, have no fear about that," he said, smiling wolfishly.

Fionna regarded him briefly, not a trace of amusement in her blue eyes.

"Her needs have nothing—and everything—to do with what you intend to 'give' her, you fool. Stop for a minute and think what you're doing. If the only reason you're carrying on with this is to pull something over on Declan, back out now."

Kellan reached out and tapped the end of her nose. "Been scrying the bottom of a whiskey glass, have you?"

She gave him a look that brought him up short.

"Whiskey doesn't touch my cauldron, and that scrying once saved your life, if you recall. Last night I saw the Cailleach, and she is no one to be trifled with. You know that. The Hag will have what she requires, and if you deny her, she will twist off your wee balls and have them with her tea."

The Cailleach. Kellan zipped Beith's suitcase and shoved it deeper into the car, then slid the door shut with more force than was quite necessary. Trust Fionna to ruin his day with talk of the Hag. Yet he knew Fionna had never been wrong about things unseen. And she was also right—her timely warning had once saved his life. He owed her at least a moment's attention.

Even if he planned to ignore her advice. Hag or no Hag.

"Then why did you agree to help me with this?"

Fionna tilted her head as if it should have been obvious. "Because I dreamed of Beith Molloy, too. The Cailleach wants something from her. And it's the only reason I'm letting you do this."

"And what would the Old One want this time?"

"What she wants for every woman, Kellan. To be whole."

To his surprise, Kel's heart did a funny little flip in his chest. He turned his head and looked at Beith, and whatever expression was on his face, Fionna laughed at it.

"You're a chancer, Kel. Just do me a favor and be careful. With luck, all three of you will get what you need."

Chapter Three

Kel's dark shirt stretched across the long muscles of his back as he leaned into Fionna's car. In spite of herself, Beith's mouth went dry and her hands turned all thumbs as she tried to fit her clothing and a few essentials into the panniers.

Lulled by the singsong cadence of Kel's and Fionna's conversation, she distantly observed that all feelings of panic had subsided. For now, anyway. Her heart beat slow and steady in her chest, and breathing in the cool Ireland morning seemed effortless. Maybe a little of the old Beith, the brave Beith, still remained. For now, she would cling to this feeling as long as she could.

She allowed herself the pleasure of anticipating a ride on the back of a Harley with her legs wrapped around Kel's amazing butt. The mental image set off a rush of blood to her belly that nearly had her groaning out loud.

Well, no wonder, it *had* been over a year since she'd had any.

Then, out of the corner of her eye, she caught Kel watching her. Stomach flopping, she looked away and finished folding, trying not to think about how that gleam in his eye would change if he—or any other man, for that matter—got a look at the scars on her skin.

Yet, instead of mortification, she felt an almost forgotten sense of excitement. A tightening of her lower belly, a heaviness in her breasts. She looked up and her gaze locked with Kel's. He looked down and a wicked grin spread across his face. Her gaze followed his.

The article of clothing she held in her hands was her bra. The red lace one. Matching panties hung from her pinky finger.

Instantly she crushed the garments between her hands and turned away to roll them up and stuff them between two of the camera lenses she'd transferred to the pannier. She caught Fionna's knowing smile, but didn't have time to wonder about it before she and Kel broke back into English, maintaining the same light tone of voice.

"She'll be needin' a sweater, then," said Kel. "Got anything to fit her?"

Fionna leaned into the back and rummaged around in a cardboard box, emerging with a cream-colored Aran sweater. "This is a little big, but it'll keep out the chill. Here, Beith, it may seem warm now, but you'll be wantin' to put this on under your jacket. Especially once the sun goes down."

Beith drew in a breath and fingered the richly knit sweater. "I can't just take this, Fionna. It's gorgeous."

Fionna waved a hand. "It's one my little sister has outgrown. These Arans are meant to be used, not stored away. Wear it in good health."

"Thanks." Beith rolled up the sweater and stuffed it into the last remaining space in the pannier. "How far are we going?"

"Not far. But we'll be takin' some side roads."

Fionna seemed to have a sudden coughing fit as she reached across the driver's seat of to produce an extra helmet. Kel took it and stepped closer, propping the helmet on the bike's seat and reaching for Beith's head. Before she could blink, he slipped the sticks from her hair and ran his fingers through it, lifting it and pulling it back away from her face.

Caught off-guard, Beith could do nothing but stand still and drink in the sensation of his fingers sliding over her scalp, his clean, earthy scent wafting to her nose. His broad chest seemed to block out the rest of the world, sealing the two of them in this one moment.

Once again, as it had in the terminal, the noise of the bustling airport parking lot faded to nothing, leaving behind— not exactly silence, but a feeling like an inheld breath, waiting for the deep sigh to follow. She closed her eyes for a moment, and from somewhere in the dark recesses of her brain, a voice whispered.

Welcome, daughter.

Oddly, the voice didn't startle her at all. Instead, she held her breath and strained to hear the voice should it speak again. But she only thought she heard a deep chuckle that echoed into nothing.

In short order—too short—Kellan had her hair gathered and twisted up behind her head again. The ever-efficient Fionna produced two large, flat clips and secured it.

"To keep your hair from getting' knotted up in the wind. Now on with your jacket and we'll be off."

All the good feelings Beith had been building on for the past few minutes almost vanished in irritation as Kel lowered the helmet over her head, and Fionna slipped the jacket up her arms and reached around her to zip it as if she was a small child.

"Take Brian's helmet, Kel."

"Don't need it, I've got one."

"Take *Brian's*," said Fionna firmly, then their next words were lost in the muffling helmet. It didn't matter, it sounded like they were speaking Irish again, anyway. In the end, Kel exchanged his deep red helmet for a black one.

Kel took her hand and guided it up to the side of her helmet, where she found a small knob. A click, a crackle, and Kel's voice sounded in her ear.

"These helmets have two-way radios," he said. "Mine doesn't have one—don't normally carry passengers."

Suddenly Fionna reached out to tap Kel's shoulder, then hitched her chin in the direction of the terminal.

"Better get moving," she said placidly. "I'll drive you out."

Before Beith had time to think about why Fionna wanted to shadow them out of the car park, the Harley gave a throaty roar that startled her two feet out of her shoes. She whirled and found Kel already on the bike holding out one hand toward her.

"On you get."

Heart suddenly thumping hard, Beith took his hand and concentrated on not letting her bad leg shake with nerves and physical strain as she planted her left foot on the peg.

I can do this. Lightning couldn't strike twice.

She stepped over, straddled the bike and let her rear settle on the cushy leather seat. She shifted experimentally. Good, no weird pains or instability. Her seat was slightly higher than his, and their bodies spooned together, her knees fitting neatly under his elbows and her hands resting naturally on his wide shoulders.

I will do this.

Kel's voice flowed into her ear from the in-helmet speaker.

"Budge up and hang on to me," said Kel.

I can definitely do that.

A morning breeze lifted his auburn ponytail to brush her neck, so soft she had to resist the urge to run her fingers through it.

"And you may want to close your eyes—traffic is pretty tight and we've a ways to go."

"What's the hurry?" she started to say, but the words were sucked back down her throat as Kel put the bike in gear. It surged smoothly forward with a throaty growl. Swallowing a squeak, she hitched forward and plastered herself to his back, hands digging in to grab two handfuls of his shirt. Nearly all her tenuous self-confidence fled and she fought not to hold her breath.

You're okay, Beith. It'll be okay.

She twisted to one side to get a last look at the terminal— why, she wasn't sure, maybe to look in vain for a break in the crowd at the Aer Lingus counter. But Fionna kept her van between them and the terminal at all times as Kel maneuvered out onto the roadway.

Once clear, Fionna honked and waved at them, then veered off the roundabout they had entered and shot away down a narrow road. Beith couldn't help but think that with Fionna's parting, her last link with reality was gone.

What an odd thing to think about.

It didn't get any more reality-based than sharing a roaring city street with, oh, about a thousand other honking, fume-belching cars and trucks.

It was probably a good thing that she didn't remember any details of the terrible crash that had almost taken her life—and her leg. But she knew the story, even if she had only read about it in the newspaper. And she had lived every painful moment of the aftermath.

She fought to keep her breathing steady, and forcibly removed her nails from where they were embedded in Kel's shoulders. Inside the helmet, she heard Kel chuckle, swear at a driver who passed too close, then resume chuckling.

He wasn't kidding about the traffic. She remembered Kemberlee talking about it. *"If you hesitate or show fear, you're toast."*

Kel certainly showed neither of those traits as he accelerated and decelerated smoothly, weaving in and out of slower traffic, somehow managing to never come to a complete stop at any traffic signal.

If traffic laws were anywhere similar to those in the States, Kel clearly had little regard for any of them.

"Little roundabout coming up," came his voice. "Hold on and just lean with me."

Beith had only a second to register that they were approaching what looked like a four-lane-deep whirlpool of cars and trucks before Kel leaned the bike left and they were sucked in.

Incredibly, she felt the muscles in Kel's arms, torso, and thighs contract and release as he accelerated the bike into the maelstrom.

Holy shit. Breathe. In. Out. In...

Beith closed her eyes, lowered her head and pressed her helmeted forehead into Kel's shoulder, praying as hard as she could as one, two, who knows how many cars and trucks set up a chorus of honking.

A cramp seized in her left thigh and she ruthlessly quashed a whimper before it escaped her throat. The muscles tightened, threatening to lift her off the seat with pain.

If she didn't straighten out her leg in about three seconds, she felt sure the cramp would pull her leg apart, or break what little bone was left in her femur.

Something hot settled on her thigh, centering on the cramping area halfway between her knee and her hip. She cracked open one eye and found Kel's hand casually resting there, steering the bike effortlessly with the other hand.

"We're out of it," he said, laughter evident in his tone. "You can relax now."

She laughed, because although they were now on what a sign whizzing by told her was the M50, they were still going at a dizzying speed on what appeared to her American brain as the wrong side of the road. The lanes looked narrower, too, with barely room to allow cars to squeeze past each other, much less that tour bus looming ahead. The sound that came out of her chest must not have sounded much like a laugh to Kel, for his hand began to stroke.

Surely he only intended to soothe what he thought were nerves, but the sensation of heat through her jeans made her want to stretch against him like a cat. Again the sounds around her faded to nothing but a distant echo, the world grinding into slow motion as his hand moved back and forth. Back and forth.

He turned his head to glance back at her. "You've got a cramp, haven't you? I can feel it."

Um, yeah, but that's actually a hunk of scar tissue you're rubbing there, bucko...

Something else clutched deep in her belly, and she forgot about the pain in her thigh as another long-denied pain reared its needy head. Her helmet earphones picked up the faint sound of an old woman cackling. Afraid to let go of Kel's shoulders, she shook her head a little in an effort to knock out the encroaching channel.

"Stretch it out," said Kel. "Once we're out of the city, we'll stop for an amble to get the blood going again." He unceremoniously slipped his hand under her knee, lifted it and straightened her leg until it extended so her ankle rested his thigh. Her leg curved around his waist, forcing her groin even tighter against his lower back. Between the delicious, relieving stretch in her thigh, the heat of his body against her pelvis, and the vibration of the machine...

The roar in her ears now had nothing to do with the growling Harley. She wondered if she might be able to quietly enjoy an orgasm without him noticing. Then her leg threatened to cramp again.

"I need to get horizontal," she ground out between her teeth, to no one in particular.

"Do you now?"

Too late, she forgot he could hear her over the helmet radios.

"So I can elevate my legs," she said lamely.

"You'll have a bed soon, darlin', but you're better off awake for now." A quick glance to the rear, a lean to the left, and they zipped around the slow-moving tour bus as if no other cars existed on the crammed highway.

The green, rolling landscape flowed by as if they were a drop of water running unimpeded down a drainpipe.

"Enjoy the scenery," he continued. "We'll stop for tea in a bit. There's a little place I know."

"Where is it?"

He laughed. He seemed to do that a lot, now that the airport was behind them. "Just a mile or two up the road."

Abruptly his hand left her leg as he reached up and switched off his helmet mike, dug into his back pocket—

brushing the *inside* of her thigh in the process—and extracted his mobile phone.

The conversation was short, but she felt his body tense between her thighs.

He put the phone away, causing her to bite back a groan, and switched his helmet back on.

"That was Fionna. Apparently there's an accident up ahead. We'll need to take a detour. Can you put your leg back down for just a bit?"

She stifled her disappointment. "Yes, I think so."

"Put your arms 'round me, then."

"What?"

"Do it now—here's our turn."

Startled by his sudden command, she snaked her arms under his and clutched his shirt, feeling like she was going to catapult over his head as he braked the machine, leaned hard, dodged between two cars, then took off at full speed down an exit ramp. Something wild awakened in her chest, the urge to whoop with excitement warring with the fear-of-everything that had been her ever-present companion the past year.

O'Neill will take good care of you, Beith. That's what Paddy had promised.

For a wild second she thought, *I don't want to be taken care of.*

I want to fly.

Chapter Four

A mile or two up the road, indeed, thought Beith hours later, when Kel finally pulled the Harley over in a tiny village, in front of a row of stone buildings with brightly painted wooden doors.

The ride had gone by in a flash, and not only because of the blinding speed at which Kel drove the bike. Though there was barely a tree in sight, the stark beauty of the stony, rolling countryside had mesmerized her, and she found herself mentally photographing each land contour, thatched cottage, ruined abbey and stone fence they flew past. If she had dared let go of Kel's shirt, she would have whacked his helmet more than once to stop and let her get her camera.

But Kel had not let up on the throttle the entire ride. It was almost as if he thought someone was chasing them, by the way he had fractionally turned his head every few seconds to look in his rearview mirror.

Kel hit the kill switch, engaged the kickstand and pulled off his helmet.

"A mile or so, eh?" she said wryly as she struggled to get her own helmet off without taking the tip of her nose with it.

Kel slid off the bike sideways, leaving her front feeling cold and bereft. She wondered how his skin stayed so hot, when despite her layers, she felt a little chilled. She heard him laugh again, and then his hands brushed her neck and ears as he helped get her helmet off, back side first so that it slid forward over her face and off without taking any extra parts with it.

"I should have explained the concept of the Irish mile." His gaze darted up and down the street, then his shoulders relaxed.

"Looking for something?" she asked as she shook out her hair.

He shoved his keys into his pocket. "Just checking. I've had my share of run-ins with the Gardaí for speeding."

"No, really?" she said, mouth quirking.

His gaze fell on her scarred lip and once again that odd expression passed over his face.

She busied herself with her hair, reminding herself that it didn't matter what Kel thought of her face. He was hired to be her guide and her face was all he was ever going to see. A twinge of regret curled in her belly at the thought she'd probably never get to see any other parts of him, either.

Taking a silent breath, she looked up and found the sparkle in his eye, the half-smile and the accompanying dimple firmly in place. Her heart thumped.

"You must be hungry."

Her foot slipped off the peg and an involuntary squeak escaped her throat as she lurched sideways. Cobblestone rushed toward her face. *This is gonna hurt*, she thought, a split second before she landed on rock-solid arms. She found herself clutched close to Kel's chest, looking up into green eyes.

"Thanks," she murmured. "Klutz. I mean me. Klutz."

"Low blood sugar," he replied, the dimple on one side of his mouth reappearing, like a north star. "When's the last time you ate?"

Someone brushed past them on the sidewalk, a blurry figure in grey, indistinct out of the corner of her eye. The figure chuckled, low, husky, like rocks scraping together. The sound rolled lazily around her head and settled at the base of her skull, tickling an ancient part of her brain that was nothing but pure impulse.

Kiss him, daughter. Mark him as yours with your own mouth.

As if in a dream, she lifted her chin toward him.

Her stomach growled.

She shook herself and flicked her gaze to the left, but the figure had vanished. Shifting subtly, she made to ease out of his arms, and he set her on her feet without resistance. But with that half-smile firmly in place.

"Nothing solid since I left Cleveland," she replied, straightening her jacket. "Was that the Burren we passed through?"

He took her change of subject in stride. "So you recognized it."

"How could I not? Kemberlee described it as a place with 'not a tree to hang a man, not enough water to drown him, and not enough earth to bury him in'."

He laughed, scanning the street again. "That would be it. After I feed you, I'll take you to the heart while the light is still good."

"Then let's get lunch to go and get out there," she suggested, eager to begin photographing—and stop imagining what Kel's body looked like naked.

He cocked his head. "We could. I would. But I have the feeling that if I let go of you right now, you'd fall down."

Realizing she was still standing in his arms, she pulled free of his grasp and stepped back. Praying that her left leg would hold up. It did, without a wobble. By sheer force of her will.

Walking, she could do. Sitting for hours astraddle a motorcycle was something she hadn't planned for.

"I'm fine."

"I'm sure you are," he said without a trace of rancor. Which somehow irritated her. "But I've friends in here and I'll be stoppin' in to say hello, at least."

"Oh."

"Take a breath."

"What?"

He leaned forward and tapped her nose. "Close your mouth and inhale t'rough your nose."

What is with this guy? Mentally rolling her eyes, she obeyed. *Ahhh...*

"Smell that, do you? That, my darlin', is the best Irish breakfast in the west of Ireland."

Mouth watering, Beith allowed herself to be led toward a red-painted door. "Will there be blood pudding?"

He raised an eyebrow in obvious surprise.

"My grandmother came from County Cork," she said, feeling her scarred mouth stretch as she aimed her first genuine smile in his direction.

Kel's foot missed the step up and he fell head-first through the pub's half-open door.

Beith followed the sound of hearty guffaws and colorful insults toward her long-overdue breakfast.

ಬಂಜಾಲ

The next time Kel stopped the bike, Beith slithered off the right side on her own. She had her helmet off, pannier open, camera out and a lens attached before he could even shut the engine off. He took his time securing the bike, enjoying the view of her bum as she leaned over the drystone fence by the side of the road, snapping pictures of a large dolmen about a hundred yards distant.

The mobile in his back pocket vibrated. He pulled it out and checked the number before he answered

"Fionna."

"You feckin' owe me for this one."

"Where are you?"

"Right now? I myself am at Hook Head, enjoying the first real sunny day of the summer. Everyone else is spread out over County Wicklow."

Kel grinned. "I do owe you."

"Why am I doing this for you again?"

"Because once, a long time ago, I made you scream like a *bean sidhe*."

"Because you stepped on my foot and *broke* it, you oaf."

Kel grinned and snapped the mobile shut.

Walking up behind Beith, he slipped one arm around her waist, another under her legs, and unceremoniously lifted her over the low stone fence, setting her feet on the solid granite face of the Burren.

"What are you doing? Isn't this someone's private property?"

"As long as we don't disturb the sheep, no one will mind."

"What sheep?" she said, looking over the empty, desolate landscape.

"Exactly." He climbed over the fence and joined her.

She smiled in delight and set off, picking her way uncertainly along the rocky ground.

"Funny. The ground sounds hollow," she called over her shoulder.

In a few strides he caught up with her, his own boots ringing bluntly on the rock.

"This whole region is basically a giant granite shield, cut by millions of fissures, thanks to the wind and water. If you look at it from the air, the earth looks like the wrinkled face of the Hag."

"You've seen it from the air?"

"Oh, absolutely," he said offhandedly. "I've flown my chute over it hundreds of times."

"You mean like a parasail?"

"Something like that. Like an ultralight, only with a chute instead of a wing."

She stopped in her tracks and stared at him. "What is it that you do when you're not taking defenseless artists on joy rides across the country?"

"I work for my brother. In security."

"Security. That's rich, the way you drive that bike."

"Some very important personages stake their lives on my driving ability. Trust me, darlin', you're safer with me than driving yourself."

She tilted her head. "What kind of security?"

"Let's just say it's the kind that keeps heads of state from coming to harm when visiting-less-than friendly ground."

"Sounds dangerous."

He grinned, amused at the lines that formed between her eyebrows. "Worried about me, are you?"

She snapped her mouth shut and moved on, cheeks flushed in a way that told him she was, at the very least, intrigued. This woman was different. Most women he met, when they learned what he did for a living, well, suffice to say he had no trouble finding company when he wanted it.

This one, she was timid. It would take time, but she'd come around. They all did. Even before they learned about his second love, extreme wilderness racing.

They reached the dolmen, a three-sided structure made up of solid stone slabs. Another slab perched precariously on top, held in place by nothing but gravity. To the uneducated eye, it looked like something out of the Flintstones.

She walked around it, touching the walls with tentative fingers, as if afraid she'd accidentally knock it down. "What is this?"

"It's said to be a tomb of kings. At some point, it was covered with a mound of rocks—a burial cairn. There are some tombs not far from here, still buried. I can take you there if you like. They say this one could be older than Stonehenge."

"How does it stay standing up? I don't see any mortar."

Kel couldn't resist. "Hag spit. Stronger than any mortar."

Beith's mouth quirked. She swung her lens toward him and quickly snapped his picture.

"The Hag," she prodded, continuing to circle the dolmen, taking pictures from every angle.

"She's also called the Cailleach." Fionna's Guinness-fueled lectures came back to him as if she were speaking in his ear. "She's said to inhabit the very bones of this land."

211

"Who is she? This Cailleach?"

"The mother of all other gods and goddesses. The most ancient of all. The most primal. The most..." He gestured, looking for a word, taking a second to study a car passing by on the road.

"Feared." Beith ducked inside the dolmen. "I wonder if this place is a shrine to her." Her voice echoed from inside the chamber.

The car rolled on by without slowing down, and Kel relaxed.

"Hard to say." He followed her inside, finding it was tall enough for him to stand almost upright. "She's older than this place. So old, no one knows her true name. She's at least as old as the world itself. We don't even know how she was worshiped, what rituals they used."

"So she's been forgotten." Beith angled her knees wide and did a strangely balletic move to the floor to dip her fingers in a small pool of collected rainwater in the dim back of the structure.

"And that makes her a little wild. Unpredictable, because no one knows what will displease her. They say she's a lustful goddess and no man was safe walking the roads alone at night. About a hundred years ago, near this very spot, they found a man. Or what was left of him. Just a bag of bones—but by all reports he died with a smile on his face."

Beith shot him a look, and he almost snorted out loud at his own words. He was starting to think like Fionna, believing in these antiquated tales. Yet, in this vast, empty space, he felt smaller than he'd ever felt in his life. Odd. He'd been coming here since he was a child and knew it like the back of his hand. Every dolmen. Every tomb. Every contour of the land.

Somehow, he felt like the land was watching him. Watching what he would do next. Judging if he was worthy. Of what?

He shrugged it off.

"This is amazing." Beith wiped her wet fingers on her jeans, then rose and exited the dolmen. She walked in ever-widening circles around it, stopping every few feet to snap a picture. Of a tiny flower. Of rocks. Of the landscape. Of the miniature dolmens that tourists had built with splintered-off chips of rock.

"There are tern nesting sites here?"

"No, closer to the coast, where we'll be staying. Tomorrow's soon enough to start scouting them out."

She nodded and switched lenses to begin shooting the stony horizon.

She's hiding behind that camera.

He watched for a few more minutes, irritation growing as she continued to look at the Burren only through her lens. Finally he could take no more.

In a few strides he caught up with her. Coming up behind, he reached around and caught hold of her hands.

"Stop. Look with your eyes, not your lens."

Her body stiffened in his arms. "I work from high res photographs. The more I take, the better my final product."

"Give me the camera." He didn't know where his words were coming from, but he suddenly didn't know what he would do if she didn't obey.

She shifted, releasing the camera, and he slung it over his shoulder. She made no move to step out of his arms. Did he detect her trembling?

"Okay, now what?"

What indeed? He wasn't sure, himself. All he knew was, he'd spent the last several hours with her warm body up against his back, trying to concentrate on the road and making

213

sure they weren't being followed, all while battling a raging hard-on. He'd never felt this with any woman, ever—never this close to losing control.

And now she was in his arms, her soft body pressed against him. Her sweet scent filled his nose. The sounds around him went silent—no wind, no birds, no passing cars. Nothing but a faint noise in his ears, like someone taking a deep breath and holding, holding it. A tension that needed release. His body took up a slow throb, a drumbeat he felt from his feet to the crown of his head.

Keeping hold of her, he walked her back inside the dolmen, took her hands and placed them on the stone wall.

His better sense warned him she was going to think him completely insane.

After almost a full minute, she spread her fingers out on the stone slab.

"Do you feel that?" she whispered. "What is that?"

He felt it. The low, insistent vibration, the pulsing, like the flow of electricity along a wire.

He felt her breath quicken and realized he had a hard-on pressed against the small of her back. He cursed silently, but nothing on this green earth was going to make him move away from her. She turned suddenly in his arms, backing up against the stone. Her eyes were huge, her pupils dilated, her breathing fast. His gaze fell to her mouth, and he wanted to cover it with his, scar be damned.

For a weird second a strange weakness swamped him. He wanted to lie on the ground and beg the Hag—something. What? Release him. To let him leave this place with all his parts intact. Especially his heart, which thumped like it wanted to leap out of his chest.

Beith's hair came loose and blew about her face. Her expression was one of a woman who wanted him. All of him.

She blinked once and licked her lips. Her brown eyes turned deep gold.

Somewhere in the distance, he thought he heard an old woman laugh.

As if an unseen hand shoved him from behind, he leaned forward and took her mouth.

Her first thought was that Patrick had chosen her tour guide well.

Her second was that she was standing in broad daylight, pressed against a millennia-old stone dolmen that might at any moment tumble to the ground, trying to put her tongue down a near-perfect stranger's throat.

She felt cold stone under her hands where they were pressed flat at her sides. She commanded them to move so she could push Kel away, delicious as he tasted in her mouth. She didn't know what had driven her to allow herself to stand in his arms like this. She'd heard Ireland was full of magic, but she'd attributed it to the fanciful tourist brochures. In any case, this had to stop.

Her hands didn't move.

She whimpered into his mouth and struggled to raise her hands, but they stayed stuck fast to the stone as if glued.

Her heart began to pound, but strangely, not in panic. She tore her mouth away from his and turned her head to one side, gasping for air.

"Kel."

His mouth roamed down the side of her neck. His labored breathing filled her ears.

Even as she arched her neck to give him better access, she yanked and tugged at her hands, but they refused to move. He misread the writhing of her body and unzipped her jacket.

Before she could gasp her next breath, his hands dove under the two thin layers of shirts she wore and sought her breasts.

Oh God.

"Kel!"

Cool air beaded her nipples, and she found herself arching her back into his touch. His fingers tugged at the hard peaks, and he swallowed her raw cry as he took her mouth again.

It had been so long. But this was different. Although she couldn't move, it was she who controlled the ravenous power spiraling up from her feet through her spine, to explode with sensation along every nerve ending. She found that wherever she centered her spinning thoughts, the energy followed and created pools of almost unbearable pleasure.

Push him away? *Hell* no.

Why couldn't she move her hands? She wanted those hands on Kel, in his hair, to pull his mouth down to her aching breasts. Why were her feet planted just as solidly on the rocky ground below? She wanted to wrap her legs around him and pull him inside. Yet she could do nothing but stand there, compelled by some unseen force to do nothing but feel.

Something wild pounded in her head, exultation razor-edged with sheer panic. The same kind of panic she'd felt when she'd awakened in the hospital, weighed down by casts, IVs and miles of wire, a tube down her throat. Only this time she had no desire to break free.

His hands left her breasts to slide down her torso, and just the knowledge of where his hands were heading was enough.

The energy that surged up from the ground, centered in her groin.

She tipped her head back and screamed as she came, but his mouth followed hers and swallowed the sound.

Suddenly, her hands were free.

She wasted no time in grabbing two handfuls of his glorious hair and plundering his mouth as she rode out the waves of pleasure on his marauding hand. Finally she pulled his face away from hers. His hair had come loose from its ponytail, and the wind whipped it around his face.

"What is this place?" she gasped, the last echoes of her orgasm still shuddering her body.

Kel blinked and yanked his hands away, his face pale, but his eyes still burning with desire. His lips moved. He was saying something, but no sound reached her ears. No sound but the laughing woman. Nearer. Louder.

She wanted him right now, down on this hard stone earth, any way she could get him. The mental image of the two of them naked on the land shortened her breath.

Curving her fingers under his jaw, she pulled his face close and sucked his lower lip between hers, watching his eyes. His low growl vibrated against her lips, but instead of reaching for her again, he planted his hands on the stone on either side of her head and let her have her way with his mouth. His breath came faster, his erection pressing against her belly.

She let her hands slide down his chest, down his abdomen, which contracted at her touch, to stroke him through his jeans.

This Beith was like no Beith she had ever known. Old or new. But she could learn to like this one, the one who held this man captive with only the power of her touch.

The land changed and shifted around her. Grass growing in the rock fissures at her feet became millions of strands of mossy hair. Long, rounded slopes became thighs; the cairn-topped hills, breasts that swayed in the sharpening wind. Stony ridges, arms that hemmed them in. Rainwater pools became eyes that shimmered with lightning-hot life force.

Ah, rasped a voice, unseen, coming from somewhere below her feet, winding up her spine like a serpent to vibrate in her ears. *Long have I waited for such a man to lie on my belly.*

Beith swiveled her head around, Kel's breath hot on her neck, and found a dark shape lurking deep in the back of the dolmen. Burning yellow eyes peered out at her from the dark shape. No, not at her.

The eyes were on Kel.

Thank you for bringing him to me, daughter. He should fill my needs nicely. For a little while.

Something inside Beith shifted from apprehension to fury. "No. No, you can't have him." Kel didn't seem to hear the snarl that emerged from her throat.

A low grunt was her answer. *Now that's what I wanted to see. A moment ago you would have pushed him away if I hadn't held your hands and forced you to use your own power. Take him and enjoy him—for now. Whatever's left of him after tonight belongs to me.*

The black shape and burning eyes faded away, leaving only the little rippling pool of water on the floor. She felt Kel's hands on her shoulders.

She turned toward him. Her vision blurred and her knees buckled as she caught her left foot in a crack and her leg gave way. She found herself scooped up and on her way back toward the Harley.

"Did you see that?"

"I saw something," he said tightly. He lifted her over the fence and stood her on her feet. "We're getting out of here."

She leaned against the stones and surprised herself by laughing drunkenly as adrenaline left her limbs. "It was the Hag. The old woman of the land. The Cailleach."

He climbed over the wall and stood before her for a long moment, saying nothing, his face unreadable. Then he set his shoulder in her belly and hoisted her up like a sack of potatoes, which only set her off laughing again. The logical part of her brain observed from a distance and *tsked*.

"Can you ride, woman?"

She snorted, then clapped her hand over her mouth.

"I'll take that as a yes," he said dryly.

"She wanted you. I told her—" she paused to gasp and she kicked her feet as she laughed harder, "—told her she couldn't have you."

"Did you, now?" He sounded amused, but he didn't slow his pace. In one strong motion, he swung her off his shoulder and onto the back of the bike.

She looked back at the dolmen, and her laughter died. Suddenly, all she wanted was to get herself—and Kel—away from here.

"I need a drink."

"We need that bed." He brought the Harley to life, put it in gear and accelerated down the track without even pausing to put their helmets on. He said something else, but the wind sucked his words away.

Beith slid her arms around his shoulders, tilted her head back, and let the cool wind tangle her hair. For the first time since her accident, she felt fearless.

Take him and enjoy him, the Hag had said.

Oh, yes, she thought. *The old Beith is back and there'll be nothing left of him for you, old woman, when I'm done.*

ഇരുകൗ

The Hag let her fingers trail through Beith's streaming hair as the midnight-blue-and-silver wheeled beast streaked past in a pitiful effort to get away.

This land was her body, and anywhere they touched land, they touched her. She knew exactly where they were at every moment. She felt the pulse of their pounding hearts in her own breast. The throb of their excited bodies in her own center.

Yes. These two were exactly what she had been waiting for.

She lay back and reveled in the delicious tension between her mountainous thighs, an itch she would not scratch. Not yet. She would let it build until the ripest moment. When the time came, their cries and hers would echo in tandem.

Their release would merely shake their hearts.

Hers would take the tide that crashed against the Cliffs of Mòr and turn it back upon itself.

The Hag shifted so that a shimmering stream flowed over her aching breasts and throbbing center, letting the wetness stimulate her dreams and cool her ardor just enough to allow her to wait.

Coiled. Impatient.

And ready.

Chapter Five

The poorly maintained cattle tracks and fire roads leading to Inisnagowan Castle were not for the faint of heart nor weak of vehicle suspension, but Kel barely slowed the bike.

His heart pounded in a way that he'd never felt, not in any of his extreme sport activities. Not even when he'd launched his chute off the Cliffs of Mòr—illegally, which was the most fun—or hung upside down in a tangled rappelling harness in New Zealand with only Fionna's quick hands to keep him from falling to his death.

His mother had told him he had the sight, but he had never felt it nor believed it. Until he'd seen the primordial black creature with the runny yellow eyes crouching at the back of the dolmen, and Beith talking to it in gut-deep syllables that bore no resemblance to English.

The energy that emanated from it was female, but felt like no female he had ever known. Its power would have sent him backward several steps—he who never retreated from any challenge—if it hadn't been for Beith standing her ground between it and him. When Beith had turned and tripped into his arms, that same fiery light had burned in the back of her pupils. Then she'd blinked and it had disappeared.

In that split second, he had been afraid.

He remembered the old tales from childhood, and from Fionna's late-night bardic ramblings. Of how the Cailleach would walk among the people every so often in the guise of a ravishingly beautiful woman, luring young men into a forest. There, she would rut with them all in a vain attempt to slake her lust. Taking each one over and over again, tossing aside one lifeless body and leaping upon the next. Until they were all dead.

He shook it off. *Those were just tales. Myth.*

Beith said nothing during the ride, her breath warm and coming fast on the back of his neck as the Harley bounced over the rough roads. Her hands scrambled for purchase on the shirt covering his chest, looking for something to hang on to. He risked a few seconds with one hand off the handlebar to move her hands down to the waistband of his Levis. But instead of gripping the waistband, she slipped her small hands under it to press hard against his lower belly, nails digging in. A groan vibrated his throat. Her cold flesh and the sting of her nails only made the pressure in his groin increase. He set his jaw and tried to concentrate on the road while his imagination conjured up erotic images of her naked skin in his fire-lit bedchamber.

As the tern flew, it wasn't many miles to the castle, but there was no direct way to get there. The shadows of the late midsummer day grew long as the castle's single stone tower loomed into view. Evening mists already gathered around its base. Urgency gnawed at his gut, to get her far away from the Hag—and in his bed—as quickly as possible. Fionna would have laughed at this. Even now, they rode on the Hag's back and no doubt the Old One knew exactly where they were. Nevertheless, the quicker they got behind the walls of Inisnagowan, the quicker he would draw an easy breath.

From the outside, Inisnagowan looked like any one of hundreds of abandoned stone castles and abbeys that dotted the Ireland landscape. That was just how he liked it.

Inside...he smiled to himself. Well, Beith would soon see.

He leaned the bike into a blind curve that disappeared over a hill. He'd traveled this road enough to know exactly how it dropped off on the other side. *Too fast*, he realized, and throttled down as he crested the rise. To come face to face with a knot of about a half-dozen sheep loitering in the middle of the track.

Beith made a sound as he reflexively hit the brakes. The rear wheel skidded sideways precisely at the same moment the front wheel hit a fresh pothole. Beith screamed as she came off the bike and sailed into the steep embankment beside the road. Kel managed to jerk his right leg out from under the bike as it went down in the mud. "Bugger!" he yelled, frightening the sheep back through the break in the fence.

He killed the engine and left the bike on its side, jumping over it to get to Beith. The bank was soft, thanks to thick layers of turf, moss and grass, but he'd heard her hit it with a solid thump. She lay flat on her back, eyes huge, mouth wide on a gasp she could not take.

She reached for him, grabbing two handfuls of his shirt as her lips moved in a silent litany of *oh shit oh shit oh shit...*

He pressed her back against the slope. "Try not to move your head, darlin'. Hold on a few more seconds. Your wind'll come back. You're all right. Easy now." He knew well how agonizing those ten to twenty seconds were before the diaphragm re-engaged. He passed the time cursing himself, brushing her hair away from her face and probing the back of her head for bumps.

Finally she got one word out. "*Leg.*" Followed by several long, relieved breaths as air flooded back into her lungs. But none of the anxiety left her eyes as her hand went to her left thigh.

"Hurt?"

A quick, jerky nod. Fear in her eyes. Her throat working convulsively as she fought some strong emotion. Kel cursed himself again, looked at the leg and gently ran his hands over it, but everything seemed to be in proper alignment. Nothing moved or crunched. He grasped her ankle and carefully bent her knee. "How's this?"

"No, I think that's fine. It's...oh *shit* I can*not* go through this again..." She passed a shaky hand through her hair.

"Through what again? What's wrong?"

Angrily she dashed tears from her eyes. "I was in an accident not too long ago. My left thigh bone is pretty much nothing but plates and screws."

He closed his eyes and pinched the bridge of his nose. "*Shite,* woman, why didn't you tell me?" He put up his hands. "Never mind that now. I'm going to press on your belly. Tell me if anything hurts."

She parted her jacket and lifted her shirt, but he put her hands aside. "Don't move anything if you can help it, especially your head."

"My neck's okay. It doesn't hurt."

"Humor me," he said more curtly than he meant to. He closed his eyes and pressed the flats of his fingers around the four quadrants of her belly, feeling for anything that wasn't supposed to be there.

She laughed shakily. "You've done this before."

He nodded and kept probing her soft flesh. "In my line of work, a certain level of medical training is required."

"Is it, now?" She raised one eyebrow as her wobbly voice mimicked his Irish lilt.

"'Tis." He offered nothing else. "All right. Let's stand you up and see what we've got."

She swallowed audibly, rubbing her leg.

"Better to find out now, darlin'." He gentled his voice as best he could, what with the adrenaline surging in his veins. "Then I'll know whether to take you on to the castle, or to Galway to hospital." *At which point Declan will find us and I'll be a dead man, brother or no.*

She was just scared, he told himself. If the bone were truly broken, she'd know it.

"Castle, huh?" she said, as if glad to have a different idea distract her from her leg.

"Castle. That's where we're staying the night."

She nodded and pressed her hands against the embankment to lever herself up.

"Let me do the work," he said gruffly, sliding his arms under hers and lifting her to her feet. For a long moment she clutched his shoulders, then let her weight come down on both legs.

She shifted, testing. Then wiped her nose on her sleeve and lifted her chin.

"I think I'm okay."

Just like that, the wildish Beith who'd offered herself up to him with abandon on the Burren, who practically had him coming in his jeans on the bike with a simple touch, reverted to the Beith he'd met at the airport. Stiff and distant. The one who didn't want help, didn't want to be touched.

His heart did something else it had never done before. It ached.

The sun slipped behind the hill and she shivered in the gathering evening fog. Shock would be setting in right about now. "Don't move," he commanded. "Just stand there and I'll bring the bike to you."

"It's three steps. I can do it."

"T'ree steps you don't need to take, girl. Stand there."

𝜘𝜚𝜘𝜚

I'm going to feel this in the morning. Every bone and muscle in her body began to ache as Kel pulled up in front of the imposing square tower, which was perched in a glen between two long slopes that led down to the sea. She craned her neck to peer up at its four stories of sheer stone walls, punctuated here and there with arrow-slit windows.

He reached back and laid a firm hand on her knee. "I'll be right back."

She was getting a little tired of being ordered around. She scooted back a few inches to give him room to get off the bike, and just that small effort set off a Greek chorus of twinges and pains. Kel opened a concealed panel in the stone wall and set about punching a series of buttons. Other than that, there was nothing on the outside of the stark edifice to indicate anything other than bats lived here.

A movement at the corner of the building caught her eye, and she leaned slightly to look beyond where Kel was standing.

She was back. The shadowy, yellow-eyed figure that had spoken to her in the dolmen. Somehow she had followed them here. The Hag said nothing, just squatted in the lengthening twilight and gathering fog, fondling one of her own pendulous breasts as she stared at Kel and licked her full, shiny lips.

Breath coming fast, Beith tried to get off the bike, her only thought to get to Kel. But her leg shook as it met the ground and she was afraid to move any farther for fear of tumbling to the fog-wet turf. "Get away from us, old woman," she gritted under her breath. "I told you, you can't have him."

There is no running from me, daughter. I will have what I desire. This one may live long enough to satisfy me. The yellow eyes looked her up and down. *And you are not woman enough to keep me from what I want.*

"Watch me, Old One."

Oh, indeed, I shall.

Kel's broad chest loomed in her line of vision. Two strong arms wrapped around her as her left leg seized up in another spasm. "Dammit," she hissed through her teeth as he picked her up yet again to cradle her like a child. "Stop *carrying* me everywhere. It's getting annoying."

"It's quicker than standing around arguing with you," he shot back, shifting her so that her arms fell naturally around his shoulders. "Besides, you're so..."

"Easy?"

"I was going to say portable."

Even as he spoke, she looked over his shoulder at the Old One grinning with green, algae-covered teeth. Rubbing herself as her yellow gaze roamed Kel's broad back.

Beith narrowed her eyes at the Hag and tightened her arms around Kel's neck. To the core of her being, she sensed his life was in danger. To save him, she would have to overcome every demon clinging to her soul.

She had no time to admire the interior of the castle as Kel carried her through an anteroom with stone walls adorned only with iron hooks, on which hung heavy yellow rain slickers. Several pairs of wellies were marshaled neatly along the wall.

Through one arched doorway she caught sight of a dimly lit great room and a fireplace big enough for her to stand up in, before he whisked her on by and up a narrow spiral staircase. He paused only to hit a light switch with his elbow. Two landings swept by her vision, each with doorways leading to cozy bedrooms and sitting areas, all simply furnished.

"All right, I take back my statement about you being 'portable'," he puffed as he stepped sideways through a door at the top of the stairs. He elbowed on the light, and she gasped in wonder.

The large bedchamber was a study in medieval splendor, all stone walls and shadowed alcoves, rough-hewn wooden tables and sturdy caned chairs. The soft light of midsummer evening filtered through what had to be modern windows installed in an alcove, falling on an unadorned canopy bed loaded with pillows and tartan blankets. The bed was arranged next to an enormous carved-granite fireplace, with an iron stove set inside it and a basket of peat ready to burn.

She looked down at the floor as he set her on her feet, and laughed.

"Sheepskin rugs. You've gotta be kidding me." Nearly a dozen of them, pools of wooly cream against the coffee-colored, wood-plank floor.

"You'll come to love them in the morning when you get out of bed and your feet hit this floor," he said, sliding her jacket down her arms and depositing it in a muddy pile in a corner.

She looked down at her feet. "Kel, I'm covered in mud." She made to step off the rug, but a fresh ache in her back stopped her cold.

"Even with your muddy shoes, I daresay it's cleaner than when the sheep was wearin' it."

She laughed and looked up into his face, and the laugh died in her throat. The Kellan O'Neill before her bore little resemblance to the care-free, ready-for-anything man who had raced off with her on his motorcycle that morning. This Kellan's face was tight with an emotion he was clearly uncomfortable showing.

Tenderness bloomed in her chest, and she reached up to stroke his lower lip with her thumbs, seeking to ease the tension there. After a moment, he released a breath, took her hands and kissed each of her palms. Then he drew them up and around his neck, slid his palms down her sides and pulled her close. She went without resistance, the trace of surprise in the back of her mind melting away with a rapidity that left her wondering at how quickly and easily this land had changed her back to something resembling her old self.

"I have to know something," he rasped.

"Anything," she agreed, ignoring the soreness in her shoulders as she sifted through his thick, glossy hair with her fingers.

"If what happened on the Burren was real."

He lowered his head, and she met his parted lips with her own.

This kiss was gentler than the first, but no less charged. His taste filled her mouth, entered her bloodstream and spread fire clear out to her fingertips and toes. He hands roamed her back, gently, finding the bruised places and soothing the hurt away with his heat.

229

He pulled her hips in to his, pressing her throbbing belly against his erection. *Mmmmmmm.*

She wanted him. Right now. On the sheepskin rug, clichéd as it was.

He took one of her hands and moved it to the bulge in his jeans. "I've had this since the first moment you wrapped your legs around me on the bike," he said against her mouth.

She curved her fingers around him and felt moisture gather between her own legs. *Oh no, Old Woman, I will have this all to myself.*

She took a step back to gain access to his jeans buttons, but took a swift breath when her leg threatened to cramp yet again.

Her stomach tightened, knowing now what the Hag meant when she said she'd be watching. She'd be watching for Beith to weaken, to give her an opening to get to Kel.

Kel closed his eyes and with an effort, regained control of himself. "I think we'd better assess the damage," he said, his voice hoarse.

"I'm going to damage *you* if you stop," she muttered, shivering now that he had stepped away, robbing her of his body heat.

He lifted her chin and appeared to be reassessing her pupils. "Fixed and dilated," he pronounced, making her laugh again despite the combination of aches and unsatisfied desire warring for space in her body.

"Only because you're killing me," she whined.

"Your clothes are going to have to come off. But not until I warm this place up a bit."

She had a retort, but she forgot it at the echo of an old woman's laughter drifting up the spiral staircase. She shivered again and wrapped her arms around herself, moving gingerly to sit in one of the cane chairs near the iron grate. Kel knelt there, lighting some blocks of dried peat. Within minutes, an aroma somewhere between burning leaves and smoldering coal accompanied heat radiating from the fireplace. Against her will, her eyelids drooped. After all, it had been nearly forty-eight hours since she'd left Cleveland.

She shook her head. *If I sleep, the Hag wins.*

She opened her eyes and found Kel gone.

She lurched out of the chair, turning in place to look for him. She'd only closed her eyes for a second!

Behind a wide wood-and-wrought-iron door that stood partially ajar, she heard water running, cabinets opening and closing. She grasped the back of the chair and sagged in relief. A moment later he appeared, his own muddy shirt already off, feet bare. His Irish skin was by no means tan, but it was all sun-kissed, solid muscle.

"Let's get you taken care of," he said quietly, making to scoop her up again. Beith made an impatient sound.

He raised his hands in a peace gesture, and she walked into the bath without his help.

More rustic stone, which cleverly disguised all the accoutrements of a modern bathroom, greeted her eyes. A playground-sized tub, full of water, steamed gently under a stone arch, its brass rim just visible above the rough granite sides.

He sat her on the edge of the tub, cushioned by a fluffy folded towel, and began peeling her clothes off, layer by layer.

Since her accident, there was no part of her body that hadn't been seen by myriad clinical specialists, but none of those people had been a half-naked hardbody like Kel.

Bare from the waist up, she followed his soft, murmured commands to move all the joints in her upper body and lift her arms so he could run his hands over her ribs. At every tender spot, he apologized and kissed it.

Her nipples beaded and she fought the urge to squirm against the desire pooling in her groin, knowing nothing was going to happen until he was satisfied she was nothing more than bruised.

His hands went to the front of her jeans, and her skin went cold. She closed her eyes and lifted herself a little off her seat so he could slide the fabric down her legs.

She turned her face to one side, feeling raw and exposed under the bathroom's too-bright lights. The silence stretched. She crossed her arms over her breasts and sighed, feeling defeated.

"Jesus, woman, how did this happen?"

She swallowed and cleared her throat, refusing to look at his face, which she was sure must be twisted in horror.

"Riding my mountain bike in the Hocking Hills in southern Ohio. The trail was steeper than I expected and I couldn't brake before it crossed a park road. I got T-boned. By a motorcycle. He was speeding. But then again, so was I." She laughed at her own weak attempt at a joke.

"Holy *shite*, and you got on the back of mine? Look at me."

She couldn't quite bring herself to do it. He touched her face and turned it toward him where he knelt before her on the cold floor.

"You trusted me. I'm humbled."

Tears blurred her eyes, and she waved a hand. "Well, I figured I had to get back on the horse sometime, so to speak."

She dashed away one tear that escaped down her cheek, caught sight of her mangled leg and quickly looked away.

"I know this is my leg, but I haven't quite gotten used to looking at it yet." She tried for a lightness she didn't feel.

"It's not that bad."

She smiled at the hint of laughter in his voice, then caught her breath as he smoothed his hot hands over the roadmap of scars on her thigh. She glanced down to find him looking at them with nothing but wonder on his face.

"I'd kill to have a look at your x-rays." He ran his fingers along the longest scar, a thin pink line which disappeared under her underwear and curved into her buttock.

She released a long breath, one she realized she had been holding for over a year. Ever since her alleged boyfriend had taken one look at her battered body in the hospital bed, the scar on her face, and had turned on his heel and left.

"I have miniaturized copies in my wallet." She tilted her head in amusement at the way Kel's eyes lit up. "It's for when I set off airport security alarms. It proves I'm not a terrorist."

"Where's your wallet?" he asked eagerly.

For the next several minutes, still perched on the side of the tub with a towel wrapped around her body, she took Kel on a tour of her reconstructed femur and pelvis. What kind of man got excited about a picture of bones held together with plates and screws?

Only a special one, she thought. Or a weird one.

"Ah, so that's why you did that pliét move in the dolmen." He turned the picture sideways to study her mended hip socket.

"That's right. If I bend over like a normal person, the joint might pop out." She was surprised at how matter-of-fact her own voice sounded. It had to be the way he was sitting cross-legged on the rug at her feet, the hot skin of one shoulder casually rubbing up against the puckered skin on her thigh. She felt her shrunken heart grow a little bigger as admiration—and maybe even a little affection—crept in.

"I have bigger copies of these at home," she said as she slipped the pictures back into her wallet and dropped it in the open carry-on bag on the floor. She extracted a clip and quickly twisted her hair up on top of her head.

Then she surprised herself by adding, "You'll have to come visit and I'll show them to you."

He turned his head and looked up at her. For a long second, the off-hand invitation hung in the air between them. Almost long enough for her to think she shouldn't have issued it.

The corner of Kel's eyes crinkled.

"Want to see mine?"

"Your what?"

"My scars. Here, look." He rose to his feet, turned his back on her and dropped his pants.

For the next several minutes Kel enjoyed her shrieks of laughter as he pointed out every ding, dent and scar on his well-used body from head to toe, including what he claimed was a bullet hole in his bum.

This woman, he concluded, hadn't had near enough laughter in her life. At least not for the past year. His decision to sneak her out from under Declan's nose had been the right one.

His decision to drop his pants in front of her was also the right one. Even though he had surprised himself almost as much as Beith when he'd done it. If he'd gazed into her soft

234

eyes, filled with something akin to gratitude, for one more second, he might have started feeling for her what he'd never felt with any woman before.

So he'd broken the tension by doing the first thing that came to mind. Compare war wounds. While she had many scars but only one story, each mark on his body had its own tale. The more tales he told, the brighter the sparkle in her eyes, a sparkle that looked like it belonged there. Like it had been lost for a long time, but had finally found its way home.

She showed no hint of embarrassment as she leaned close and squinted at the round scar on his right butt cheek.

"There's no way that's a bullet hole," she declared.

"'Tis," he replied, pretending offense that she'd doubt him.

"I bet it's from a piece of rock salt."

"On my mam's life, it was a shotgun pellet. If you don't believe me, ask Fionna."

"Oh, Fionna was there for this one, as well?" Beith raised an eyebrow.

"She's the one who put it there."

Beith laughed. "Now *that* I don't doubt."

They grinned at each other, and once again Kel had the sensation of everything in his life clicking into place. He wasn't sure what to make of that feeling. He wasn't a man who was big on comfort. He liked things fast and loose. On the edge.

Still, things had never moved this fast with any woman. Sure, and he could go out and find someone to warm his bed for a night. And had. But that had been years ago and he'd quickly grown tired it. These days, he enjoyed the chase. The game. Choosing a woman and dancing the dance of seduction. For a few weeks. A few days, at the very least.

But Beith, she'd taken to the game more quickly than he would have hoped.

Trouble was, he wasn't sure he wanted to play it this time. And that worried him.

He cleared his throat. "The water's going to get cold."

Beith covered her mouth and made a coughing sound that sounded suspiciously like "rocksalt".

"That's it."

She giggled madly as he swooped in, scooped her up and made as if he was going to simply drop her into the water.

"Okay okay okay! It's a bullet hole! I give!"

"Good choice," he grumbled, stepping into the steaming tub and lowering both her and himself into the water.

She let out a sigh of pure enjoyment as she settled in and leaned forward to give him room, scooping hot water in her hands and sluicing it over her shoulders. The tub was plenty big enough for them both to sit in it without touching.

At the sight of a few tendrils of hair curling at the tender nape of her neck, something in his throat seized up and the urge to keep her laughing died. He busied himself with a wash cloth, lathering it up and reaching out to gently wash away the travel grime and road mud from her body.

She stilled at the first contact, but then relaxed as he rubbed the nubby cloth across her back. His fingers brushed smooth skin and glided over the ridges just under it. Her ribs. He made a mental note to feed her again after their bath was finished.

"You know," she said hazily, "twenty-four hours ago I was in a flying tin can, trapped in a window seat by two football players on my left. Drinking warm diet Coke and wishing they hadn't stuck me in front of a screaming infant."

"Mmm."

"Planning ahead on how I was going to get back home with my sketches intact."

"And now you're naked in a tub being felt up by a strange man."

"Strange just about covers it," she said wryly, and from behind he could see by the curve of her cheek the exact instant her smile faded. The muscles in her neck stiffened. "Like what happened at the dolmen this afternoon."

Kel's hand stilled. Fionna's warning echoed in his head, and it was on the tip of his tongue to tell Beith what his friend had dreamed about the Hag.

"Ours wouldn't be the first strange experience out on the Burren," he said instead. "Whatever it was, even if it was the Hag herself, it can't get to us in here."

Her shoulders lifted an inch toward her ears. "I don't know about that," she said slowly. "I...I think I saw it again just outside the castle."

She doesn't think. She knows.

Kel dropped the cloth into the water, took her tense shoulders and eased her back against his chest. He folded his arms around her and felt a fine tremor under her skin.

"There's iron on the doors," he said, as much to reassure himself as her. "They say the other crowd won't cross it."

She was quiet a long moment.

She doesn't believe me.

With each breath, her skin moved fractionally against his, friction eased by the warm water. His cock responded, but he found himself loathe to set her away from him.

Before, out on the Burren, the Hag's magic had overwhelmed them. Some part of him wanted to know if what

237

had happened between them out there was all the Hag—or something more.

He let his erection press against the small of her back. And waited.

A soft, shuddering sigh escaped her mouth. He closed his eyes and hoped like hell it meant what he thought it did. She shifted a little, arching her back against the pressure. He couldn't contain his low groan.

He felt her muscles relax, and she turned her head and lifted an eyebrow.

"So...is that a shillelagh in your pocket or are you just happy to see me?"

Kel rolled his eyes. "That was probably the worst line I've ever heard."

She shrugged and levered away from him.

"I've always wanted to use that word in a sentence," she teased, smiling despite the fatigue shadowing her eyes.

The huge tub let her turn around with ease, and once she was facing him she picked up the cloth to return the favor of a bath. He watched her breasts float in the water, and his mouth went dry. She passed the cloth over his skin, cleaning mud off his arms, face, and chest, leaning forward to playfully flip his hair aside and scrub at his ears and the back of his neck.

Eventually the hot water seemed to sap her energy, and he reached for her and laid her against his chest again. This time she melted into him, her too-thin body almost disappearing when he put his arms around her.

Something fierce reared up in his soul, a wholly unfamiliar emotion so strong he closed his eyes against it.

Kellan O'Neill loved women. No doubt about that. But until this moment he had never felt so certain that if anything threatened to harm *this* particular woman, he wouldn't hesitate to kill in order to protect her.

Careful, boyo, warned a voice in the back of his head. *You only laid eyes on the woman a few hours ago. This is supposed to be a casual summer fling, remember?*

He watched his own hands move over her skin, as if they had minds of their own. He let them do what they would. She writhed slowly, graceful in the water, raising her arms over her head and running her fingers into his hair as he traced slippery circles over her breasts. He avoided her nipples, torturing her until she groaned and arched her back so that the aching tips finally brushed his fingers.

He kissed the tender, sensitive skin on the side of her neck, just under her ear. She smelled of soap, and of the wind that had whipped through her hair all day on the Harley. He closed his eyes and drank in the scent, and let his hands wander down over her soft belly and between her legs.

She opened her mouth on a soft, breathy "oh" and let her thighs drift apart in the water. He slipped his fingers under her panties, parted her swollen, sensitive flesh and let his fingers stroke in and out of her cleft, one thumb zeroing in on her clit.

She gasped and arched, and he opened his eyes to the incredibly erotic sight of her own hands on her breasts, teasing her own nipples, while his darker hands worked the flesh between her legs. His cock grew harder and he pressed one hand against her belly to tighten contact with her back.

Her hips bucked once against his hand, and her vagina pulsed around his fingers.

"Yes," he whispered in her ear.

Her head thrashed restlessly from side to side.

"No," she groaned.

Shuddering, she turned and lay with her breasts pressed against his chest, sucking his lower lip into her mouth while her hand closed around his hard cock. He feasted on her mouth for a few moments, then let his head fall back against the tub rim. Her lips trailed down his neck as she stroked him.

She closed her lips over his flat nipple and flicked the nub with the tip of her tongue, then gently set her teeth on it. His breath hissed as he ran his hands into her hair, removing the clip and letting the sunlight-colored strands fall into his hands. He held her there, lifting his chest out of the water to give her better access. His hips began a slow, involuntary pumping against her hand.

Through slitted eyelids he enjoyed the primal scene—the two of them surrounded by ancient stone, her head moving over his chest, hand disappearing below the water to alternately stroke his cock and cup his balls.

Sweet Jesus, she's beautiful.

She grasped his shoulders and pulled her buoyant body through the water over him, sliding along his skin until her face loomed over his and her slightly parted legs allowed her swollen flesh to settle over his cock.

It leapt against her satin-covered opening in response, and with a groan she slid up and down, up and down along its length.

Desperately needing something to distract him from the agonizing need to come right then and here, he lifted his chin and caught her lips with his.

Their tongues dueled as Kel grasped her hips and pulled her tighter against him, bringing her clit in white-hot contact with the head of his cock. An involuntary keening sound rose from her throat and she rocked urgently against it.

He slipped his hands under the waistband of her panties and helped her slip them off. Opening her legs a little wider, she sought and found the head of his cock with her opening. She threw her head back and bit her lip as she took just the first inch of him into her body.

He filled her ear with urgent words in Irish as he slid his hands over the wet skin on her buttocks and pulled her down farther.

A warning bell went off in the back of his head.

"Wait, darlin', I have to put on a—"

But it was too late. With a second to spare, he let go of her delicious rump and lifted her away, ignoring her cry of protest, and pressed his fingers against a spot under his balls.

Keeping his hand there, he reached for her with the other, pulling her close as he sat up straighter and set his mouth over the tip of her breast. She wrapped her arms around his head, threw her head back and cried out as he suckled her. Her breast, pressed against his mouth, muffled his growl as his orgasm rumbled through him.

Crisis averted, he released the pressure point and stroked the wet flesh on the inside of her thighs. She shuddered and looked down at his face, and he met her gaze even as he continued to lave her nipples.

"What was that?" she asked, breathless. "What did you do?"

With a last lap at her nipple he released her and lay back in the tub, pulling her with him.

"A delay tactic," he said. "I forgot the condom."

"Oh." A smile curved her lips. "Are you okay?"

"Brilliant." He guided her hand down to his still-hard cock to prove it to her.

"Good. Because I want you in my mouth."

In an explosion of water, Kel came out of the tub, somehow carrying Beith with him. He carried her through the now-warm, peat-scented bedchamber, detouring only once to retrieve a condom from his jeans and toss it on the bedside table. He laid her out on the bed, following her down, parting her legs with a muscled thigh.

Reality hit cold and hard in her belly. She'd been told she could walk, but no one had mentioned anything about the rigors of healthy sex.

Because she'd never been good at keeping her face from revealing every thought, every emotion—and because Kel was Kel—he pulled back and looked down into her eyes.

"Don't worry, darlin'. We'll figure this out." He laughed. "God, we'd better figure it out or it could be fatal."

Oh, Kel, if you only knew.

After a few abortive attempts looking for a position that didn't press on her bruises or risk putting her leg at an extreme angle, they wound up on their sides, facing each other, her good leg draped over his hip.

By this time their bodies were slick with sweat, not water, and Beith was nearly crying with need. The head of his cock nudged her flesh, and he closed his eyes and set his jaw. "God, Beith, I can't wait. I'm sorry." With one hand at the small of her back to steady her, he entered her in one smooth thrust. He pressed his forehead against hers and groaned with a sound almost akin to relief.

She cried out at the sweet sensation of being filled with Kel. God, it was so *good.* She flexed her leg around his waist and tilted her hips, thrusting to meet him. Low sounds she didn't recognize as her own erupted from her throat as her walls clenched around him.

At the edge of orgasm, she shut her eyes and breathed hard.

No, not yet.

"What's wrong?" His warm breath in the delicate curve of her ear nearly pushed her over the edge.

She bit her lip and shook her head, gripping his hips tighter with her leg and stroking him with her flesh. If anyone was going to drop nearly dead from orgasmic overload tonight, it was going to be Kel, not her. She knew he could probably make her come until she passed out, but not this night. Not now.

"Shite," he muttered. "I feckin' did it again." Abruptly he pulled out of her without coming and rolled her to her back. She looked down, confused, and found his dark head between her legs, his powerful shoulders parting her thighs. In one hand he grasped the condom he'd forgotten to put on. Again. She started to laugh at that, but at the touch of his tongue to her clit, she gasped. She couldn't help it; she surrendered, tangled her fingers in his hair and rolled her pelvis against his mouth.

He kept up the onslaught until she offered up her orgasm, sweat beading her body and strands of her tangled hair sticking to her face.

The ancient scent of the peat fire drugged her senses. With strength she didn't know she had, she pulled him to her, rolled him to his back and scooted down to take his hard cock into her mouth. She tasted the bead of liquid at the tip, tasted herself on him, and moaned. The vibration of the back of her throat against his tip had him groaning and sifting his hands through her hair, muttering something low in his throat, in Irish. She didn't need to understand the words to know what he wanted. She took him deep, reveling in her ability to keep this powerful man helpless beneath her touch.

His cock grew rock hard in her mouth and he gripped her hair to pull her mouth away from him, but her quick fingers found the same spot she'd seen him pressing before.

"What the hell—" he gasped.

She let him slide out of her mouth and sat up, maintaining pressure on that spot while stroking him with her other hand.

"I learn fast," she said huskily.

"Jaysus, woman, are you tryin' to kill me?" He groaned, uncharacteristically flailing his hands until he found a spot on the ironwork in the headboard to wrap his fingers around.

No, Kel, I'm trying to save you.

She made him suffer through another release that wasn't quite a release, watching in fascination as he came, his tortured groans grinding out from clenched teeth. It was the biggest turn-on she'd ever experienced, controlling this big man's pleasure with just the tips of her fingers. Her breasts grew heavy, and she released his cock to touch them as she lazily watched him ride it out.

Finally his jaw relaxed, and he breathed heavily as he watched with hooded eyes as she toyed with herself, exulting in the power flowing through her body. Power she'd never felt, even before the accident.

"Enough," he ground out, reaching down to lift her and settle her on top of him, pausing just long enough to roll the condom on. With one hand he supported her weak thigh while his other hand, on her hip, urged her to ride him.

No longer caring if she cracked every bone in her body in order to have him, she guided his cock to her entrance and sank down on him, slowly, carefully stretching her thighs apart until she had him seated within her to the hilt. Her breath quickened as she felt another release building within her body. She rode him in excruciating slow motion, enjoying every second of it, every inch of him.

She opened her eyes and found him watching her, his green eyes dark and glistening.

"Hold still." He grasped her waist, lifting her just an inch or two. She braced her hands on his shoulders as he began to thrust. Slow. Strong. Deep. His breath rasped out on her name, pronounced in soft Irish syllables.

Beh-yeh, Beh-yeh.

"Kel!" Beith shuddered and cried out, her orgasm rolling through her in long, intense waves of pleasure that seemed to have no end in sight. Seconds later, Kel's back arched and she felt him pump deep inside her, his groan driving her to yet another peak.

She collapsed onto him, and he rolled her to the side. They lay in the darkness, breathing hard, arms and legs tangled together.

"Check my pupils," he mumbled into her hair.

Barely able to move, she lifted her head and peered into his eyes, just visible in the midsummer evening light sifting through the windows.

"Yep. Fixed and dilated."

He sighed in contentment. "I'm officially dead, then."

Beith smiled and closed her eyes. Just as she drifted off, she thought she heard hands clapping in a slow rhythm, and an old woman's voice whispering in the darkness.

Well done, daughter.

Chapter Six

Morning was bright in the sky when Kel padded into the first-floor kitchen, intent on brewing coffee for himself and Beith. He grinned to himself, thinking of how she looked with her hair spread out on his pillows. Snoring.

"You're getting sloppy, Kellan."

Kel pivoted and banged his hip into the stove, already annoyed with himself because he knew that voice.

"Declan, you feckin' shite hawk! How'd you get in here?"

"I can't be givin' away all my secrets, now can I?" Declan removed his feet from the kitchen table and rubbed his dark-circled eyes. "I ought to be givin' you a dig in the snot locker. Where is she?"

Kel leaned back against the counter and crossed his arms. "Sleepin'. I'll be thankin' you not to wake her up just yet."

Declan's mouth twitched. "Long night's ride, eh?"

"None o' your feckin' business." Inwardly he cursed himself for not closing the bedroom door behind him. No doubt their voices were echoing right up that spiral staircase.

He spied his Harley's panniers sitting by the kitchen door. "What's this?" He pointed at them.

Declan leaned back in the kitchen chair and clasped his hands over his flat belly. "She'll be needin' to pack her things—"

246

Kel's eyebrows slammed together. "No, she won't."

"—as soon as Fionna and Airdinn get here."

"Airdinn is on holiday."

"Not anymore."

"Then why is Fionna—"

"I'll be collecting her keys and her security badge. I'm sacking her. And I'll have the distinct pleasure of doin' it in front of you."

"What! Fionna had nothing to do with—"

"Airdinn will take Miss Molloy on her tern tour," Declan went on. "She has a job to do."

"Wait, you can't fire Fionna. I own half the business and I have a say—"

"Fionna let her friendship with you compromise the safety of a client. She's gone," Declan declared, never moving from his chair.

"Beith was never in danger," Kel roared, then snapped his mouth shut, irritated with himself for letting Declan's studied calm get under his skin. Again.

Declan cast a pointed glance at the shiny blue panniers, one of which was crusted with fresh mud. "So you *didn't* lay the bike down sometime in the last few hours?"

Kel rubbed his hands down his face.

"It's clear you learned nothing about her. You missed the little details—like her medical condition. Like I said, Kellan. Sloppy." He got to his feet. "Plus, you wasted the time and resources of the search team looking for you. That'll be coming out of your earnings for this quarter."

Kel shrugged. "Keep it all. I quit."

Declan narrowed his eyes at him. "You can't quit, you're my feckin' brother."

"Fionna and I will start our own business."

"And Miss Molloy's to be your first client, I suppose? Stolen from your own brother?" Declan stuck out his jaw.

"If that's what she wants." Kel set his own jaw.

Declan's gaze moved to the kitchen doorway, and his lip curled in a half-smile. "Why don't we ask Miss Molloy?"

Kel looked at the door and cursed roundly under his breath.

Beith stood there, hair rumpled sexily around her face, a pair of his clean socks sagging around her ankles and one of his shirts hanging from her slim shoulders. Eyes wide, she clutched it closed at her throat with one hand and tugged the hem down over her scarred leg with the other. The vulnerability that once again shadowed her eyes nearly killed him.

He took a step to move between her and Declan, but his brother, ever the courtly one, stood up and inclined his head toward her. "Miss Molloy." His gaze slid back to Kel, murder written clearly in the grey depths of his eyes. "Aren't you going to introduce us, brother?"

I am so dead.

"What is it? What's going on?" Beith's gaze bounced between the two men, her eyes widening even more when she caught the resemblance between them.

"I'll leave you to explain, Kellan, while I wait outside for Fionna. Excuse me, Miss Molloy." With that, Declan left the room and exited through the anteroom door.

"Kel?"

He sighed. "Maybe you should sit down."

She stayed where she was. "No. Tell me what's wrong."

No point in softening the blow, not now. Not with Declan right outside, ready to take Beith out of his life. *Shite.* She was already gone. And he had no one but himself to blame. He took a deep breath.

"Fionna was supposed to be your tour guide, not me."

"What?"

"Declan and I own the security business together. I was in his office when Patrick faxed over your schedule. And, um, I saw your photograph. I..." He spread his hands. "Just wanted to meet you. Show you the real Ireland—and have a bit of fun. And I knew Declan wouldn't have let me within a mile of you. So I, um...talked Fionna into—"

"Letting you kidnap me?" She gasped and went pale. "You mean, people have been *looking* for us for two days? Thinking I was *missing*?" Now she did sit down. "Oh my God, Kem and Patrick must be worried sick."

Kel, his knees strangely weak, pulled up a kitchen chair and sat facing her. "I'm sure Declan has already called them."

She swept one hand over her head, dragging hair away from her face and hanging onto a handful of it as she propped her elbow on the table.

"I should have found a way to let them know I was all right. Found a pay phone and used a credit card. Something." Her eyes darkened, haunted with some memory that had Kellan clenching his fists to keep from reaching out to hold her.

"They're the only family I have, the only ones who stood by me when my leg and my life was in pieces. They helped the deputies look for me while I lay in a ditch for almost eighteen hours..."

Kel winced.

"...and I ran off like some irresponsible teenager with more hormones than sense."

"The mobile won't work out here. You can use my land line—"

"Did I hear your brother say he's going to fire Fionna?"

He felt his face redden and he nodded. "She agreed to help me with my plan." He made a helpless gesture. "Said she had a dream about it. About us. And the Cailleach. She actually tried to talk me out of it, said it was dangerous, but I wouldn't listen. Not once I laid eyes on you."

Beith straightened and rubbed her arms as if cold. "It *was* dangerous. We could have been killed, racing around on the Harley like that. And the Hag—she wanted *you*. Your life. I made love to you until you collapsed, to protect you from her. Because in one short day, somehow I actually started to care about you. But the truth is, I don't know you. And you don't know me. All along this was nothing but a game...." As if aware she was babbling, she snapped her mouth shut and swallowed hard.

Something within him cracked. He reached out and took her hand. "No. What we experienced was real, Beith—"

Beh-yeh.

She pulled away, brow knitted. "I have to go. I have to think." Tears filled her eyes, and she again tugged the edge of his shirt down over her scarred thigh. "Where are my clothes?"

"I'll help you," he said, his voice strangling on the wholly unaccustomed feeling of being completely helpless.

"No," she said firmly, getting up. "Let me know when Fionna gets here. Maybe I can talk Declan into letting her keep her job."

She opened her mouth to say something else, and he braced himself. Nothing came out, but her conflicted emotions were clearly written in her eyes.

How could you do that? How could I do that?

And Kellan O'Neill experienced another new stab to his heart. Shame.

Fionna had been right—he should have backed out when he had the chance. He had underestimated the fragility of Beith's battered spirit. Suddenly afraid of doing more damage than he'd already inflicted, he resisted reaching for her and kissing her senseless in an effort to change what he knew was coming. He could sense the progression of her thoughts behind her pretty brown eyes.

She turned to open a pannier and the first thing she pulled out was Fionna's sweater. She stared at it a long moment, the emotions of the last two days playing across her face. "Hopefully she won't mind if I keep this."

"She won't," said Kel softly.

Beith hung up the phone in Kel's bedroom and remained still for a moment, perched stiffly on the edge of the bed where just a few hours before she had thrashed like a wild woman underneath Kel's straining body.

Who was that woman?

At the remembered relief in Kemberlee's voice, Beith allowed the pain in her heart to overshadow the physical aches the last twenty-four hours had bestowed.

Something about this land had swept her out of her good sense as much as his ability to give her mind-bending orgasms.

Her stomach felt hollow, that afraid-of-everything quiver that had been her comfortable, constant companion for far too long. She thought of the regret she'd seen in his eyes, and for one wild second all she wanted was to run down the stairs and still that trembling thing in the pit of her belly with his intoxicating scent, the warmth of his arms. She clamped down hard on the impulse.

No. Too easy. Things had happened too fast. She needed time to get her spinning emotions straightened out. They both did.

You disappoint me, daughter.

Beith closed her eyes and leaned one hand on the edge of the bed. Her flailing thoughts gladly latched onto the reason she had come to Ireland in the first place. The terns. The endangered birds who needed her talent to help them survive.

She shut out the Hag's voice, finished putting on her clothes and left the bedchamber.

But not without one wistful glance back.

Chapter Seven

Four months later

Kemberlee Shea stood at the back of the exhibit hall in the Cleveland Museum of Art, watching the charity auction in progress. And sighed.

Sure, she'd be getting her cut from the sale of Beith's newest wildlife paintings. But Beith herself had refused to take more than a token amount for the project, insisting the conservation organization that had commissioned the paintings needed it more than she did.

Kemberlee had almost been shamed into giving up a chunk of her cut, as well.

Almost.

But when she'd gotten a look at the collection, she knew instinctively how much they were going to fetch when they hit the auction block. Only a fool would give up that big of a chunk of change.

Okay, okay, so she'd donate a portion of it. But hell's bells, she also liked to eat. And pay her rent. When the mass market designer collection hit the stores, they'd all be eating better. A lot better.

The lush, passionate canvas on the block at the moment nearly took her breath away, she who never lost her breath over anything that didn't have a dollar sign sitting in front of it.

Steady, girl. Don't be going soft, now.

The door next to her eased open, and a dark-haired man slipped quietly through it, catching it before it clicked shut behind him. The moment his grey-eyed gaze found the painting at the front of the room, an eyebrow went up in appreciation and he switched his numbered auction paddle to his right hand.

Good. I hope your wallet is as big as I think your package is, she thought, letting her approving gaze pass over his custom-tailored grey slacks and crisp white shirt.

She snagged a champagne glass from a passing waiter and watched the man out of the corner of her eye. He bid unobtrusively, without hesitation, seeming to have an almost telepathic connection with the auctioneer.

Kemberlee had hand-picked the auctioneer herself for his uncanny ability to sniff out the bidders who had the real money. This guy, whoever he was, had it in spades.

Yep, eating regularly was looking real good this year.

She turned to the far back corner of the room, caught Beith's eye, and gave her two thumbs up.

Beith, sitting in a folding chair, chicly dressed in black and her hair pulled back smoothly from her disgustingly make-up free face, smiled back and raised her own champagne glass. Then her gaze moved past Kem, and her expression went blank.

Abruptly she set her glass down on the floor, bolted out of the chair and left the room.

Kemberlee, brow furrowed, set her own glass on a table and went after her friend. Just as she reached for the door, the gavel smacked down and the auctioneer declared the work sold to a Declan O'Neill.

Declan O'Neill?

Kem did an about-face, but the man was striding through the door, mobile phone to his ear. Making a frustrated sound, she about-faced again and went after Beith.

She found Beith in the interior courtyard, staring at a small water fountain tucked in between some towering potted plants. She moved to stand beside her friend and client, reached into her handbag and brought out a small silver flask. Unscrewing the top, she offered it to Beith.

Beith's eyes, which weren't really seeing the fountain, shifted at the flash of silver. She snorted a breath out of her nose, accepted the flask and took a swig.

"You miss him."

Beith shrugged and contemplated the flask in her hand, saying nothing.

"Your work is done for now." Kemberlee poked Beith with an elbow. "Take a break. Get on a plane."

Beith shook her head and handed the flask back to Kemberlee. "It's been too long. He's not the kind of guy to wait around."

Aha. So she has been thinking about him. "You know this for a fact?"

"He's reckless, and irresponsible, and..."

"Name one reason why you shouldn't go to him right now."

She threw up her hands. "Oh, I don't know, Kem. How about the fact that I knew him for maybe twenty-four hours. Oh, yeah, then there's that little thing about kidnapping me—"

"Please. Like that's not every woman's wet dream."

"Almost got me killed on that motorcycle—"

"Mmm," Kem said dreamily. "Harleys."

"And...things happened, Kem."

"What things?"

A long silence. "You'd think I was nuts if I told you."

Kem leaned in, squinting at Beith. "He made you scream like a banshee, didn't he?"

Beith blushed.

Kem pumped both fists in the air in a silent *yesssss!*

"Shut up."

"The man's brother shows up to buy your painting. Doesn't that tell you anything?"

Beith's eyes rounded. "Declan bought it?"

"Hell yes, he did. What he paid for it will keep me in Jameson for a friggin' decade." She watched as a new light ignited in Beith's eyes, then just as quickly faded.

Beith shrugged. "So maybe it's Declan's way of apologizing for his brother's bad behavior."

"Shit, Beith, when did you become such an old lady?"

Beith's mouth snapped shut.

Bull's eye, thought Kem. She took a deep draught from the flask and took her time putting it away, planning her next words carefully.

"I think that for a little while, Kellan O'Neill made you remember who you were before the accident. The woman..." Kem ducked her head and cursed herself as her throat tightened. "My friend who was not only my partner in crime, but knows where all the bodies are buried. Hell, even helped me bury some of them."

Beith laughed, a strangled sound.

"I miss that friend," Kem said simply. "I want her back. And if knocking her in the head with a baseball bat and forcibly sticking her on a plane back to the man she loves is what it takes to bring her back, I'll do it."

If possible, Beith flushed even redder. "I don't—"

"You can lie to me all you want, dearest. But for god's sake, stop lying to yourself. You have all the signs of wanting that bad boy back. And can I tell you something else?"

Beith waved a hand. "Don't hold back now, Kem."

Want warred with caution behind Beith's eyes, and Kem wracked her brain for the words that would give "want" the edge.

"Look. If Declan O'Neill is the kind of man who'd fly three thousand miles to buy your painting as an *apology*, maybe his bad-boy little brother isn't as bad as all that. Maybe—and if you tell anyone I said this, I swear to God I'll take out a hit on you— maybe he's worth another chance."

Beith shrugged a shoulder, and Kem grinned to herself. Her friend was fast running out of excuses.

Beith tilted her head, deep in thought. "Maybe I—"

"Miss Molloy." From across the courtyard, a soft, Irish-accented male voice floated.

Both women nearly jumped out of their shoes and peered through the dim light at the figure standing in the door.

"Declan," Beith breathed.

"May I speak with you a moment?"

Kemberlee squeezed her friend's arm and stepped away.

Maybe she wouldn't need that baseball bat, after all.

Beith focused on the man as he approached, then wished she hadn't.

Declan's smooth, athletic stride reminded her so much of Kellan, she suddenly felt as if something solid was lodged just under her breastbone. Something wild that had been stuffed down tight for four long months.

Oh, yeah. Kemberlee was right. She still had it bad.

She caught sight of her friend lingering at the door, blatantly checking out Declan's backside and fanning herself with one hand.

"Good*bye*, Kemberlee."

Kem winked and slipped out of sight.

Declan, startled look on his face, turned sideways in mid-stride, as if he didn't want his back to the door Kem had exited. Beith couldn't help but smile—Kem had a way of bringing out the deer-in-the-headlights in any man.

"That was Kemberlee?"

"Yes. Don't worry, you're safe with me."

Relief relaxed his features. "My apologies, Miss Molloy. I didn't mean to chase you away from your own celebration." He slid his hands into his pockets, as if he wanted to offer one of them to her, but thought better of it.

Beith lifted her chin and stuck out her own hand. With a glint of respect in his eye, Declan shook it.

"Just caught me by surprise. What I should have done is thank you for buying the painting. The money's going to a good cause."

"You're welcome. It was the least I could do."

Beith crossed her arms. "For...?"

"You did what I've been trying to get my little brother to do for a very long time. Grow up."

A bark of laughter escaped her before she could stop it. "I knew him less than twenty-four hours."

"Whatever happened in that one day, well..." His mouth lifted in an enigmatic smile and he let the sentence drop. "But to buy your painting is not the whole reason I came."

"Oh?"

"I'm here to offer you a job. If you're willing to take it on, that is."

"Uh..." It was the only sound she could make.

"Five minutes. I will consider it a favor if you just hear me out."

For the first time, Beith noticed the dark circles under his eyes and the weary lines around his mouth. The cocksure CEO who had dealt summarily with his wayward brother in the castle kitchen was gone. The man who stood before her now looked like one who wanted a chance to make amends, but who wasn't accustomed to coming right out and admitting he was wrong about anything.

Much like a certain Kellan O'Neill she knew.

The wild thing trapped under her breastbone stirred.

"I'm listening."

Chapter Eight

Kel and Fionna stood back to admire the brand new lettering over the door of their office. Granted, the hole in the wall on the back streets of Galway was a bit spare, compared to the plush offices they'd shared with Declan in Dublin, but it was a start.

"The web site is up, and we're getting calls already," she said. "With luck, we should be solvent within a year."

"I hope so. I have payments on a castle to make."

"So, you're no longer a renter, now you're the landlord?" She poked him with her elbow.

He grinned and bumped her back. "We all have to grow up sometime."

But the grin didn't quite reach his eyes. No smile had, not since the day Beith Molloy had walked out of his life.

A FedEx truck pulled up to the curb, brakes wheezing. The delivery man got out and opened the side door. "You Kellan O'Neill?" he called, hauling out a large, flat, rectangular crate.

"That would be me." Kel signed for the package and peered at the return address.

"What's this all about?" he muttered.

She helped him maneuver it through the office door and found a screwdriver to pry the crate apart. Inside it, they found something wrapped in brown paper. Kel held it while she tore the paper off.

"I believe you'd call it a peace offering," she said. It was a canvas, an original. A flock of endangered little terns in flight over the Cliffs of Mòr. In the lower left-hand corner, small, slashing brush strokes spelled out *Beith Molloy*. Fionna watched Kellan's expression with growing tenderness as his gaze devoured the painting, as if looking for something of the woman who had created it.

"Here's a note." She handed him an envelope that had slipped out onto the floor.

Kel opened it, and Fionna unabashedly read over his shoulder.

Every new business should have one brilliant piece of art. Makes clients think you're respectable. Good luck. —Declan.

PS—Close your mouth and look at the back of the painting.

Kel snapped his mouth shut and tilted the canvas. A large manila envelope was taped loosely to the frame.

"What's that?" said Fionna.

Kel opened the flap and looked inside.

For the first time in months, she saw a smile that reached his eyes.

He pulled out an x-ray film and held it up to the light. And laughed.

She peered at it. It was of a long femur bone, patched together with countless plates and screws. She gave a low whistle and stood back to watch as he angled his head to look at the Post-it note stuck on the top right corner, which he read aloud.

"Fionna told me about the alleged bullet hole in your ass. Get over here before she puts another chunk of rock salt in the other side."

He turned to look at Fionna, who stood ready with his Harley keys dangling from her finger.

"Get out of here, ya wee chancer," she said, silently thanking Declan for listening to reason when it came to his little brother. And the dreams that had told her that bringing Beith back into Kel's life was the right thing to do.

Kel's smile froze. She squashed the urge to laugh out loud. He had the look of a man caught cold between sheer joy and sheer terror.

"Where the hell am I going—and what do I say to her when I get there?"

Fionna rolled her eyes. "You, at a loss for words? That'll never happen. And if you can't find one wee woman, we might as well close these office doors right now."

"But—"

Patience wearing thin, she gestured toward the painting. "Look at the evidence."

She waited while he crouched in front of the canvas, and knew the exact instant he figured it out. Without a word, Kel grabbed her shoulders, planted a solid kiss on her cheek, snagged his keys and charged out the door.

Fionna smiled.

Kellan O'Neill would shortly have all he'd ever needed.

If he didn't wreck his feckin' bike on the way.

The Cailleach stretched and smiled as a familiar set of motorcycle wheels raced across her curved back.

The magic stirred, growing ever stronger as he closed the distance between himself and his love. A magic that had lain cold for a while, but sparked anew the moment the woman had made the decision to set herself free.

She shuddered, pressing the long, smooth mountains of her thighs together in anticipation of the night to come.

Smiling indulgently, she flicked one bit of fingernail casually in the direction of a speeding lorry approaching the motorcycle at a right angle from a blind curve. Its tire flattened, and the vehicle shuddered to a stop just before the Harley streaked by, missing it by mere feet.

The Hag closed her eyes and whispered to the wind, knowing it would carry her words to the right ears.

Prepare yourself, daughter. It's your time to fly.

Kellan stood at the top of the rise, looking down past the cottage he had seen in Beith's painting. She had obviously counted on the fact he knew this land like the back of his hand. She had been right.

She stood at the tip of the headland, her back to him, wrapped in a green ruana. The fringed edges of the garment whipped in the wind, echoing the way it lifted her hair, which was lighter than he remembered it.

She must have been spending more time out in the sun. She had been eating better too, he noted as he ran his appreciative gaze over the fuller curves of her body under the tightly wrapped shawl.

Then he frowned as she leaned forward a little, letting the strong sea wind support her body. She was too close to the cliff; one wrong step would send her tumbling into the waves below. He opened his mouth to call to her, but the words died in his throat.

Best not to startle her, he reasoned. If she jumped at the sound of his voice, her bad leg might trip her up. That was the reason he'd parked his Harley on the other side of the rise. So he'd not startle her.

Yeah, he'd go with that.

He refused to consider that she might have locked her door at the sound of the Harley's growling engine. That he might not want to see the look on her face should she catch him coming down the fells toward her. That it might be better to wait until the last moment—like ripping a plaster off quickly instead of peeling it in slow, painful increments.

He wasn't sure what to make of the hollow sensation sitting in the pit of his stomach.

This must be what fear feels like.

He quashed the feeling, shoved his hands in the pockets of his leather jacket and stepped off down the long slope, boots swishing through the thick, tall grass.

A grazing sheep raised its wooly head to look idly at him as he strode by. He narrowed his eyes at it.

"What are you lookin' at?"

The sheep belched and went back to grazing.

Beith leaned into the cold October wind as it bit at her ears and carried a faint whisper to the back of her mind. She let a smile lift the corners of her mouth.

I hear you, Old One.

A delicious shiver ran over her skin, and it had nothing to do with the chilly air. The scent of the ocean, crashing far below at the base of the cliff, seemed to fill her entire body. She drank it in and sighed deeply. She closed her eyes and lifted her face to the late afternoon sun, which held little warmth, but lit the back of her eyelids with red and gold.

Without looking, she knew the thatched-roof cottage behind her would be glowing like a dollop of new snow on the still-green slope, so bright as to hurt the eyes. She knew, because in the short week since she'd rented the place, she'd photographed and painted it as it stood bathed in all kinds of light. Even at this time of year, Ireland was rich with colors she could find nowhere else.

If Kellan never showed up—and there was a distinct possibility he wouldn't—she wouldn't regret a thing. Not her decision to return here, and not the short time she had spent with him. She curled her toes toward the earth and silently thanked the Cailleach for the magic that had brought them together. Those electric twenty-four hours in his arms had stimulated more healing within her body and soul than an army of therapists could have achieved.

Her bones were stronger. *She* was stronger.

If she was lucky, she might get another session. If not, she would live.

Oh yes, she would *live*.

In her next breath, the hard wind supporting her body abruptly died. Her eyes flew open and Great Blaskett Island reeled past her eyes as she lurched forward. Intellectually she knew she had a good six feet of solid ground between her feet and the cliff's edge, but still her heart rocketed into her throat.

What felt like two hot bands of steel coiled around her body and pulled her backward. She heard a muttered "Whoops" and the world tilted again. His scent—remembered, cherished— enveloped her, augmented now with the rich aroma of a leather jacket.

Laughter bubbled up in her throat before the two of them even hit the ground.

"Oof!" Kel grunted as he sat up, one arm still around her and the other hand rubbing his stomach. "You're not nearly as portable as you used to be."

"Now there's a fine greeting after all this time." She leaned back on his supporting arm, her gaze devouring his face. The north-star dimple on one side of his mouth was the same, as was the sparkle in his eye. But the devil-may-care air he'd always carried about him had been subdued by a steady, quiet confidence. Her mouth watered.

"I've got a better greeting." He levered himself up off the ground and brought her with him, pulling her several more yards from the edge of the headland.

"I'm not going to fall, you know. I'm stronger now."

"Humor me."

She rolled her eyes, but let him lead her, her lower belly tightening at the sight of his jeans hugging his butt. She hadn't realized how much she missed that until just now.

He turned to her and took up both her hands in his. But instead of speaking, he looked at her with such concentration it brought a smile to her face.

"About this alleged greeting?"

"Hold on now, I'm thinkin'."

"Don't hurt yourself."

He stuck out his chin. "I've been working on this every blessed second since I got your note. So will you be quiet, woman?"

She wasn't sure if the tears forming in her eyes were from emotion, or from mirth. She ruthlessly squashed them, pressing her lips together to keep a laugh—or was it a sob?—from erupting.

Less than one minute in Kel's presence, and she'd already smiled more than she had in the last four months. Tenderness welled up in her chest.

He let one of her hands drop and pressed the other one between both of his.

"I'd like to introduce myself, miss. My name is Kellan O'Neill. You can be callin' me Kel, if you like."

Her voice strained with suppressed emotion, she managed, "Pleased to meet you, Kel. I'm Beith Mol—"

"Wouldyouliketogoouttodinnerwithme?"

She let her hand swing his back and forth playfully, pretending to think hard.

"No."

At the look on his face, she finally let go of the giggle she'd been holding down. "I've got a better idea."

She marched up the slope, towing him behind her. When they reached the cottage, she led him around back to an outbuilding, opened the door and led him inside. Then she stood back and watched his expression.

He stood still for a minute, then pointed at the machine in the middle of the storage room.

"This is my ultralight."

"'Tis." Her heart pounded at what she was about to ask him to do.

"What's it doing...did Fionna do this?"

"The one and only. But Declan loaned her the lorry to get it here."

"Um..."

"I'll go out to dinner with you, Kel. After you take me for a ride."

"In this?"

"It carries two, last time I checked."

"But it's cold. It's dangerous. And—"

She approached him and slid her hands up his leather-covered arms. "Illegal? You're damned right it is."

His set his hands on her waist and pulled her close. He was hard under his jeans, pressing against her belly. The heat of his body made her shiver with anticipation.

His gaze burned down onto her face. "I know we just met, Miss Molloy, but I have to say I think I could love you."

She leaned back and grinned up at him, her heart skipping a beat.

"Could you, now?"

He began to sway back and forth, grinding his erection against her. She moaned at the contact.

"Do you think..." He lowered his head and grazed her lips with his, "...we could...fly later?"

She opened her mouth and took him deep, nearly weeping at the taste of him in her mouth. She ran her hands into his hair and released it from its tie. It flowed over her fingers, remembered silk. She broke the kiss only to grab a much-needed breath.

"It's really good to see you, Kel."

He lifted his head and stared down at her, his eyes dark with regret. "I'm sorry for what happened before."

She framed his face with her hands. "I'm sorry I didn't stick around long enough to get the whole story. I let fear get the best of me. What we had was magic. *Is* magic. I should have fought for it."

His expression relaxed, and the dimple reappeared.

"There you go shouldin' on yourself again." He grasped her rear and lifted her. With a gasp, she wrapped her legs around his waist as he carried her out of the storage building and made a beeline for the cottage's red-painted front door.

It had one room. The bed wouldn't be hard to find.

His strides were quick and long, one hot hand caressing her scarred left thigh as if in wonder at the new strength he felt there. She wiggled in delight, adjusting herself to cradle his erection between her thighs.

He groaned and staggered to one side, bumping both of them lightly against the cottage's outer wall. She squeaked then snorted in a very unladylike laugh.

"Be careful, woman. You're treadin' dangerous ground."

She dipped her head close to his ear, smiling at the way his whole body shivered at the touch of her lips, her breath.

"Oh, I'm counting on that."

About the Author

To learn more about Carolan Ivey, please visit www.carolanivey.com. Send an email to Carolan at books@carolanivey.com. Join her Yahoo! group at http://groups.yahoo.com/group/wild-ivey. Visit her blog at http://www.carolanivey.blogspot.com.

Look for these titles

Now Available

Abhainn's Kiss

Coming Soon:

In The Gloaming Print Anthology
Beaudry's Ghost

GREAT
cheap
fun

Discover eBooks!

THE FASTEST WAY TO GET THE HOTTEST NAMES

Get your favorite authors on your favorite reader, long before they're out in print! Ebooks from Samhain go wherever you go, and work with whatever you carry—Palm, PDF, Mobi, and more.

Samhain
Publishing ltd

WWW.SAMHAINPUBLISHING.COM